# Surrender Sweet Stranger

## DeWanna Pace

PAGEANT BOOKS

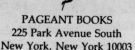

PAGEANT BOOKS
225 Park Avenue South
New York, New York 10003

Copyright © 1988 by DeWanna Pace

Printed in the U.S.A.

First Pageant Books printing: July, 1988

10  9  8  7  6  5  4  3  2  1

When an author's first book is published,
there are many people to thank.
To all of you who have taught me the craft
of writing—thank you.
To my agent, Sandi Gelles-Cole,
my editor, Arlene Friedman, and the
wonderful editors at Pageant Books
who helped in focusing this book,
I give my deepest gratitude.

Most of all to Roy Pace and all other
husbands of women writers—
who are man enough to help with the dishes,
clean the house, and babysit while
his wife follows her dream.

# Surrender Sweet Stranger

# Prologue

✦ ✦ ✦ ✦

*July 1864*

NIGHT GRIPPED THE city with darkness as intense as
Octavio Cordoba's thoughts. His carriage teetered back and forth on its rocky progression
toward the hilltop castle of Chapultepec.

"Seems all of Mexico is going to the bastard's
ball," Octavio muttered as another buggy veered
dangerously close. It had not been the first
near-accident that night. With invitations going
out to every highborn man and woman in the
province, the traffic was monumental.

A stream of colorful oaths from the driver who
sat atop the carriage urged a brief smile to
Octavio's lips. It was one of the few moments he
had relaxed since his meeting with Benito Juárez
two weeks ago.

He had known something important was
about to happen the moment Juárez handed him

1

a letter sent by the European agent known only as Zerman.

The letter said the new emperor of Mexico, Maximilian of Austria, and his wife, Charlotte, were hosting a ball in Mexico City. A perfect moment to put their assassination plan into effect, Juárez had said. And what better instrument of fortune to complete the daring plan than Don Octavio Diego Cordoba of Córdoba province? A lightning-fast escape would be necessary. The agility Don Octavio had learned in the bullfighting arena would serve him well.

The churning of wheels and pounding of hooves brought Octavio's thoughts back to the present. *The ball.* How easy it had been to insure his appearance at the elaborate affair. He had merely informed his betrothed, Modesta Hidalgo, of his arrival in the capital. Modesta's beauty and charm guaranteed her an invitation to every important social function, Imperialist or Juárist. Only hours after his arrival, Modesta presented him with an official invitation.

"It was simple, querido," she told him, tossing back her raven tresses. "I simply said that Don Cordoba was visiting our city. The empress herself extended the invitation. She has seen you fight in Brazil and is much taken with such a handsome matador."

Modesta's sultry eyes smouldered with simmering passion. "Should I worry that she desires you more than her own fair consort?"

Octavio laughed and took Modesta in his arms. Certainly he had missed the soft curves of her slim waist and hips, the taste of desire upon

her lips. But her insistence upon a long engagement had placed a wedge between them.

The civil war between the Juárists and the
French, who were aided by the Mexican Imperial
Army, had delayed the marriage still further.
Modesta relished the excitement the conflict
afforded her. She loved being adored by two
social circles. Octavio had a different view: The
war was an instrument of his personal destiny.

For years he had traveled from arena to arena,
challenging the bulls to the dance of the death.
When Napoleon decided Mexico should be gov-
erned by the French puppet, Maximilian, Octavio realized the true challenge of his life. He
would serve the choice of his people, Presidente
Juárez. For all his faults, Benito Juárez was the
true father of Mexico, and Octavio was determined that he be recognized and rule.

Finally, the night of destiny had come. Thank
everything that was holy, it was *he* who had
been chosen to assassinate Maximilian.


Garrett O'Malley watched the tall, dark-haired
matador with a careful eye. Something in the
man's manner alerted his senses. Was it his
arrogant entrance into the stately ballroom,
which demanded and received the entire company's attention? Or was it the way his blue eyes
seemed to meet every gaze and measure its
worth?

"You are jealous, señor?" asked the plump
governor from Monterrey.

Garrett arched a sandy-colored eyebrow at the

man beside him. "You mean jealous of Cordoba's affect on the señoritas? No, Vidaurri. I've had my share of the ladies tonight. And every other night I've spent in your country," he added.

Vidaurri rocked back on his booted heels. "As well you should, compadre. One so broad of shoulder and narrow of girth should not let these Mexican fires simmer too long."

"Yet even these beauties cannot compare to the sweet belles of the South," Garrett stressed with pride.

"*That* you will have to prove to me when our plan is completed." Vidaurri's serpentine eyes glinted with anticipation. "I expect the hospitality returned."

"As it will be, señor," Garrett assured him. He'd kill the man before he ever allowed him to touch one pore of sweet southern womanhood. But why not let the bastard have his fantasies? "The South never forgets a kindness."

Garrett excused himself and headed toward the sultry señorita who had turned every head when she entered the ballroom.

Hidalgo. Modesta Hidalgo was her name, if he remembered correctly. Daughter of Benito Juárez's most efficient generalissimo. Maximilian was a fool to allow such brazen spying in his own court, Garrett scoffed. He probably thought he could win the love of the Mexican people with these well-intentioned galas. But the people wanted reform, not parties. Garrett hated dealing with someone so foolhardy, but Maximilian held the key to Jefferson Davis's plan.

Less than two months ago, President Davis had instructed Brigadier General Hardeman to choose a man from the Arizona Brigade to be a courier to Maximilian. With Maximilian's men and the Apache battling in every corner of the countryside between Hardeman's camp on the Red River and Mexico City, only the best-trained Indian fighter could make the journey. Garrett O'Malley came from Apache country: he knew the Indians' every trick and wile. He had been only too glad to accept the assignment.

Fortunately the journey had been easy. It had been more challenging to gain an audience with the pompous emperor of Mexico. Yet when Garrett finally succeeded in getting past Maximilian's army of advisers, he had been more than accommodating.

"Of course I will enlist the French and my own army to help in the Confederate fight," the emperor told him. "However, you must remember that even as I stand here, Juárez is receiving guns and ammunition from the Yankees in the port of Acapulco."

"Why do you allow this?"

"We cannot fight the Juárists on one hand and the raiding Apache on the other. We do not *allow* it; we cannot prevent it! Our supplies are being stolen as quickly as we send for them, and our debt to the French is as great as the monthly taxes we collect from the provinces." His ruddy cheeks flushed with anger. "And the church cannot help us. All over Mexico Juárez is torching churches and carrying off the gold and silver."

"You're telling me that if we keep the Apache in line so you only have Juárez to contend with, then we could be assured of help from your Imperialists and the French?" urged Garrett, trying to draw the spoken promise from him rather than an assumed one.

"At Juárez's surrender, we are at your disposal," Maximilian confirmed.

Certain his mission was accomplished, Garrett set about enjoying the ball. And now that he had settled on the beautiful daughter of Hidalgo for his companion, he was sure his last night in Mexico City would be a memorable one.

The Hidalgo woman was alarmingly alluring. The red lace gown adorning her petite figure sharpened her waistline to an intake of breath and hinted at the firm bosom protected by its layers. What a delight it would be to peel away each layer and see the true secrets of her beauty, Garrett mused as he neared her.

"Why, Garrett! Garrett O'Malley, of all people!" A familiar voice interrupted his thoughts. "Whatever are you doing in Mexico?"

Garrett was more irritated than surprised to see Shelly Kate McCandless standing beside him. Shelly Kate's father, Thorne, was his rich and powerful neighbor in Arizona. And his future father-in-law. He was engaged to Shelly Kate's older sister, Gila.

So much for his plans to seduce the Hidalgo woman, Garrett thought, hoping his annoyance did not show on his face. He didn't want to do anything to jeopardize his wedding plans. One night in this delightful señorita's arms was nothing to the wealth and power he would gain from an O'Malley-McCandless alliance. He forced a cheerful tone into his voice. "I might ask you the same question. How are you, Shelly Kate?"

"Well, thank you," she said, tossing back her near-white braid. "May I present my friend, señorita Modesta Hidalgo?"

Garrett bowed politely and met Modesta's frankly appraising look.

"Mo and I were schoolmates," Shelly Kate continued, "in Boston. She invited me for the summer and Father agreed to let me come. He didn't want me home with all the trouble with the renegades. So he sent me to visit dear sweet Mo, and here I am in the middle of a civil war. A lot of blarney if you ask me."

The lilt of her laughter revealed her Irish heritage. It was charming but did not fool Garrett. Shelly Kate was spoiled by her father's wealth and his indulgence. More than likely she had demanded the visit to her friend. And Thorne McCandless had catered to her whim as he did to his younger daughter's every fancy.

But what of my bride-to-be? Garrett wondered with some apprehension. "Gila did not accompany you?"

"No," Shelly Kate said flatly. "You know my sister would *never* leave her cactus field during harvesting season—except when she's herding horses with Father. It seems the Texas Mounted Rifles have given their contract solely to my father." Raising her voice, Shelly Kate boasted,

"His pact with Cochise is making him the only horse dealer in the entire territory who delivers on time."

Shelly's news made Garrett run one hand irritably through his sand-colored hair. So he would have Thorne McCandless to deal with if he were to rid the country of the Apache! McCandless was the most powerful man in the Gadsden. To win Maximilian's help for the Confederacy, he would have to proceed more carefully than originally anticipated.

"Your sister sounds like an unusual woman," Modesta declared. "If she is as tiny as you, Shelly, how can she manage a remuda of horses?"

Shelly Kate waved a dainty gloved hand. "Oh, she is nothing like me. She's much older . . . almost nineteen. And much taller and bigger boned. She reminds me a little of rimrock walls. Her will is immovable when she's riled, and her coppery hair is only the first indication of her temper."

"I would like very much to meet such a one," Modesta said sincerely.

"Don't be too sure," Shelly Kate replied. "No offense intended, but she has a deep hatred for Mexicans. I doubt she would ever consent to meeting you."

"We have a saying for such people," Modesta's voice was hard-edged.

"And what is that?"

"The tongue that spites shall ever taste the lips of prejudice. Which means that your sister shall one day fall prey to a countryman of mine."

Shelly Kate threw back her head and laughed. "Gila? With a Mexican? Never! Never in a million civil wars. Why, not even your glorious Don Cordoba would catch her eye!"

Garrett's gaze went to the object of Shelly Kate's admiration. After the emperor himself, the matador was the most sought-after man of the evening. Who was he? Why was he so sure of himself?

Garrett looked closely at the matador's attire. Black velvet vest and pants elaborately trimmed in gold braids. Suddenly he caught sight of the abnormally large bulge at the base of Cordoba's abdomen. That's it! That's why he is so aloof, Garrett realized. No wonder the señoritas pursued the man. They must think he is the sire of all sires!

Yet Garrett recognized the true nature of the bulge. He had frequently hidden a knife in his trousers. More than once he had prevented himself being taken prisoner by plunging his dagger into an unsuspecting enemy's stomach.

Who was Don Cordoba's intended victim? The matador's manner and gaze had been unchanging except for one moment. When Maximilian announced that he and his wife would heretofore be called Maximiliano and Carlota, Cordoba's blue eyes had flickered with something, some quickly masked feeling Garrett had not noticed until now.

The victim was none other than the emperor himself, Garrett realized. Though he knew he must stop the assassination attempt, he began to respect the matador's boldness. How could he attempt such an incident in a crowd this size? Either the man was foolhardy, or he had cheated death in the arena so many times that he no longer feared anything.

Garrett watched Cordoba's slow, calculated moves toward Maximilian. He had to do something but could not draw attention to himself. Jefferson Davis did not want the Confederacy's association with Maximilian known, so someone else would have to be the emperor's savior.

Garrett excused himself from the ladies and hurried toward Vidaurri. Quietly he whispered a warning as he pointed toward the matador. Vidaurri signaled for his men, and Garrett rejoined the ladies.

Octavio Cordoba's watchful eye noted the gathering of the soldiers. Someone must have discovered his intention but that did not deter him. He made a desperate lunge at the emperor. But the knife was knocked from his hand and Vidaurri's men wrestled him to the ground.

Modesta screamed and rushed toward Octavio, but the onlookers would not part to allow her at his side.

"Who is the impudent swine who dares attack me?" bellowed Maximilian, pointing a pudgy finger at Octavio.

Octavio stood, arrogance flaring his nostrils while his captors chained his arms. "Don Octavio Diego Cordoba dares to rid Mexico of Napoleon's nursemaid!"

Maximilian jerked to his feet, rage hampering his words. "A—a—a French nursemaid, am I?

Who would you have rule this . . . this . . . nation of cactus and mesquite?"

A hush fell over the crowd and resentment of the emperor's words rose and thickened the air into a dangerous, living thing. Octavio's pride made him bolder. "The true president, Benito Juárez, will show our people how to make bread from the mesquite and sweets from the cactus. He will not teach us laws we cannot live by. We *will* govern ourselves. No foreign rule. Viva Juárez!"

"Viva Juárez!" the crowd echoed.

Maximilian's face turned livid with rage as he ordered his palace guards to his side. "Let all who oppose me know this. I deal harshly with my enemy. Those of you who are yet undecided in this must decide now, this very night. Do you follow me or oppose me?"

Tides of opposing loyalties washed over the crowd and came crashing back in competing shouts of "Viva Maximiliano! Viva Juárez!"

"Let this be a warning," he said, waving his hand as if encompassing the masses of Mexicans who stood outside the palace gates. "Should you choose against me, there will be no mercy or even the luxury of death. I will send you to the Sonora, to the dungeons of La Carsel. So will be the fate of Don Cordoba."

"No! No!" Modesta wailed as the soldiers escorted Octavio out of the ballroom. "Not La Carsel. Please, not La Carsel!"

Shelly Kate tried to comfort her friend. "Don't cry for the likes of him. He deserves his fate for trying to murder the emperor. There will be others. Cordoba's no good, no good at all."

Modesta removed tear-stained hands from her eyes. "Beware, Shelly, or you will share your sister's lot. You will have a man as bad as you claim Octavio is, and Gila will marry a man of Mexican blood."

# Chapter One

✦✦✦✦✦

*March 1865*

"AGAIN?" GILA MCCANDLESS argued as she looked up into her father's stern hazel eyes. When he was this angry, they darkened to match the deeper shade of her own. Gila thumbed back her sombrero over the straggling ends of her auburn hair and blinked away the hot afternoon glare of the Arizona sun. "No wonder we don't have any water holes left. If everybody took a bath every time they came to a mudhole, the whole Gadsden would've dried up a century ago."

Thorne McCandless loomed in the saddle above her, his massive proportions filling the leather between horn and cantle, dwarfing the roan. Gila wished she hadn't dismounted before the argument. It was hard enough to meet the giant Irishman's gaze at equal level, much less in the position she now held.

He repeated the command. *"Bathe."*

Gila sighed. Another word would only nudge his temper one notch higher; in the scorching heat, she didn't think she could bear it.

She and Thorne had argued for two weeks before the roundup started, but her father's will had been stronger. Gila knew she should have been home bottling her cures to sell at San Xavier's Easter pageant, as she did every year. Instead she was having to ride all over hell and back herding his blamed horses. Horses provided for a war of which she highly disapproved. Let Jefferson Davis fight his own battles; she had other problems to attend to.

If only Shelly Kate would take her turn, Gila fumed. But as usual, her little sister had sweet-talked Thorne out of making her go. If Shelly's skin weren't as white as milkweed, or her hair as fair as the July sun, their father might have decided differently. The youngest McCandless looked frail to those who chose to see her that way, but to Gila she was a strong-willed, impudent beauty who unceasingly took advantage of her position as favorite daughter of the richest and most powerful man in Arizona.

Gila sighed. Why should this be any different from any other time? Her father never thought she was right. Why should he now?

She watched as Thorne dismounted with an ease uncommon to men his size. His white linen shirt looked even whiter against the deep tan that was burned into his skin from more than twenty years of desert sun. The forearms that grasped the saddle horn were as powerful as those of a man twenty years his junior.

Gila heard his horse's grunt of appreciation and thought the animal well deserved its rest. Thorne McCandless was more burden than any man, beast, or daughter should have to bear. She returned her attention to her father's physique. She'd seen him knock a man out by backhanding him with one of those mighty arms and remembered too well the sting of the razor strop on her own behind when she'd tested his will against her own.

He looked as if he were carved out of the mountains themselves, except for the crop of curly hair that hung to his shoulders. The flame-colored mass shone brightly in the blistering sunlight, reminding her of a bonfire with gray ashes around the edges. His beard and mustache were of identical shading—red peppered with silver.

Thorne's voice vibrated over the countryside. "You're a McCandless, girl. Act like one and take a bath."

Gila brushed the trail dust from her britches in irritation. She and every settler, soldier, and Indian in the territory knew the respect her name demanded. Sometimes she wanted to forget she was a McCandless, but how could she?

Almost twenty years ago, Thorne had brought his family all the way to Fort Yuma across what was now the Butterfield Overland Mail route. Her mother, Kathryn MacGregor McCandless, had insisted that if she were expected to live in

this godforsaken Indian territory, she would
choose the place where they settled. Thorne had
backtracked the Gila River toward an outlet of
the Aravaipa Creek in hope of finding a piece of
ground that would please his pregnant wife.

Gila was born near Gila Bend on the way to
Kathryn's paradise. Later she learned that her
father had named her for her birthplace. But her
parents had not known the Spanish pronunciation of her name. They didn't call her *Hee-la*, but
pronounced the *l* as *y*, the *g* as a hard *g. Geeya*.
She liked her name. It suited her.

Correct pronunciation or no, her father often
called her his little "gila monster." That suited
her, too. She knew she was a monster at times.
She meant to be. She had learned quickly that if
she didn't throw tantrums, cuss, scream, be
downright stubborn, her father would simply
ignore her presence the way he might brush
away a pesky gnat.

When she was small he had been proud of her
bad temper, had boasted to everyone who would
listen that she had inherited his Irish nature. But
now that she was grown, she knew he found her
stubbornheadedness exasperating.

Gila began to hobble her paint, Wee-People.
More out of habit than need, she tied the reins to
the gelding's left foreleg. Arizona soil was notorious for not providing ground brush or trees to
tie a horse to.

"Why'd you do that?" Thorne asked. "There's
plenty of buffalo grass to stake him. We're near
the Santa Ritas now. Quit your stalling, lassie,
and get your bath 'afore the men ride in." He

wiped the sweat from his brow. "Why do you think I said we'd scout ahead of the remuda? So be done with it or I'll take a switch to your arse."

"You and what cavalry?" she blurted before thinking. Then she ran to the water's edge, knowing she had said too much. But the words had been there on her tongue tip, and she bore too much Irish blood not to say them.

Thorne picketed his roan. "I'll be choosing camp while you get your bath. And I'm guaranteeing you it won't take the Dragoons to dunk you either, lassie. So get yourself clean. And mind you, don't take too long. The drovers are about an hour south." He stretched both arms high in the air, clasped them behind his back, then bent backwards to relieve the ache of a day's journey on horseback. "I'll be catching a few winks since it's my watch tonight. I expect Cochise will honor our treaty, but there're always renegades about. We'll have to court caution from here on in."

Gila trudged off to the rocky bank of the seep. Like most of the sinkholes, the land around it was level on three sides. On the fourth side a low-rising dune blocked the water from view. Unless a passerby knew what to look for. And in this landscape there wasn't much else to see.

Southern Arizona looked much the same for miles—a brown haze of saguaro cactus and buffalo grass. To the north, back home on the Aravaipa, the landscape was different. The paloverde trees had already flooded the foothills with yellow blossoms. The refreshing odor of greasewood drifted amidst the flame-colored

prickly pears and the red caterpillar-tips of
shaggy ocotillos. There, it was as if the desert
had washed itself of winter and was dressing for
a summer rendezvous.

Gila closed her eyes to the shimmering, sun-
bleached horizon. How she longed for home and
privacy. She stripped off her dusty shirt and
britches and looked around at the land. Sand
and cactus, cactus and sand. No wonder the
Mexicans sold this territory to the United States.
Imagine, ten million dollars for this! She bet
there was some *bandido* in Mexico laughing his
sombrero off. Gila shivered, her hatred for the
nation to the south almost as fierce as her hatred
for her overlarge breasts, her handicaps, as she
called them. The Gadsden Purchase had been a
fool's folly as far as she was concerned.

She unlaced the sombrero from under her chin
and tossed it with her clothes near the base of a
treelike saguaro. Her nose wrinkled at the musty
smell of the muddy water and she wondered
which was worse, the stench from the mudhole
or the odor from her hard day's ride.

Gila shrugged, then plunged into the pool's
watery depths. Surfacing, she felt her aggrava-
tion wash away. Thorne had been right, of
course. He was always right and everyone told
him so. She *was* hot and dusty. If only he had
told her to bathe because he was concerned for
her comfort. Instead, she knew it had only been
to prove his own superiority.

Gila had learned quickly that Thorne wanted
his name branded on Arizona history. Not only
did he own the territory's largest sheep ranch,

but he'd also accumulated large mine holdings of silver and gold. In the last few years, he'd rounded up and sold wild mustangs to the Texas Mounted Rifles. Gila knew of no one who lived in or visited the Mogollon Rim who did not know about her father and his influence on the settlement of the Gadsden.

Thinking back, Gila could remember only one time Thorne had been deliberately kind to her. That incident reminded her that Thorne *could* be persuaded in her favor, if she gave him profitable reason. Three years before, on her birthday, he'd awakened her and demanded that she come out to the corral. Afraid she had done something to displease him, she took her time getting dressed.

"I'll take it away before you see it," Thorne had threatened when she tarried too long. *It* had been a newborn albino buffalo. Its mother had strayed in that morning and caused a ruckus among the horses. The older animal died within minutes of giving birth.

Thorne passed instant judgment. "You'll need to find a home for the likes of him, lassie. I'm not seeing any reason to tarry with him."

Gila took one look at the doleful calf as it stared mournfully at its lifeless mother. "Let me be responsible for him," she pleaded. "He'll not get in the way. I'll take good care of him. *Please*."

Previously her pride had always stood in the way of her begging her father for anything, but she desperately wanted the calf. She searched her mind for a reason that would convince Thorne to let her keep it.

Didn't the Indians revere the white bison? What if she taught the white calf to pasture with the remuda? Then the Indians would be less likely to rustle the horses. She presented the plan to Thorne and was thrilled by his instant approval. She kept the animal and named him Dublin, after the city of her parents' birth.

Now, as she floated in the water, Gila grew anxious for the buffalo's arrival. Dublin was always the first to smell the sweet water, so the horses gave him plenty lead. She had scolded him on many occasions for acting like a true McCandless, for staying ahead of the pack. Gila had always managed to be one of the fellows and was grateful she had not inherited the McCandless arrogance.

A billowing dust cloud on the far horizon urged Gila toward the bank, though she doubted that her appearance, even naked, would cause much of a stir among the men. Her almond-shaped eyes, slightly round chin, and auburn hair were attractive enough, but nothing compared to Shelly Kate's beauty. Her little sister had certainly blossomed this last summer!

Gila studied her reflection in the muddy pool. It was a good thing she couldn't see herself too well or it would have put her in an even worse temper. Without her willing it, her left cheek creased and she splashed her image away angrily. How she hated that dimple! Sometimes, when she was mad enough to spit arrows, the darned thing would indent and no one would take her seriously. It gave her a cherubic expression that made her more attractive than she cared to be.

Worse than the cheekhole were the two large breasts nature had given her. She liked being built like a sod house—stocky, large boned. She could ride, shoot, and wrestle to her heart's content without fainting from the desert heat. But to have breasts almost twice the size of those of many well-endowed women was downright ridiculous and unfair!

Men were forever asking for her hand. Her full figure seemed to defy the desert and its ability to shrink even the most determined of wills. The combination of her physical fortitude and her fortune made her much sought after. Many women would have been pleased by the attention, but she wasn't.

Though she constantly protested, Thorne had made her entertain her various suitors by threatening to send her to boarding school back east. Eventually Garrett O'Malley's visits became more frequent than the others'. She had always been suspicious of her father's motives where her suitors were concerned. He actually expected her to marry the insufferable man! The thought of Garrett's hot lips on hers made her shake with anger, and she scrubbed herself with hard, resentful strokes. She must get Garrett out of her mind. How she hated him, yet she must stifle that hate. Soon Mr. Lincoln's war would be over and Garrett would be coming home . . . home to be her husband. *Damn Thorne! Damn McCandless! Damn Garrett!*

An angry tear trickled down her cheek, and
Gila brushed it away, hating her feminine weakness. She was tired of being a pawn to the will of
men—first with her domineering father and
soon with a husband she hated with every
breath.

Gila waded out of the water and walked
briskly to the multifingered cactus where she
had tossed her clothes. She stooped to retrieve
them.

Suddenly a rough palm cupped her mouth,
almost choking off all air. The jagged edge of a
sharpened rock pressed hard against her throat,
muffling her scream of fear. She struggled to
break free, but the crude weapon sliced deeper
and drew blood.

# Chapter Two

**✦✦✦✦**

A HARSH ANIMAL odor assaulted Gila's nostrils. The
stench grew stronger and she fought to control
the waves of fear and nausea that threatened to
overtake her. She must stay conscious and fight.
But the pain in her throat made breathing difficult. She longed to close her eyes and give in to
the sweet oblivion that threatened to engulf her.

Suddenly a thunderous noise sounded from
the creosote bushes nearby. Her attacker cried

out in alarm. The jagged blade was jerked from her throat and flew through the air. Ignoring the fierce pain, Gila turned her head in the direction of the commotion.

In the distance loomed a monstrous hulk of white mountain, so big it dwarfed the mighty saguaros. The mountain edged toward her. Twin peaks sharpened into horns, massive shoulders plunged to hooved valleys. "Dublin," Gila whispered gratefully.

The flint had sliced expertly into the bison's left shoulder, staining his white fur a deep crimson. The animal's one blue eye flickered with pain. Inwardly Gila cursed the heavens for Dublin's injury. Had he not been born blind in his pink eye, he might have dodged the blade.

She whistled as hard as her throat permitted. A look of terror passed over the haughty face of the Indian who knelt beside her, frozen with fear. Dublin answered her call with another grunt and began a labored run toward her. The Indian screamed as if possessed and scrambled to his feet. Gila curled her body protectively and rolled over onto her side, catching only a brief glimpse of her attacker's moccasins as he raced over the jagged desert rocks, leapt onto Thorne's roan, and rode off.

Dublin moved toward her, his steps faltering. His moist, bulky nostrils nudged her gently, his warm tongue licked her arms. She lay helpless, gasping for breath, willing her uncontrollable shaking to stop. The awful moment finally passed; her mind cleared and she was able to think once again.

All she could think about was how dirty she felt. She grabbed a handful of sandy earth, and began furiously wiping away the foulness of the Indian's touch. When she had rubbed away some of the filth she thanked God and all the saints for Dublin's timely rescue.

She stood and wiped away the dampness that had formed in her eyes. With a handful of earth she made a crude poultice for her neck. It wouldn't last long, but it would do until she could bandage it properly.

She turned to minister to Dublin, who was waiting patiently beside her. She gripped the flint that was lodged in his shoulder and jerked it out with one clean motion. The wound bled freely for a few seconds, cleansing itself. Then she applied the same poultice she'd used for herself.

Gila stroked the white buffalo's nose with one hand and peered into his one healthy eye. "Are you all right, Dub?" she asked. He nudged her, and she knew he would recover after the injury had time to heal.

"We've got to find Thorne," she said, resolutely putting the terror behind her. "He could be in trouble."

She retrieved her white blouse and tore a strip from one sleeve for a makeshift bandage. She wound the linen cloth around her neck and dressed as fast as her dizziness allowed. Then she stumbled back to where she'd last seen Thorne. There he lay, spread-eagled, staked, his mouth gagged, but every inch of his muscular frame screaming with insult.

Why had the Indian spared them? Gila wondered. Wee-People had not been taken. Why
would the Indian take Thorne's horse and not
her own?

Quickly she untied her father's gag. The bellow which followed sounded like the thunder
that often threatened their Arizona sky. "Did
you kill that son-of-a-coyote? I'll cut out his
tongue and chop off—"

"He got away." Gila's voice was barely above
a whisper as she tugged at the rawhide that held
her father captive.

"Got away? Got away, did he? And you the
best shot in the territory, lassie! Were you blind?
Get a knife, dammit! Get these damned bindings
off me and let me up from here!"

Gila suddenly went blank for a moment. What
was her father saying? Cut him loose? Knife? Get
the knife?

Then memory washed over her and the words
began to make sense once again. She returned to
the cactus and searched the surrounding area.
Where had the flint landed? Over there. Yes,
that way. The same direction as *he* took.

Gila stumbled to the rocky bank of the mudhole and recovered the flint, gripping it with a
vengeance that left her shaken. She hurried back
to her father and cut the rawhide with a jagged
motion.

Thorne McCandless struggled to his feet, grabbing her roughly. "Just look. Look where that
bastard got me."

Thorne turned and Gila saw the bloodstain on
his right buttock. A nervous giggle escaped her

lips, making him whip around. She didn't know why she had laughed, only that it had somehow kept her from crying.

Thorne shook her. "Did you even *try* to stop him? How could you let me be insulted like this?"

"What about me?" Gila asked, staring defiantly into his flashing eyes. A tear rolled down her cheek. "I was nearly raped and you can do nothing but yell at me!"

Thorne grabbed her harshly. "Don't lie to me, girl. Did that savage lay his . . . *hands* . . . on you? I won't have the McCandless name sullied! Tell me exactly what happened."

Gila told her father the story, then laughed bitterly as she met his intense gaze. "Don't worry, Father. The bastard was more interested in stealing your horse than molesting me. Your precious name is saved."

"I said, don't lie to me, girl. This is not Garrett O'Malley we're talking about!"

Gila jerked away from her father's grasp. Her one and only indiscretion had been with Garrett, and Thorne hadn't let her forget it. Not even after four years.

She and Garrett were hardly more than children when she let him talk her into making love with him. She'd done it out of curiosity and bravado, not love or even lust. But then she had learned that Garrett had made a bet with a few of the O'Malley ranch hands, a bet she'd let him win easily. Any feelings of friendship, any liking for him quickly turned to a deep, abiding hatred.

Garrett had made a fool of her; she'd never forgive him for that.

Then Thorne had found out. Overheard a boozed-up O'Malley hand gloating in the cantina. Thorne had confronted her. She lied at first. She knew she'd tarnished the McCandless name, knew Thorne would thrash her within an inch of her life if she told him she'd been foolish enough to let Garrett O'Malley take her virginity. But Thorne kept at her until she admitted she was lying. Then he'd announced her engagement to Garrett. Luckily the War Between the States had intervened, and she had so far escaped having to marry the man she had come to hate.

"I'm not lying this time. The Indian didn't touch me, I swear. Would you have *preferred* that he did? Would you believe me then?" She stared defiantly back at her father, challenging his look of disapproval.

But McCandless pride, McCandless honor had been soiled—once again because of her—and he meant to avenge them.


The desert night was almost unbearable to Gila. Organ-pipe cacti and shrubs formed hard black shadows, looking as if their prickly fingers reached up to strangle the sky. In the distance, the Santa Rita peaks faded into dark patches of ebony. The moon shone eerily across the white desert sand, and the March wind set shadows in motion. Gila wished desperately for morning, though she knew she was safe for the moment. Apache did not attack at night, supposedly believing that ghosts wandered after sunset. She peered out into the night, certain they were right.

She scooped the last ladleful of beans into Book's tin as they sat within the circle of men around the campfire. Her hand continued to tremble even as the fire crackled its warmth, and she knew her shiver was not from the cold.

"Are you all right, Gila?" Book asked in Japanese. "I heard you were thrown very far."

Gila was grateful for the concern in the old samurai's face. She answered in his native tongue, which he had taught her when she was barely old enough to speak. "I'm all right," she assured him. Then, realizing the others needed to hear the explanation Thorne demanded she give, Gila switched to English. "Wee-People got crazy on me again. Always said I should've done that dad-blamed horse in months ago. But you know me, once I get to liking you, I don't let loose. That old paint's got me blind to his mean streaks, is all." She cleared her throat against the hoarseness caused by the wound. Her hand automatically went to the bandana she had tied around her neck to hide the injury from questioning eyes.

"Does your neck hurt very much?" Book asked. From his tone Gila knew her friend had already guessed the falsehood. The samurai missed little. He had an unfailing instinct for the truth. She wished she didn't have to lie to him.

Book finished the frijoles, wiped his mouth on

his sleeve, and let a loud reverberation rumble up from the pit of his stomach.

Gila laughed. "Trying to keep the coyotes away, Book?"

"I've told you often, a healthy burp is the greatest compliment one can give to show appreciation for good food." Book's voice was gently reproving.

Gila instantly regretted her sarcasm. "I know, Booker, I was just joking."

Another of the wranglers, a new hand, brought an empty tin to Gila. "Give him a coupla hours, and he'll be doin' them ol' polecats real justice, too." The rail-thin man laughed at the insinuation.

Newcomers learned all too soon that baiting Book raised Gila's dander real fast. "At least he comes by his prairie odors honestly," Gila retorted. "You stink from the inside out."

Several of the other wranglers sitting around the campfire chortled in appreciation of her quick defense of the samurai. Book had earned the men's respect on more than one occasion.

The conversation around the campfire grew loud and lewd as it always did. Gila had heard it all before. To the ranch hands of the Circle-Shamrock, she was just one of the fellows, and that was how she liked it.

Normally she would have joined in their yarn spinning, but tonight she needed to keep her mind and hands busy. For hours she'd fought back the torrent of rage welling within her. To think that Thorne still refused to believe she had not been touched by the savage. His belief so

strong he had forced her to lie to Book and the
others about her injury.

Making camp had provided enough busywork
to dull the angry thoughts that rumbled in her
mind. But the strain of deceiving Book had taken
its toll. The idle chitchat caused her head to
throb like a hundred tom-toms echoing from the
Santa Ritas. Her hands shook and she dropped
the tins.

Book hurried to gather them for her. She
smiled but refused to let him help. "Guess I'm a
little skittish after that fall."

"You want me to braid Wee-People's tail and
cut it off?"

Gila laughed, grateful for the old samurai's
attempt to amuse her. She could imagine him
out there trying to braid the paint's tail. That
cantankerous cayuse would kick her old friend
clear to heaven.

"Really. It wasn't the horse's fault," Gila lied,
hating every word. But Thorne's word was law.
Embarrassed, she repeated the falsehood.
"Snake scared him. He didn't mean to throw
me. Honest, I'm all right. A little stove up is all."
She nodded toward the tins. "I've got to get
these washed."

Gila headed toward the mudhole, hesitant but
determined. She'd only gone a few yards when
a shadow fell on the path in front of her and
demanded, "Gila . . . wait."

She froze. The scream died in her throat as she
recognized Thorne's looming silhouette. He
looked more ominous than usual in the flickering
firelight.

"It's all right. I wish everybody would quit worrying about me. I'm not scared. Besides, If you treat me any differently, they'll know something's happened." In a more hushed tone she added, "Apache don't usually hit until dawn. You know that." She had taken a few more steps before she was halted by his iron grip upon her elbow. What had she done now to make him angry?

"I know, lassie. But evidently some Indians have no respect for the time of day. I won't be made a fool of again, I tell you. You were lucky no one else saw. 'Twould be shame you'd bring on the McCandlesses if anyone knew."

Gila looked at him, resenting his stone-faced expression. Her hands shook with the rage that surged inside her. "The God-Almighty McCandless name, is it! I wish to God he had ra—"

The bearlike palm struck swiftly, jarring the dimple and every tooth behind it. "I won't have you rowdying the Lord's name, lassie, no matter what Satan has inflicted upon you."

Gila wiggled her jaw to see if the teeth were still rooted. Much to her surprise, they were. She knew she had gone too far using the Lord's name in vain in front of her father, but she was mad. Damned mad!

Normally she'd scream to get his attention, but tonight her tone was hushed. Despite her anger, she didn't want anyone else to know what had happened. It would make the lies she told at supper unforgivable. But she had much to say to her father and she meant to say it.

Gila began, pronouncing her words very care-

fully, making certain Thorne understood each
one of them. Even this was difficult, for her teeth
still smarted from the slap. "You don't care that
I was frightened out of my skin, do you? What if
it had been Shelly Kate? Would you still be so
quick to disbelieve *her?*"

Pacing back and forth, she continued. "My
hands are still shaking. Then you try to knock
my teeth down my throat after it's been sliced to
the bone. Is it my reputation we're arguing over
or your pride? What kind of man . . . father . . .
are you?"

"I'm a McCandless, lassie. I won't be arguing
over what I cannot change."

Gila sagged. She'd argued too many times
about the family pride. As usual, he was right.
They could not change what had happened.

She reached the edge of the mudhole. "I'll
wash up these tins. My neck hurts and I'm tired.
I feel as though I've been galloped over. I'd like
to scout again tomorrow, if it's all right. I want to
get to Tubac before the others, so I can have this
seen to." Gila winced as she untied the scarf at
her neck. "It's too bad I don't have any of my
salve here," she said. "Maybe I can farm enough
saguaro pulp for a small batch when we get near
Tucson."

The pulp made a potent medicine that had
enabled her to cure many a sickness. But for
now, Tubac was the closest settlement with a
doctor, even though he was trained to nurse
animals, not people. Still, her wound needed to
be attended to, and it was in a place that she
couldn't see to herself.

Thorne reached out to touch the injury, but Gila moved away. "Not much good at weaving, am I?" he said.

"It'll do till we get to Tubac," she assured him. Thorne had sewn up the jagged cut as best he could, but the wound needed to be restitched.

"We're not going to Tubac. We're heading back to Nogales."

"Mexico? Why?"

Thorne turned away, facing the Santa Ritas. "That cut's too bad for a horse doctor to tend to," he said gruffly. "I've told the others to push on. Book will ride with us. I told him I want to see about that fall you took. Good thing none of the laddies cared for a closer look at Dublin. They'd know it wasn't any saguaro he ran into with that blind eye of his. Book's already asking me about that shoulder, and he's noticed that my backside hasn't been sittin' too friendly the past few hours. Man's too smart."

Wondering why the Indian had spared them, Gila asked, "Why didn't he kill you instead of tying you up?"

Thorne ran a hand through his thatch of red hair. "I'm sure he was a renegade. If he killed me in Cochise's territory, the Apache nation would be riding down on him within the hour. Since he took my horse and raped you, I'd say he was trying to warn me to keep my eyes open, even though I'm under Cochise's protection."

"But he didn't rape me!" Gila repeated in frustration. Meeting his stoic gaze, she bent at the water's edge and began to scrape the utensils. A few minutes later, a strange feeling itched across her shoulders and caused her to turn. For the first time in several years, she smiled at her father.

Why dwell on the anger between them? At least he was willing to take her to a real doctor. There had to be some love in that decision. It had been a very long time since they'd spent a day together that didn't involve work. Perhaps she could use it to ease some of their differences.

Gila finished her chores and rose. "Just think," she said, linking her elbow with his. "Once we see the doc, you and I can spend the rest of the day taking it easy together—doing things we haven't done in a long time. It'll be a day like no other."

" 'Twill be like no other," he echoed solemnly. "Like no other."

The journey to Nogales the next day was loud in silence, finally broken when Thorne complained to Book about his injury. Gila had been worried about her father ever since they had left the other wranglers, who would take the horse herd on into Tucson.

As the miles trailed behind them, Gila had seen Thorne's painful grimaces the few times he couldn't contain his discomfort. If it were apparent to her, she was certain Book had noticed, too.

She almost choked on her laughter when the broad-shouldered samurai demanded, "Get off your horse, Thorne."

No one, absolutely no one, but Book ordered Thorne McCandless about. He was the only person on earth who could get away with it. She wasn't exactly sure of the reasons, but everyone in the territory speculated about the secret between her father and Book, a secret that Thorne McCandless did not want anyone else to know.

She did know that a deathbed wish from her mother had kept the two men from killing each other. But she had never learned why. Now, more than fifteen years later, Thorne and Book were better friends than most. Each was the first to defend the other in times of trouble. Still, there was a barrier between them.

Thorne dismounted carefully, his face etched with pain. Wiping away the sweat that moistened his forehead, he tossed back the unruly, flame-colored mane. "Get your hide down from there and let this be done," he called to Book.

Book lowered his own bulky frame to the ground. He was not tall, only five-foot-three, but he was wide in the shoulders. Powerful calf muscles held the broad-chested physique at a precarious balance. He's like a buffalo, Gila thought as she watched her old friend, large and bulky on top, but small and solid on his feet.

Gila dismounted and led Wee-People a few feet from the men. She turned away. There was a brief silence, then came a round of cursing.

"Damn you, Book! Be careful. That's not rawhide you're stitchin'. Ouch!"

Gila giggled.

Book interrupted Thorne's tirade with one of

his sayings. "The wise man who lies still while an arrow is yanked out of his saddle may get the point."

Gila laughed again, unable to stop herself. Somehow the mirth helped relieve the pent-up tension of the last few hours. Suddenly tears of frustration welled in her eyes and she turned away from Book's penetrating gaze, permitting the stream of self-pity to flow.

"What troubles you?" The gentle old samurai hurried to her side and lifted her chin. "Tell me." She felt his next question burn deeply into her soul. "Has someone hurt you?"

She could not return his stare and turned away, wiping the tears from her face. "No, nobody's hurt me," she lied.

"Thorne?"

"No!" Gila insisted.

"Then who?" Book persisted.

Gila was silent. She wanted to tell Book about her quarrel with her father and his refusal to believe her about the rape, but the thought of Thorne's rage stopped her. McCandless arguments were for no one's ears but their own.

Book patted her shoulder kindly. "When you are ready to talk, I will be ready to listen."

Their private moment was broken by Thorne's bellow. "What the devil are you two doing? We've got to get moving."

Exchanging wry smiles, Gila and Book rose and mounted their horses. Moments later the three were back on the road to Nogales.

# Chapter Three

✦ ✦ ✦ ✦ ✦

OCTAVIO CORDOBA'S EYES opened with a jolt. He sat upright and kicked furiously at the gnawing teeth that penetrated one ankle. Scampering feet eluded his blows. "Not today, amigos. Not today," he mocked.

As he scratched an itch in his ebony locks, Octavio blinked the remainder of sleep from his eyes and stared at the damp earthen chamber that had been his home for nearly eight months. Where were his drinking tin and spoon? He reached to his side. Yes, they were in their usual place. Quevera is consistent, he thought. Octavio clanged the metal together violently and hollered, "Good morning, Mexico!" Then he waited.

Soon the muffled echoes of a hundred other spoons clanged against tin cups. He struck his own again, grateful for even a token of companionship in this dungeon of horrors.

Once again he glared at his cell, then let out a long sigh. "What shall I do today, I wonder? Perhaps count the rats' teeth marks on my posterior? No, it would probably take more time to count the lice in my hair."

A tickling sensation inched its way up his leg. He looked down. "Ahh . . . Angelita, my friend, shall I count your babies today?" The cockroach began to investigate the seeping wounds made by the rodents. He lifted the insect and watched its antennae twitch either in fear or anger, he was never certain which.

Thick chains hung heavily upon his wrists, but he willed the strength to hold the roach upright. "Go along, señora, and deliver my compadres in sin, if you please. It is my birthday today. Invite everyone. The rats may feast on my sallow flesh, while your family and I eat that gruel Ignacio feeds the imprisoned." He lowered the roach to the ground and it zigzagged away, as if hurrying to do his bidding.

"Necessities first," Octavio muttered as he lifted the tin spoon. He raised the scrap of cloth that had once been a black velvet pant leg and pressed the utensil deep into his right thigh. His strength was not what it had been yesterday, he realized with futility. He pressed further and drew blood. After twisting the spoon just enough to leave the scar he sought, Octavio tossed the bloody utensil to the floor. The pain was only a dull ache, and he let it pass without even a curse.

Octavio counted the scars. "Yes, I'm correct. Today *is* my birthday. March twenty-fourth, eighteen hundred and sixty-five. Thirty-five years old, *madre Santísima!* How time is passing." He started to chuckle, but the sound from his throat soon rose to an hysterical pitch.

"Stop that hellish howling, or I'll give you reason to wail."

Octavio squinted, narrowing his sapphire blue gaze upon the bulky form of Quevera, the keeper of the keys. The man reeked of stale tequila. But Octavio's patrician nose did not turn away in disgust on this day. Aged liquor smelled much better than his own rotting flesh.

Octavio was shaken when he realized that the Mexican had opened the large creaking iron door without his having heard it. Even his jungle sense was leaving him, the sense that had helped him survive many a quick thrust from a *bandido*'s blade, many a thundering hoof in the arena.

He waved his chained arm in a grand sweeping gesture. "Did you come to pay Don Octavio Diego Cordoba his birthday respects? Let's see . . . thirty-five lashes with the whip is the usual, is it not? And of course, one to die on."

Quevera cursed. "Mother Mary herself must watch over you, Cordoba. Today, no lashes for your stinking flesh." He motioned for his men to enter. "Gonzales, Ortega. Unchain the bastard and take him to Ignacio."

Two Mexican guards came toward Octavio and he felt a moment of dread. Was this the day he would truly die? Had they chosen to execute him on his birthday? He could only define the outlines of their frames, his eyes having grown accustomed to the dimness of his cell.

One of the two guards spoke as he unlocked Octavio's chains. "*Madre mia*, he stinks!"

Octavio spit at him. "Swine."

The other guard jabbed him in the stomach with the butt of a rifle. "Do you wish me to tell Don Ignacio you were already dead?"

The guard drew back to hit him again, and Octavio glared at him with all the defiance and anger his imprisonment had instilled in him.

"Stop!" bellowed Quevera. "Ignacio said he must be alive. Do you wish to share this chamber with him, Ortega?"

Octavio rubbed his wrists, thankful the shackles had been released. "Yes, by all means, Ortega. What a birthday present that would be. The rats could feed on your ankles instead."

Quevera took another swig of liquor and demanded, "Take hold of him. Let's get this over with."

The two guards jerked Octavio to his feet and balanced his towering height between them. He would have been grateful for the jailer's thoughtfulness, but he realized the help was merely to prevent him from slowing down the procession. He gasped as his ankles felt the pressure of his body weight. In the past few months he had been unable to walk more than a few steps due to the shortened length of the chains.

"So!" mocked Quevera. "The great matador, Cordoba, cannot walk, can he? I would wager on the bull today, señor," he added with a cruel laugh.

Octavio swore softly at the jailer and was rewarded with a powerful slap. The jolt knocked him to his knees. His head spun. Pain pulsed in his upper lip as salty blood burned his tender flesh.

Quevera motioned to the two guards. "Pick him up." He stared at Octavio and sneered. "Another word and I'll tell Ignacio that I found you dead. Believe me, Don Cordoba, if I have to risk the governor's anger over your stinking

flesh, you will wish you were meeting El Diablo
in the ring instead."

As he passed their iron doors, his fellow
prisoners offered condolences and cheers. Some
prayed for his soul, some for his deliverance.
One braved Quevera's wrath by asking, "When
the firing squad asks for your last request, what
will you say—tequila or cigarro?"

"Neither, señor," Octavio jeered. "It will be to
aim their guns at Quevera."

A loud round of laughter echoed through the
dungeon as Octavio was led up toward the
daylight.

Octavio greeted the day like an appreciative
badger coming out of a long hibernation. The
blazing sun attacked his vision and made him
squint at the red and black spots that danced
before his eyes. Yet the heat felt good against his
skin. Warmth seeped in and thawed the chill
that had settled into his bones during his confinement.

As his eyes grew accustomed to the glare, he
glanced at the adobe structures where freedom
dwelled. Trash and animal dung littered the
roadway.

With the searing sun overhead, everyone
would be inside, either refreshing themselves at
the local cantina or taking a short siesta. The
town was the same as it had been even before
his imprisonment. He remembered well that
Nogales in midafternoon was always one of the

hottest settlements in the sun-baked Sonora desert.

Octavio winced inwardly as his bare feet trod the graveled sand of the earthen street. His swollen soles tore with every step, yet he would not permit an audible sign of pain. If he'd learned one thing in this hellish place, it was that only honor and pride had saved his sanity. He would die in front of the firing squad with a sneer on his lips, his head held high. Maximilian's wolves would long remember Don Octavio Diego Cordoba.

The small procession moved away from the impoverished section of the city and headed toward the office of Sonora's district governor.

Octavio breathed a sigh of relief as his feet left the heat of the sand and met the wooden steps that led up to the governor's office. The wood felt cooler to the touch, but he hoped the governor would not make him wait outside, as was his usual custom with prisoners. Even the cool planks did little to lessen the pain of his injuries.

The procession came to a halt. Octavio noted the guards stationed at either side of the entryway to the whitewashed adobe structure. Their crossed rifles barred the entrance.

"Prisoner Cordoba and Sergeant Quevera to see the governor," Quevera announced. "I have orders."

One of the guards examined Quevera's papers. "All is in order, Sergeant. You and the prisoner may enter."

*     *     *

Don Ignacio's massive office was elegantly furnished. The chairs were made of polished mesquite. Richly stained cowhide upholstered the
furniture. Palm-fiber lampshades gave the room
a mellow-toned light. The brick tile floor and
hearth were waxed to a deep tobacco brown.

Octavio took a long, estimating look at the
faces of the three men seated in the office. Don
Ignacio sat in the oversize chair behind a mahogany desk. He looks like the same three-chinned,
bald, mustached pig I saw last summer, Octavio
thought as he eyed the governor. A shame he
hasn't eaten the slop I've had to. The official was
dressed in full regalia, including the governor's
sash that slanted proudly across his broad chest.

Octavio's attention turned with interest to the
gigantic red-haired American and the barrel-
chested Oriental who sat on the other side of
Don Ignacio's desk. Ignacio would not have
gone to so much trouble about his appearance
unless the strangers were worth impressing.
Were they here to witness his death, and if so,
why?

The American turned his hazel eyes on Octavio. The pupils did not flicker, the lids unblinking. Octavio felt as if every pore of his being
were being searched. The redhead was the largest man he had ever seen in his entire life. The
massive shoulders reminded him of the bulls he
had met in the arena. The man's powerful
muscles rippled as he breathed. And that hair!

That hair looked like Guadalupe Peak spitting fireballs into the heavens!

When the giant spoke, his voice was a deep rumble. "Is this him?" he asked skeptically.

Ignacio beckoned Octavio closer. "Yes, Señor McCandless. This is Don Octavio Diego Cordoba."

"He's thinner than you said," McCandless continued. "And what's all that blood on his feet? You said he'd be healthy."

Octavio bowed gallantly. "I beg your forgiveness, señor, but I hurried here without my bath."

Quevera poked the rifle in Octavio's side and warned, "Shut up or you *will* see the firing squad before the day is through."

"Let him sit," the giant commanded. "He looks as if he might fall any second."

Quevera nudged Octavio toward a chair, and he sat. At last! To sit in a real chair. His feet throbbed with relief. He looked at McCandless and said, "*Gracias*, señor."

Ignacio told Quevera to leave, but the keeper of the keys protested.

Octavio smiled. "It's all right, amigo. I will not share your secrets with just anyone. Only the rodents, and perhaps my favorite roach, Angelita."

Quevera's curses were audible as the guards prodded him through the doorway.

"Well, it looks like a sense of humor is all the man has left. Are you sure there's no better?"

Ignacio's forehead wrinkled into a scowl. "I wish there were better, Señor McCandless. But he is the only one of proper family, as you requested. Most titled gentlemen do not end in La Carsel. But this one is bad. Maximiliano himself had him locked away. And if the emperor learns what I have done, I may be the next to enter that hellish place." He paused as if he were reconsidering something. "Do you have the gold?" he asked.

McCandless lifted one bundle and set it on the rawhide table. "It's all there. Count it if you wish. But first, have you asked him?"

Ignacio ignored Octavio, as if he were an inanimate object incapable of hearing the discussion about himself. "I knew he would accept. However, I thought he would understand the offer better if it came from you, señor."

Octavio was puzzled by the conversation. A decision had been made about him, but he wasn't about to let the American think he was so weak he would agree to anything. "Excuse me, gentlemen, but just what is it I'm supposed to be asked?"

McCandless stood. He's almost a head taller than me, thought Octavio, and I am taller than most.

McCandless's presence commanded respect, if not awe. The redhead took a cigarro out of the rawhide container on the governor's desk. He offered it to Octavio, who nodded his acceptance. The American lit the cigarro, then took one for himself.

"*Gracias.*" Octavio inhaled deeply and savored the cool taste of tobacco. But his enjoyment was short-lived. His stomach seemed to roll forward, then up. Blue and gold sparks danced before his eyes, making his head swim. Still, the nicotine tasted good enough to make his mouth water. He took a second, shorter puff and felt his long-denied body start to relax.

"I am Thorne McCandless, owner of the Circle-Shamrock Ranch in the Gadsden territory. You may or may not have heard of me."

Octavio had heard of a McCandless who ruled the Arizona territory with an iron fist. Even the great Chiricahua Cochise was said to revere him. Octavio gave a nod of recognition.

Thorne continued, "So you have, have you? Whatever you've heard, I'm a fair man. I'll need your word as a gentleman to the agreement, or I'll go elsewhere."

"And what agreement is that, señor?"

"If you marry my pregnant daughter, give her child a name, and stay with her until a few months after the wee one is born, you have bought your freedom. You can go at the end of a year. Do you agree?"

Octavio looked hard at Thorne. Certainly Mc-Candless must know he would risk exposure by giving his name to the Irishman's daughter and grandchild. "Mexico will have been told I have died," he reminded.

"Should the authorities discover the truth, you will be beyond their jurisdiction," Thorne assured him. "Until your year is completed and you return to your homeland."

Being out of prison under honorable circumstances was more important than the danger it posed. This was better luck than he thought possible. At last! A way to get out of this stinking hellhole. A way to get out and help Juárez overthrow Napoleon's nursemaid, Maximilian. But then . . .

To marry an American full with child, he would have to give up his holiest of obligations to the Church. He could not later enjoy a sanctified union to the woman he chose to love. Could he give up his rights to a holy marriage just to be free?

Yes! He could never serve the Juárist cause from La Carsel. He must take this opportunity the Holy Mother offered him. His personal happiness would always be less important than the happiness of the Mexican people.

Octavio rose to his full height. "You may be making a poor bargain, señor. I'm afraid my last owners cared little for the upkeep of their property."

Ignacio gave an indignant grunt.

Octavio stared at the governor until the obese man lowered his eyelids. His fat cheeks blushed with vexation. "I'm curious, Ignacio. What is it *you* gain from all this? How will you explain my whereabouts?"

The governor's three chins lifted as the mustached lips blew out a ring of smoke. "I will replace you with the body of one of your compadres and say that you died of the plague. And, of course, Señor McCandless has paid well for my services."

"Quevera?"

"He will be paid well also."

"And if I refuse?"

Ignacio smiled. "Then you will make a meal for the buzzards, señor."

Though Octavio despised the thought of Ignacio and Quevera making money from the deal, fate had given him a chance at freedom. He would have to wait several more months to be really free, but at least he could walk in the sun and breathe clean air. After that he could devote himself fully to his beloved Mexico. "We have a deal, señor."

Thorne offered a massive hand and Octavio grasped it firmly. He knew he'd lost much of his strength in the last few months of confinement, but he was determined to match the power of his future father-in-law's handshake.

Octavio decided then and there that he trusted the giant, although he wondered why he felt so inclined. "I do have a few questions."

Thorne released his hand. "No more than I, Cordoba. But like you, I will only answer those I care to."

Honest enough, thought Octavio.

Thorne turned to the Oriental man who had remained silent and seated. "Book, see that Señor Cordoba is prepared for the wedding."

The man called Book stood. Octavio examined the unusual man closely. His short yet powerful frame was covered by a gray tunic with long curving sleeves and a black sash at the waist. His bulky gray trousers struck him at midcalf. Oddly, the man's feet were bare. Octavio knew of no one who chose to go without shoes. Could this man be a slave?

No, he decided. Book could not be a slave.

And yet there was a bond between the strangers he could not define.

Book spoke. "I'll take him to the doctor first."

Thorne protested, but the Oriental held his ground. "The doctor first."

Thorne turned to Octavio. "Señor Cordoba, this is Book, my top hand at the Circle-Shamrock."

Octavio bowed low.

The Asian returned the compliment. "I, too, am honored."

"We need to get on our way," Thorne interrupted. "You can get acquainted later." He nodded curtly to Ignacio. "Take your gold and get out. I'll let your guards know when we're finished."

Ignacio started to protest but thought better of it. With as much dignity as he could muster, he hefted the bag of gold and left the office.

After the door shut behind the governor, Octavio stared at Thorne McCandless. The Irishman was indeed someone to reckon with, if he could get the vain Ignacio to leave the stately surroundings of his own office.

Octavio's attention turned to Book. The Oriental stood, arms folded across a broad chest. He looked like a short mountain overshadowed only by Thorne. Octavio waited.

Thorne waved one powerful arm toward the chair. "Please sit. I appreciate the gesture, but I'll be needing a bridegroom able to stand up to marry my daughter. So sit."

Octavio sat.

Thorne lowered himself to the edge of the

rawhide desk. "First of all, the governor's told me most of your background. I know you were arrested for trying to assassinate Maximilian."

Octavio could not conceal his surprise.

Thorne continued. "There's no love lost between Maximilian and myself, Cordoba. I don't like a French dictator putting an Austrian puppet over Mexican people. It reminds me of the damned Tories and my beloved Ireland."

Octavio's respect for the American grew. "What will you expect of me during this year, señor? I would like to know the full bargain, so there will be no misunderstanding between us."

Thorne looked at Book. Octavio felt as if the Oriental had spoken, yet he had not.

Thorne glanced about the room, then headed for the far wall. Behind him, Octavio heard the soft ring of crystal and the light sound of liquid being poured. Thorne moved to Octavio's side and handed him a glass of clear liquid.

Octavio drank slowly, enjoying the bitter shock of the tequila as it slid down his throat. *Ignacio knows his liquor,* he thought.

Thorne returned to the desk and sat in the same position. He drank the shot glass of liquor. "You must marry my daughter and give her unborn child your name. I expect you will want to work for your keep, so you can help break in the horses. I don't know how much like bullfighting it is, but I expect you'll take to it."

"I enjoy hard work," Octavio replied.

Thorne nodded his approval. "Good. I will pay you the same as any other hand. My daughter Gila earns her own money, selling her cactus potions. I don't know how the lassie manages, but she won't take anything but food and a roof over her head from me." He cleared his throat. "Faith and begorra. I didn't mean to wander off like that." He brushed back a handful of flame-colored hair and continued.

"I expect you'll be wanting to know about your husbandly rights. You'll have the rights owing to you, but I'd advise a bit of caution with my Gila. She's not a fan-flicking, eye-batting lassie. She's a virago of the first order. If her fists don't get you, her tongue-lashing will. Another word of caution. Book is very fond of the lassie. He doesn't take kindly to anyone annoying her."

Octavio looked at Book. The Asian's stony face assured him that Thorne spoke the truth. "I am not a woman beater," Octavio replied.

Thorne nodded. "Good. I expect you to consummate the marriage, Cordoba. I feel you to be an honest man, and I think you wouldn't lie to me about the consummation." His hazel eyes twinkled. "But I know my own daughter, and she will fight like a she-bear to keep you from taking your husbandly rights. So I insist that Book witness the act."

Octavio felt the shock register in his eyes. He thought he saw the same in the Asian's as well.

"Oh, I don't mean she has to know he's there," Thorne continued. "Listening will be all Book has to do."

Octavio sensed an undercurrent of rage passing between the two men. Book would make Juárez a fine compadre in battle, he decided.

Though he obviously disagrees, he holds his counsel. His admiration for the Oriental grew.

Thorne frowned. "Mind you, Cordoba, you're marrying a McCandless, and I won't have our name trampled in the ill-fame houses of the district. So practice your manly rights on Gila. If you can make her enjoy them, so much the better. But I doubt it."

Thorne chuckled. "She comes from Irish stock, and her temper shows it. She's a fighter, she is, and stubborn in the bargain. And she doesn't care much for Mexicans," he added with a challenging smile.

Octavio straightened. "I will not allow anyone to insult my homeland," he said stiffly.

"Tell her that, son. Tell her that." Thorne chuckled again. "Why don't you go with Book? He'll take you to the doctor and get you patched up and cleaned up. I'll wait for you two at Carlos's cantina."

Book moved toward the door. Octavio followed, wondering what manner of woman he was marrying. Apparently she was prejudiced, ornery, foulmouthed, and pregnant by another man. It sounded as though he had a rough year ahead of him. Had he made such a good bargain after all?

Thorne laughed out loud behind him. "You be sure to tell her not to insult Mexico, son."

The sound of the Irishman's laughter ran like a spider up Octavio's spine.

# Chapter Four

✦ ✦ ✦ ✦ ✦

GILA LIT THE oil lamp, her hands trembling with rage. "He did what!" She could not believe even Thorne would do such a thing. How could he insult her this way? How dare he! She wanted to call him everything but . . . but could not think of the right word. For once she was struck dumb.

Her awe and fear of her father, which once had simmered in youthful resentment, ignited into a full-blown blaze of hatred. Gila steadied herself as the emotion overtook her, shuddering with its ferocity. Finally the words came. She was surprised to hear herself speak with deadly calm. "I will *not* marry him!"

Gila studied Book's stoic face and waited, knowing he would offer no explanation until her temper ran its course. This time she was determined to have her way. She must. She *must!* She would fight for her very freedom: freedom to be whatever she wanted to be, no longer a puppet with man-held strings, but a successful woman of property. And for this she would battle will against will with the great Thorne McCandless.

But first she must know how Book truly felt about the marriage. "And you, did you agree to this lunacy?"

Book turned and looked at her. No emotion marred his expression. "Yes."

"Why? Because you know the whole story

now? Thorne must have told you what really happened."

"Yes. But that is not my reason."

Her fear knotted itself into despair. If Book were against Thorne she had a chance, but she could not fight them both. She stared at him, feeling as if she were standing on a canyon floor and wishing desperately to reach the top of its sheer-walled cliffs. A new dread washed over her. "The property?"

Book folded his arms across his broad chest and nodded.

Gila sank onto the edge of the bed, rubbing one eyebrow in irritation. "Damn him! He has no right, Booker. It's *my* life! It's *my* right to pick and choose who I marry. All he's worried about is the God-Almighty McCandless name."

Book reached out gently and lifted her chin. She tried to avoid the intensity of his gaze, but she'd never been able to hide the depth of her feelings from him and now was no different. "He does this for you."

She pushed his hand away and rose. "Thorne does nothing unless he himself benefits from it. He just doesn't want anything to ruin his reputation, that's all." Tears of defeat came down in steady drops.

"Do not act like a weak woman."

Gila blinked back the tears. "How can you say such a thing? You of all people!" She began to beat her fists upon his chest, pounding harder and harder until, at last, her anger weakened into despair.

Book's black gaze visibly softened as he

stroked her auburn tresses, calming her as he would a child. "Insult was not my intention, Gila. I only wished to put this rage back into you. You will not overcome Thorne's decision if you've the mind of a woman."

She flung her hands up in vexation. "Sometimes I don't understand you, Booker. Speak straight."

"I have spoken straight," he replied evenly.

Gila thought for a moment but still did not understand. She tried another argument. "What will happen when the nine months are up and there is no baby? All Thorne's plotting will be for nothing. What will he say to my husband? Sorry, I made a mistake. I *thought* she was raped by a Chiricahua?"

Concern filled Book's face. "You are certain the attacker was Apache?"

Gila nodded soberly. "Yes. When I turned to look at him, I saw a red slash on the heel of his moccasin. He was Chiricahua Apache, all right."

Book's forehead wrinkled with a frown. "This is not good. Others must not learn of this."

"Hell no! The others won't learn of it!" Gila yelled, stiffening with resentment. "I gave my word. Save the precious name, I will. But I thought you'd feel different. I thought *you'd*—"

"I am not concerned for the McCandless name, Gila. If others believe a white woman was ruined by Chiricahua, retaliations will come upon the entire tribe. Thorne has a thin-edged peace with Cochise. The Indian who attacked you was a renegade, not of Cochise's authority."

"How do you know that? You weren't there."

"Cochise does not permit his men to rape. If a captive gives herself to one of his warriors, that is different. The brave who attacked you was alone. According to Thorne, there were no signs of a war party. Apache seldom move alone. Your attacker was almost certainly renegade. You were fortunate your buffalo arrived when he did."

Gila looked at him in surprise. "The Apache didn't seem very concerned about Dublin's white hide. He didn't blink twice before he threw the flint right into Dub's shoulder."

"Do not think in haste, Gila. The sight of the white buffalo *did* save your life. The Apache acted on instinct when he heard Dublin. He must have seen the sacred omen only after he injured it."

"Now that I think of it," Gila paused, "I wondered why he looked so afraid when I whistled and Dublin moved toward me."

"Ahhh. That explains much."

"What?"

"The whistle. The whistle prevented him from finishing the deed. According to Chiricahua beliefs, a whistle calls back a ghost from the dead. When Dublin moved to answer the call, the renegade believed a spirit had entered the white buffalo and was angry about the injury. That alone saved your life. To kill the white buffalo is to bring many blessings upon the tribe, but to injure it will bring ill fortune to the hunter. You must beware the Indian's vengeance for bringing such anger among the spirits."

Gila rubbed her brow. "Hasn't he done

enough? What more can he do?'' She refused to think about it anymore and returned to the one possibility that might change Thorne's mind. "Just suppose the Indian had knocked me unconscious long enough to have raped me. Not that he did, but just suppose. I don't believe I could have been left with a child by so short a tussle, especially since I wasn't willing.''

Book reached to brush away a wisp of hair that nudged her cheek. "Ahhh, my little foolish one, so strong of will, but so weak in worldly ways. If a man's release occurs, whether a woman is willing or not, she may be with child.''

Gila felt a blush burn her cheeks and turned away in embarrassment. "But we don't have to worry about it one way or the other. He didn't touch me!''

Book reached out to steady the tremble that had begun in her shoulders. "We must do as Thorne wishes.''

"You mean as he *commands*, don't you?'' Gila jerked away. "No! I told you I wasn't unconscious. It all happened too quickly. There simply wasn't time for him to do anything.''

"And if you were unconscious and don't remember?'' Book asked calmly. "Thorne believes this to be a strong possibility.''

Gila lifted her chin defiantly. "Then it will serve Thorne right to have a bastard grandchild.''

Book turned to leave. "Now, you act as a child.''

Gila ran to him, grabbing him by the waist. "Please, Booker, please! I can't marry someone I don't know. Please don't let Thorne do this to me. If you'll talk to him. If you'll—"

"I will not intervene."

Gila felt the set of his strong back muscles, knowing he braced himself against further pleas. Angrily she released him. "Then to hell with you! To hell with you and my father. I will not go with you. I will not! You'll have to hog-tie me and drag me down there."

"Gila." He spoke her name low, but with deadly authority.

Recognizing the tone, she calmed her temper and stood quietly. Only once had he ever spoken to her in that way. It was so long ago she'd almost forgotten the day she'd sneaked into the cave and rummaged through his belongings. She had possessed an eight-year-old's natural curiosity and was more daring than cautious.

She'd found the trunk quite by accident. She and Shelly Kate were playing near the cave's entrance. They thought they heard someone coming. Shelly ran, but Gila hurried into one of the passageways that led deeper into the mountain, backing up slowly until she bumped against something hard and cold.

Stifling a scream, she turned to await the dreaded cave monster she was certain would eat her in the next moment. Instead she found a beautiful trunk. The outer surface was black and painted with various-sized lotus blossoms on the top and sides. There was no lock. When she opened the lid, the aged hinges creaked.

Gila caught her breath and listened. There was

no sound of anyone coming. She sighed with relief as indecision washed over her. She almost closed the lid, but curiosity ruled, and she began to inspect the trunk's holdings.

On top lay two gray tunics and two pairs of short britches. The next layer contained several ancient books—the very ones she had seen him read so frequently. Because of the thick tomes, she called him Book. His real name, Bukamoshi Minamoto, was much too long to say for an eight-year-old.

She would have searched no further in the trunk had she not caught sight of a withered lotus blossom and the strange saber beneath it, two feet long, the blade curved like a machete.

Gila raised the sword, paying little attention to the yellow paper that fluttered to the ground. She swished the weapon here and there, practicing swordplay. The metal was heavy and she almost lost her balance several times.

"Gila." The fierce command echoed through the cave.

She twirled around to find Book towering above her, anger clearly written on his face.

She tried to gulp down her fright and embarrassment. "Y-y-yessir."

He had scolded her unmercifully that day, lecturing her on the evils of handling others' belongings without permission. She remembered, too, the look on his face when he bent to retrieve the yellowed paper. "Did you read this?"

She had not, and she told him so, but she

could not bring herself to tell him that in one glance she had translated the Japanese symbol for assassinate.

She still had no idea what the paper meant, but she had never forgotten that day, or the tone of Book's voice. It still had the power to silence her into respect.

Now he repeated her name in a more gentle tone. "Gila. You know I will let no harm come to you. And you know Thorne's mind is set. If the man brings you heartache, I will squeeze the life from him with these hands."

Defeated, Gila stared at the planked floor. *Saint Peter preserve me!* She suddenly relaxed as she noticed that Book's toes were curling upward. Book's still on my side, she thought. His only outward show of emotion was the way his toes curled when he was unhappy. She doubted even he knew of the indiscretion, for he was a stern practitioner of *Bushido*—the discipline that demanded total indifference to emotion.

The sign convinced Gila she must concede to the plan. Perhaps later Book would help her devise a plan to shorten the term of her "marriage." But for now, she would have to be very careful, very cunning, if she were to keep her beloved property. "All right. Go get the outlaw, I'll marry him."

# Chapter Five

♦ ♦ ♦ ♦ ♦

GILA FINISHED OFF the last of the tequila and felt the warm blush of it spread across her cheeks. She flopped down on the bed and swore for the thousandth time that day, "Damn you, Thorne McCandless."

The yellow-lace ruffles of her wedding gown swished with every motion. She reached up and scratched between her bosom. "Damned rash, anyway. Gotta get married and suffer with this all at the same time."

She tugged at the lace that formed a modest barrier across her breasts, then sat upright and looked around the room, searching. A red bandanna lay on the table beside the bed, and she grabbed it, then tucked it between her cleavage.

Gila stared down at the leather boots sticking out under the layers of petticoats. The boots, which she had bought to spite her father, were too large and yet more suitable than the pair of shoes she was supposed to wear. "Be hanged if I change 'em!" she spouted, glancing across the floor at the yellow deerskin slippers that completed her wedding ensemble. "Heck no. I won't wear 'em. Nobody can make me. I've got some pride left, and I'm *not* going to get married in any deer-gutted Indian moccasins."

A knock sounded on the door. "Gila. Thorne's ready."

"Oh, he is, is he now?" Gila jerked open the door with the force of her anger.

Book's gaze inspected her from head to foot. His gaze halted at her neck. "Won't you put something around your neck? Thorne sent these to help hide the wound." He lifted a necklace made of mother-of-pearl and another of turquoise and silver.

She stood and took a deep breath, steadying herself as the liquor took its toll. "Tell him no thank you. I've got just the thing to hide his shame."

She pulled the red bandanna from between her breasts and tied it around her neck. "Tell him to hold his saddle horn. I said I'd be there, and I will. I'm going to stop off at the bar and get some more tequila." She blew out the flame lighting the lamp and stumbled to the door through the darkness. "Let's get this over with."

In the cantina, Gila ordered a fresh bottle of tequila. "The best in the house, Carlos. Tonight's my wedding night, 'tis," she said in her best imitation of Thorne.

Carlos set the liquor in front of her. "On the house, Señorita McCandless. Is it anyone we know?"

Gila laughed sarcastically. "Hell no, Carlos. It's nobody *I* know."

Carlos laughed. "Ahhh, señorita, always the joker."

"We must go, Gila," Book urged. "We'll be late."

Gila saluted the cantina owner. "I mustn't keep the bridegroom waiting. He might run off." She took another swig of the clear liquid and staggered into the street. "Where're these fireworks supposed to take place, anyhow?" she asked Book. "The only church I saw is somewhere off that-a-way." She pointed in the opposite direction.

Book motioned to a lighted window ahead of them. "We go there."

"Not even a church, eh?"

They crossed the distance and entered one of the many pottery shops lining the main street of Nogales. Gila felt a nervousness begin to settle into her stomach. She had not eaten earlier and shrugged off the weakness as the effects of liquor on an empty belly. Too late to worry about it now, she mused and took another drink.

Book looked at her, a frown creasing his massive forehead. "Inebriation will not delay your destiny."

Gila sneered. "No, but it sure as hell will put a burr under Thorne's saddle, won't it? Which is nothing compared to what he's putting under mine."

Thorne stood in the dimly lit hallway. "What kind of foolery is this, Book? I thought you said she bought a fittin' dress."

Gila looked down at herself. She must look quite something in her yellow lace and ruffles, red bandanna, and oversize boots. "This is a fittin' dress. Fittin' enough for a *ruined* McCandless. Yellow 'cause I'm too yellow to give up my property. And by the way, I want all that in writing. I don't plan on being lassoed by you again."

"I gave you my word, lassie. That's enough."

She stared him straight in the eye. "Not for me it isn't." She figured he would hit her, but he didn't.

Thorne stood there a few moments, his jaw stretched tight with anger. Then he pulled a document from his shirt pocket and announced, "I knew you'd ask for the title."

Gila snatched it and held it close, squinting to control her half-drunken vision. She was able to decipher ONE THOUSAND ACRES, NORTHERN BORDER, CIRCLE-SHAMROCK RANCH, TERRITORY OF ARIZONA. At last! The giant saguaros finally belonged to her, only her!

Satisfied, Gila announced, "All right. I'm ready." Thorne offered his arm, but she declined. "I want Booker to give me away. You're *selling* me." She watched both men's expressions and saw anger rising in her father's face.

Thorne cursed. "Have your headstrong way, lassie. In the morning, you'll belong to a husband, and before this night is over you'll be gentled a notch or two, I expect."

"Like hell I will!" She grabbed Book by the elbow and marched forward. But when she entered the potter's living quarters, her bravado slackened. Thorne stomped across the room and disappeared into a corridor. Candles offered the only light, giving the scene an eerie haze.

An old Mexican couple stood next to the fireplace. The man clutched his sombrero and bowed. The woman nodded solemnly, her features veiled behind black lace.

"Who are they?" Gila whispered, then realized the clandestine atmosphere had urged her lower tone.

"Witnesses to the marriage," Book explained.

Gila felt embarrassed for a moment, hating that anyone would view the ridiculous affair. But then why should she care? Thorne had probably paid them well for their services.

Thorne stepped through the archway, followed by a priest. Her father motioned to someone in the hallway. "It's time, son."

A tall, gaunt man moved into the light. His black shaggy hair fell to wiry shoulders. In the flickering candlelight his skin had a sickish pallor. He was dressed in what looked to be one of Book's tunics and a pair of britches.

Gila took in the sight of her future groom and was aghast. His feet and ankles were bare and bandaged. A pungent smell emanated from his direction. She took a deep breath. What was it? Coal oil?

The ghostly flickers of candlelight made it hard to make out his features. She could discern dark eyebrows that stretched above a large nose. And those eyes! Blue, like the depths of the clear mountain springs that pooled into the Aravaipa and snaked their way toward the mighty Colorado River. Despite those intriguing depths of sapphire, the man's unhealthy condition promised nothing as a bridegroom other than someone to test her cactus cures on. "Are you two plumb loco? Couldn't you choose someone a little more healthy looking?"

Her intended bowed. "And *buenas noches* to you, too, Señorita McCandless."

Gila could not believe what she'd heard. Revulsion ran up her throat and sharpened the edge of her tongue. "A *Mexican!* You plan to marry me off to a Mexican!?"

Thorne chuckled.

Book started to speak but was interrupted by the bridegroom. He lifted his head proudly, nostrils flaring below an icy-cold stare. "Don Octavio Diego Cordoba, at your service."

"Hah!" Gila said and took another swig of tequila. "Move into the light," she commanded drunkenly. "Or are you afraid to face your bride?"

Octavio's jaw stiffened with resentment, but he bowed gallantly. "Why, of course, *dulce mia.* Whatever you wish. I will gladly show the goods your father has bought you."

Gila felt the slap of his words. "Arrogant bastard, aren't you?"

Octavio only shrugged and Gila's anger mounted. The nerve of the man! Just who did he think he was? She looked at Book, hoping the samurai would set the insolent beggar straight. But one glance told her she was sorely mistaken. She caught the glint of merriment twinkling in Book's eyes. He was laughing at her! She looked to Thorne and then back at Book. They were both grinning. "Well, I'm real happy you think this is so gall-darn funny."

She glared hatefully at Octavio, allowing the full extent of her anger to focus on her bridegroom. "I'll make you earn every cent he paid you."

Octavio cocked his head coyly. "Only that much, eh? You act as if you're worth more."

"Sweet Mary McDonough," Thorne said as he slapped his knee. "If you aren't a match for my lassie after all!"

Gila hated the look of smug satisfaction upon Thorne's face. She moved toward Octavio with a vengeance, drawing back the bottle, ready to strike. "Why you . . . I'll—"

"You'll not do a thing, lassie," warned Thorne as he blocked the blow with an ironlike grip. Liquor splattered his face and clothes, making him curse. " 'Tis the land you'll be forsakin'."

Her hand dropped slowly to her side. She stared at Thorne in stony silence. Moments passed as she allowed the tide of rage to settle into a dull undertow of bitterness. She spoke in a mocking tone, but with determination. "You've won this one, Thorne, but you'd better be watching from here on in. I'll have the last say. You can bet on it."

Gila took another drink, then looked disdainfully at Octavio. "What's my new name, Mexican?"

Octavio repeated his title.

"Well, come on October, let's get this over with." She raised her bottle in salute and drank the rest of the liquor down. "Viva tequila!" she shouted and threw the bottle against the flagstone wall.

The solemn ceremony began. The padre's monotone echoed in the background of Octavio's mind as he mulled over the day's events.

He couldn't believe his eyes. He had never seen anyone quite like his bride. Her rebellious auburn hair looked as if it had been combed with a cactus. Her cheeks were blushed from the effects of the tequila rather than any female deliberation, and the whites surrounding her hazel eyes were redder than her cheeks.

She was definitely not pretty, but there was something striking about her. All that wildness and yet something innocent, too. Possibly it was the dimple in her left cheek. Yes, that's what it was. It made her look like the angel adorning the arch of Our Lady of Guadalupe mission in Madera.

Then he looked down and noticed the leather boots sticking out from under the yellow lace ruffles. *Madre Santísima!* The Apache would see her coming for miles, such big *zapatos*. Was there nothing small about her? He had never seen such large feet!

Yet Fate had not totally disfavored this McCandless woman. Destiny had seen fit to give his unorthodox bride a pair of breasts that any man, woman, or infant would be grateful for.

Gila felt his eyes on her breasts. "Don't get any funny ideas, October," she warned.

The padre looked at her in surprise and stopped his prayers.

Octavio leaned close and whispered, "We shall see, *dulce mia*. What was once yours is now mine."

Gila gave him a resounding kick in the shin with the tip of her boot. "Next time I'll kick a little higher. *Comprende?*"

His leg throbbed so badly that he reached down to massage it. The next thing he felt was a swift kick to the seat of his britches, which sent him sprawling. With little care for his bandaged feet or throbbing leg, Octavio jumped up and grabbed her violently, crushing her to him. "Do not make a fool of me, *dulce mia*, for I too can play the game."

Gila glared at him defiantly. "I'm not afraid of you or anything you think you can do. Book will break you into tiny pieces if you hurt me."

True to her word, Book had moved closer to her, his every muscle at the ready.

Gila laughed. "See. What did I tell you."

Once again Book spoke her name in the low, deadly tone. "Gila. Do not act like a heathen. Cordoba will be your husband. Treat him as such. Do not disgrace yourself."

"But he's a damn Mexican!"

"As I am a damn Japanese," Book said calmly. "Does that make me less human than you? Can any race or country claim superiority to another?"

Gila hated Octavio at that moment, hated him for being Mexican—a long-standing hatred that came from the death of her mother. Mexicans had killed her. She hated him for the memory he evoked.

Thorne and Book had been off herding horses the day her mother died. They'd thought the McCandless home was impenetrable, having been dug into the side of the mountain. But Mexicans had found a weak spot—the kitchen chimneys. They'd shimmied down and begun to ransack the house. Hearing the commotion, Kathryn had acted upon instinct. She'd hurried the three-year-old Gila into the bathing chamber and told her to not let anyone else in.

"I'll bar the door behind me," her mother had said. "Now, hurry! And no matter what you hear, don't cry, don't scream. Don't let anyone know you're here except your father, Book, or me. If Shelly starts to cry, cover her mouth with this." Kathryn placed a portion of the swaddling blanket in Gila's pudgy hands and showed her how to cover the baby's face properly. "Not too hard or you'll smother her. Just enough so no one can hear her. Do you understand?"

Gila hadn't understood all that took place that day, only that her mother had died two days later from the awful things those Mexicans had done. Hatred toward the Mexican people had raged within her ever since.

Now that same ill will made her seem prejudiced against anyone who was different, even her beloved Book. But she loved Book. She never judged him inferior, never thought of him as belonging to another race. He was simply Book.

Octavio's eyes flashed blue fire. "I do not wish to harm you, señorita, but I will not be treated as an animal."

Thorne ordered the padre to finish the ceremony. "Let's be done with this and get to bed. Tomorrow we ride to Tucson."

\*   \*   \*

When the padre pronounced them man and wife, Octavio pulled Gila close and slowly untied the red bandanna from around her neck. To him it was a symbol of her defiance of their marriage and he wanted to remove it. But he was shocked to find that the red cloth covered a nasty wound, jagged and sloppily stitched.

Gila trembled, yet the shiver did not seem to stem from the anger. She was frightened! Why this sudden knowledge should make him feel protective of her, Octavio was uncertain. Yet it did.

"Make it legal, Cordoba," Thorne ordered. "Remember your end of the bargain."

His bride swayed against him drunkenly. Octavio caught her in his arms, then bent and kissed her fully.

His touch brought Gila to her senses. She tried to break the embrace, struggling to free herself. As the kiss intensified, she grew rigid with fright. His body arched closer to hers, and she felt the first hint of his desire.

A spoiled child, he thought. Obstinate. Ill-tempered. Innocent. Had she played a woman's game and gotten into trouble? If so, drunkenness would not solve the problem. Long-forgotten sensations pulsed through Octavio. It had been so long since he'd tasted the sweetness of a woman's lips. The tequila she'd drunk added a salty taste to hers. The contrast in tastes was like the contrasts in his bride. So womanish, yet so childish.

Gila grew rigid, her hazel eyes widening. "No!

No! Don't touch me," she screamed, lashing out at him.

Octavio grabbed her flailing fists, barely able to control the insane pounding on his chest. Her scream died to uncontrollable whimpers. He backed her toward the potter's worktable, resisting her struggles. She clung to him in desperation. He smoothed the tangle of her hair, petting her as he would have a two-year-old child.

The trembling faded. Still she clung. Within moments Gila's breath became even. Octavio curved a finger beneath her chin and gently lifted her face. To his amazement, she'd fallen asleep.

Octavio faltered with each step as they headed to the cantina. Why had Gila screamed? Was she truly asleep or had she passed out from the liquor? Whichever, she felt as if she weighed as much as a year-old buffalo. He struggled to shift her to a better position and almost fell to his knees.

Book took Gila from Octavio's arms. "I will carry her." The Oriental slung her up over a massive shoulder as if she were a flour sack.

Octavio stretched. Her weight had borne heavily upon his injuries, and he felt the warm blood ooze through the bandages.

Thorne came up beside him. "You won't be forgetting the consummation, will you, son? It must be legal and binding."

Octavio sighed irritably. He was tired of being

reminded so often. "I have not forgotten, señor."

Thorne thrust a bag of coins into Octavio's hand. "A wedding dowry. It wasn't part of the bargain, laddie, but you'll need money to throw around with your title, or the locals will be suspicious. There's more where that came from. You can pay me back by taming the lassie."

Octavio stumbled to an abrupt halt. "Señor McCandless, I come from a wealthy family. I, too, have my own fortune. When the year is over, or if I can contact my father sooner, every cent will be repaid. This I swear. Until then, I will work as hard as any of the others for my room and board."

Thorne slapped him good-naturedly on the shoulder, almost knocking him off his injured feet. "Son, you'll work the hardest, 'tis for sure. 'Tis *your* wife she is and no other's." His hearty laughter echoed down the silent streets.

When they reached the cantina, Octavio was led upstairs and into a small room. A lamp had been lit. Gila lay sprawled across the bed, whether asleep or unconscious he was uncertain. He glanced about the sparse room. She wasn't the frivolous sort, that was certain. There was no baggage, only a war bag. No vanity jars, parasols, or frilly dresses. A well-worn pair of nankeen britches, a white linen shirt, and a sombrero graced one corner post.

Octavio wondered if the hat were hers. Perhaps it was a clue to her deep hatred for Mexicans. Was her baby's father some caballero who had wandered in and out of her life, leaving only his hat and his seed as reminders of their passion for one another?

"We set out early in the morning, son," Thorne reminded. "Don't be keeping her up too late." He took another look at Gila and shrugged, then held out a massive hand toward Octavio. "The saints be with you, October. I like the lassie's name for you, if you have no objections."

Octavio nodded in agreement. His name was of little matter. He was going to a strange place, with a strange woman, under even stranger circumstances. It was only fitting his name be equally so.

Thorne and Book prepared to leave. "Book will be stationed outside the door."

Octavio bowed with a sweeping gesture of one hand. "I will do my utmost to provide the necessary confirmation, señor."

The door closed behind the two men. Octavio glanced at his wife and shuddered. The wound on her neck was most certainly recent, for it was swollen and red. Who or what had done such a thing to her? And why?

For a moment Octavio allowed himself to think of Modesta. His beautiful Modesta! Never again would he touch the silkiness of her ebony tresses or smell the sweet fragrance of honeysuckle that clung to her golden skin. No more would he feel the curve of her petite hips beneath his fingertips as they danced or taste the dewy lips beneath his.

With determination, Octavio shook off his

regret. Modesta was lost to him forever. The price he had paid was high, but well worth it. If he could hold to his end of the bargain for the next several months, then Mexico might be saved. Juárez would thrive and win!

Octavio leaned over the bed and bent to kiss Gila's pouty, heart-shaped lip. Gila snored loudly and turned over. *"Madre Santísima!"* He retreated to the dresser where he noticed a pitcher of water, washbowl, and fresh towels. "At least someone has manners," he muttered, giving Gila a look of reproval.

Octavio stripped carefully. The tunic and britches were clinging to wounds that had continued to ooze. He eased into a hard wooden chair and began to unbandage and wash his feet. His dirt-caked soles throbbed with each cleaning stroke.

Octavio glanced about for liniment and found none. He reached up and rubbed his hair briskly, then stroked the bottom of each foot. If coal oil could kill lice, then it would probably do the same for infection, he decided.

Octavio continued his grooming, savoring the cleanliness that had been denied him for eight months. When he was finished, he threw the filthy water out the opened window. The splash was followed by the yapping of an indignant dog. He leaned out, staring into the darkness below. "Forgive me, *perro*." He did not wish to inflict injustice upon another innocent soul, especially so soon after his own release from such cruelty.

Octavio stood tall and stretched his long, wiry

frame. Placing his palms around to midspine, he bent forward as far as possible and felt his aching joints groan their relief. Then he straightened and walked a few steps to the mirror that hung above the dressing table. He gave himself a long, appraising look.

He'd grown thin during his confinement, not so much from undernourishment as from lack of exercise. The prison gruel had provided him with enough stamina to remain alive, but the dirt from the earthen walls provided more. He knew his family would be horrified to know he had eaten dirt, but it was true. One of Juárez's best lessons in survival concerned the life-sustaining minerals found in the earth. It was one of the many secrets Mexico's greatest nationalist had taught him, and for this, Octavio owed Benito Juárez his life.

Gila's snoring interrupted his cogitations. "Contain yourself, *dulce mia*," he jeered. "It will not be long."

While in prison he had often wondered if his manly thirst had been taken from him. Earlier tonight he had been surprised at his unsolicited response. Evidently his fear was unfounded.

Octavio studied himself closely. Prison had not beaten him, he thought with pride. A few weeks of ranch work and some time in the sun would revitalize his sallowed skin and bring the tone back to his muscles. He stared down at the gruesome scars that lined both thighs. For the first time, he regretted the manner in which he had kept track of the term of his imprisonment. "I have ruined my own body because of Maximilian." He shook his fist high into the air and swore, "I shall not rest until your body lies heaped at the end of a firing squad and Juárez rules from your throne. I swear this!"

Gila's eyes parted, her vision distorted. She felt her clothes slip over her head; the coolness of nudity made her shiver. She closed her eyes once again and drifted into the numbing pleasure of liquored sleep.

She dreamed of a tall, dark lover kissing her ever so gently. "You love me?" he asked.

She threw her arms around him and returned the kiss, the answer more certain than if she'd spoken.

He caressed her, his hands exploring wildly. She moaned in delighted agony as his blistering mouth set hers afire.

Gila stirred in the cool depths of the linen sheets as the dream became more vivid. She felt the thrust of her lover's intentions and was suddenly, purposefully, awake. She tried desperately to steady her mind as alarm coursed through her. This was not a dream! What was happening?

She struggled to get away. "Get off me. Get off!"

"That's it, *dulce mia*," Octavio whispered as he moved slowly above her. "Tell the world I make you mine." He braced her hands with his own.

She bit him.

His curse was loud, his passions halted for the moment. "So you do not wish to allow me husbandly rights?" he asked, pinching one of the rosy pinnacles at her breasts.

A different type of gasp escaped Gila and she found it was both pleasurable and infuriating at the same time. "I d-damn sure don't! Isn't it bad enough to have your name? I don't want you, too." Oh, why had she drunk so much? She should have been prepared for this. He was just a crude, lusting Mexican.

Yet the lazy, hot circle he was tracing with his fingertip sent a shiver of pleasure to the pit of her belly and Gila felt a curious tightening there. Was her loose hold upon her will the result of too much tequila?

"You may not like it, but you are mine, Señorita McCandless."

She could not contradict him. What difference did it make? He would be gone in the morning. Gila wanted to feel cold and somehow apart from the room, the man whose body claimed hers in the most intimate possession, yet she couldn't. Perhaps if she kept talking, she would bore him, and he would hurry. "I am Señora Cordoba now, remember? And if you would be so kind as to remove yourself, Señor Cordoba. Your hair smells like buffalo chips." She struggled again but fell back in frustration.

Gila became angrier by the moment. She was tired of being used. First by Garrett, now a Mexican husband. "Get off me, now!"

*I only wish to put the rage back into you.* Book's voice echoed from her memory.

"Scream all you like." Octavio nodded in the

direction of the door. "We have an audience, *dulce mia*."

Gila stiffened and craned her ears. Sure enough, there was a slight creaking of boards as the eavesdropper shifted positions.

It was all she could do to keep from screaming, but she managed a crisp, "Who would dare?"

Octavio's tone lowered. "Thorne stationed someone outside to hear our consummation."

Gila could not contain her disgust. "Oh, he did, did he?" She struggled once again to get up. "I'll show him . . . ooohh." Her head fell back against the pillow.

Octavio placed a finger against her lips. "Sshh. You'll do nothing. In the first place, you're far too drunk. And in the second, we must finish the act or you will not receive your beloved property."

"You know about that?"

Octavio nodded and she was given full view of the sharp contours of his face. He was more handsome than the candlelight had suggested. "My end of the bargain is to complete the marriage, so your baby will have a 'true' father, as the Irish chieftain dictates."

Gila felt the blush rising in her cheeks, uncertain if it was from rage, embarrassment, or the tequila. Stubborn pride kept her from telling him there was no baby. "Is this why the witness is outside the door?" she asked.

Again Octavio nodded.

Gila trembled. Witness to the consummation? This was the lowest form of ridicule from her

father. Father? What kind of father did such a
thing?

Gila recalled the old man and woman who
witnessed the wedding and assumed they stood
in the hallway. They would never see her again,
nor she them. Why should she worry? Why not
make an elaborate joke of this whole situation
and be done with it?

A joke? A deep sadness washed over Gila as
she realized that her decision brought an end to
the fairy-tale dreams of a knight in white armor
swooping down to carry her off to the rapturous
world of lovers' ecstasy. To men sex was like
washing their faces, or combing their hair. They
had to do it once in a while to be considered
normal. "You'll have to show me how," Gila
whispered in a low voice.

The surprise registered in his face. "The baby's
father did not show you? You did not enjoy?"

The accuracy of his question sharpened her
tongue. The time with Garrett had been a quick,
clumsy fumble. "I'm sure all men are not as
good at this as you think you are."

Octavio began to caress her with his lips, his
body moving seductively against hers. He whispered huskily in her ear. "Then, *dulce mia*, I must
show you that I am the best."

His arrogance strengthened her determination
to withstand his tantalizing attack on her senses,
but she realized within moments that there was
one undeniable truth. He knew exactly what he
was doing.

Every place his lips touched, her flesh burned

with a heat greater than the hottest day of July. The slow circular motions of his hands sent tiny shivers of delight up her spine.

She felt dizzy, uncertain if it were due to the liquor or the headiness brought about by his exploring hands. She sought to steady herself and reached up and found the sinewy muscles of his back. He released the rosy peak of one breast, then made a similar assault upon the other. Gently yet urgently he began to carve out his possession.

As in all things in her life, Gila learned quickly. Her ears rang with the passion-filled moment, and she tried to restore some semblance of sanity. October was taking control of her senses, of her entire being. Trying desperately not to reveal the passion that coursed through her veins, she blurted out, "Let's give them something to remember."

Octavio chuckled, and Gila wondered if she had sounded as carefree as she had intended. What manner of woman was she? Had she lost her mind? No, insanity could not make her feel as free as she did at this very moment. Even her wildest dreams could not have prepared her for the ecstasy she felt in Octavio's arms. As her desire mounted to its peak, her last virtuous thought was of Book. What would he say if he could see her now? Unable to control herself, she cried out the confirmation the witness had waited for.

\* \* \*

A soft, steady rapping woke Gila from a hazy dream. Outside the closed door Book's voice ordered, "Gila. Time to get up. We ride out in an hour."

She yawned and rubbed the sleep from her eyes. "Do I have to?" She rolled over and snuggled deeper into the bed covers. Her palm came to rest on the warm flesh beside her. She bolted upright, startled into alertness.

Octavio chuckled. "Even witnesses must sleep, my sweet. But if you wish, I'll be happy to wake them."

As he turned toward her, Gila hastily pulled up the covers. She looked into his blue eyes and felt her hatred for Mexicans rise up sharply. "That won't be necessary."

Octavio propped his head on one arm, his elbow resting against the pillow. He reached over and playfully teased a breast, sending Gila into flight. She scrambled to her feet, untangling Octavio from the quilted folds that covered his nudity. In her haste, she accidentally flipped him off the bed.

He landed with a thud. "Control yourself, wife! Do you mean to level all of Nogales!" He stood, limped over to the chair, and picked up his clothes.

Just who did he think he was talking to? She started to yell at him but couldn't. His painful limp caught her attention. She looked closer, her gaze traveling his full length. It was all she could do to forget last night's ecstasy in those arms— arms she hated with every fiber of her being.

Yet the sight of the terrible scars on the

Mexican's inner thighs had touched an unbiased curiosity—and a sympathy that came from years of tending wounded animals and people with her cactus remedies. Gila cleared her throat, shamefully aware of the husky tone. "What's wrong with your legs?" she asked as she waited impatiently for him to dress.

He gave no hint of modesty, even stopping to admire himself in the mirror. "Did you hear me? I said, what's wrong with your legs, Cordoba?"

"You would not be interested, señora."

She hurried to the bed and sat, making certain the quilt covered everything but her face. "The hell I wouldn't! I've got a right to know if you've got some disease I need to have doctored."

Octavio laughed. One eye winked as male pride sneered his lip. "You weren't worried much about it last night, *dulce mia.* You will not have to see a doctor on my account. It is an injury of the soul, nothing more."

Gila felt relief, but anger quickly settled in its place. "Last night will never happen again, I assure you. You gave me what I needed—a husband's name. And you got your freedom. I'd say we're even. I suppose one night was a small price to pay for all I've gained." Her haughty gaze defied him to request any more than what he'd already received in the bargain. "All of Thorne's conditions were met."

Octavio picked up the sombrero, walked over, and plopped it on Gila's head. "Haven't you read the contract, my sweet? You are mistaken. We have much time ahead of us together."

Gila bent and lifted one of the boots that lay at

the edge of the bed. Blood rushed to her head as
she felt the aftereffects of last night's liquor. The
room rushed in, and she had to lie back against
the pillow to steady herself. The sombrero slid
down over her face, and she brushed it aside. "I
don't know what you're talking about."

After a moment, Gila sat up slowly and shook
the boot's contents onto the bed. A money
pouch, contract, and knife fell against the covers.
She unfolded the document and read. The string
of curse words that followed would have embarrassed even a foul-mouthed ranch hand.

Gila bolted to her feet, unmindful of her own
nudity. "One year!" She was furious. That was
not part of the bargain. Just the marriage. Only
the marriage. She had assumed it would be a
one-night affair, then home to the Circle-
Shamrock.

The more she thought about Thorne's plan,
the more agitated she became. She pulled the
nankeens up to her waist and buttoned them,
then bent to put on one boot. "I suppose you
knew this last night, didn't you, Mexican?"

"The name is Octavio Diego—"

Gila finished dressing and inspected herself
in the mirror. After a few haphazard strokes
with a brush, she set it down lightly. There. She
looked her ugliest. The Mexican would rue the
day he thought marriage to her was better than
prison.

Prison. She remembered that she had not
undressed herself the night before. She spilled
the contents of her war bag out onto the bed.
There was more money in it than there should

have been. She looked at Octavio in surprise. "Where did this come from?"

Octavio rose, pulled her to him, and kissed her fiercely. Gila's resistance died in a brazen rush of desire. Even the air around them seemed charged with excitement. She pulled away, breathless.

Octavio's male pride twinkled his blue eyes. "Let's just say that's payment for services rendered, señora."

The slap came hard and fast. "Don't you ever lay a hand on me again, you Mexican. You don't have enough money to buy me."

Octavio walked to the door. "Don't worry, my sweet. The next time we make love, you will ask me. No, you will *beg* me for it."

Gila screamed her contempt as she grabbed the brush and threw it at him. She cursed Octavio's luck when it banged harmlessly against the closed door.

# Chapter Six

✦✦✦✦✦

AT DAWN THE McCandless party rode away from Nogales. Thorne took the lead, Octavio followed Gila, and Book brought up the rear. The Irishman's rendition of "Sweet Katie McCall" echoed over the Sonoran countryside.

Gila's temper was ill-turned this morning, partially from the tequila torment, but mostly from her anger at her father. "If you insist on singing, could you please try singing on key for once?"

Thorne pretended not to hear. She knew he had and was deliberately exercising his McCandless prerogative. Her head hurt enough without his bullheaded bellowing.

Octavio's horse cantered alongside Gila's. "He is your father, Gila. Be respectful."

Thorne turned halfway in the saddle and peered at them, his fiery brow arched in amusement. "By all means, daughter, be respectful."

Gila felt the flush that rose with her temper. She pointed one finger at Octavio. "Don't you ever try to tell me what to do, October! You may be my husband, but you damn sure aren't my trail boss. So the best thing for you to do is leave me be."

Octavio shrugged. "What is it to me if you act like a bad-tempered burro?"

Thorne's chuckle filtered back, pricking Gila's pride. "That's it. Take his side, why don't you?" She reined to a halt and waited for Book. Octavio rode ahead.

"Something wrong?" asked Book as he reached her.

"Nothing," she denied, nudging Wee-People into a trot alongside the Oriental's Appaloosa. She was thankful Book never demanded conversation. This morning what she needed most was time to think.

Already the sun's blazing heat attacked the

pinkish white desert sand, making it shimmer on the horizon in a scorching haze. The early spring day would be a scalder. A bead of sweat formed along Gila's hairline and trickled down her temple. Her breasts became itchy with moisture.

Even as the land baked, so Gila's anger simmered. How could she have been such a fool? She should have known there was more to the bargain than just one night. How could Thorne do such a thing to his own flesh and blood? But then, Thorne had never been a real father to her. Never. Book was more loving than Thorne had ever been.

She glanced at the Irishman and then at October. Thorne's spine was covered with patches of sweat dampening the white linen shirt. October seemed undisturbed by the heat. Don't Mexicans sweat? she wondered.

Yes. He had definitely sweated last night. Gila closed her eyes and felt her breath catch at the thought of his warm, moist skin moving rhythmically with her own to a tune of unthinkable pleasure.

Now, through barely parted eyes, she watched October. His horse's gait, the hazy atmosphere, played seductively upon her senses. She shook her head, as if to wake from a dream. The movements of horse and rider continued to seduce Gila, sending shock waves of desire through her. Her temples pulsed with unquenchable need. Her breath came in short, inaudible pauses. She felt her breasts grow taut with the want of him.

"Gila. Are you all right? You look faint." Book steadied her with one hand, concern clearly written in his black eyes.

She looked at him, not knowing how to hide her embarrassment. "I—I—I'm fine, Booker. Guess the heat's got to me." She spurred her horse away from Book.

Octavio rode toward her. "Your father wants to know what's wrong. He's going to move ahead. Is it the child?"

Gila sighed, expelling her irritation slowly. There was no child. She wished everyone would just stop talking about it. "No." She brushed back a wisp of hair. "I just got . . . overheated."

Octavio inspected her. When his gaze rested on her hardened nipples, he chuckled. With one finger he traced a line to one of the traitors. "Patience, darling."

Gila slapped his finger away. "Keep your hands to yourself. It's daylight."

Octavio reined his pinto half-quarter. "Passion doesn't know the difference between daylight and moonlight, *dulce mia*. It can happen anywhere, anytime."

"Is that a threat?"

Octavio offered a wicked smile. "No, señora. It is a fact." He left her in a cloud of dust.

"We'll see about that!" Gila choked.

Book rode up and called her name sternly, then grew quiet for a few moments. She hated it when he did that. It meant she had made him unhappy in some way. She loved him dearly, but hell, hadn't she been through enough in the last two days!

"Listen to the young man's words. You cannot control all things in life, no matter how strong-willed you are. That is the joy of discovery and the agony of grief."

The unmistakable look of utter loss distorting the Oriental features puzzled Gila. Had the massive shoulders slumped slightly or did she imagine it?

The samurai fell back to rear guard. Gila did not wait for him. He had betrayed emotion to her and needed to be alone. She had never seen him grief-stricken and wondered what had brought on this uncharacteristic lapse. But then she knew so little about him.

Book had been her mother's servant for many years. She remembered Thorne saying that Book had been a gift to Kathryn from her father. Because Thorne was away from home so often, fighting with the Young Irelanders, Kathryn's father worried about her. Times were dangerous in Ireland then and Book was hired to make certain that Kathryn was protected at all times.

Later Gila had asked her father why Book never left after her mother died. "Katie made him promise to raise you and your little sister. She thought I'd be too busy making my own name to worry about two wee ones. I can't say as she was wrong."

Book had been more father than friend to her and Shelly Kate through the years. He'd taught them to read, write, cipher, and think for themselves. He was a stern disciplinarian but equally praised them when they acted wisely.

Again Gila wondered what had provoked the

look of such devastating loss in Book. Octavio
had joked about passion happening anywhere,
anytime. Then Book offered one of his sayings.
She had the feeling that her mother was tied up
in this somehow. But what could passion and
not controlling things have to do with Kathryn
and Book?

Even as the questions entered her mind, a
shock of realization washed over Gila. She
turned in the saddle to look at the man she had
loved all her life. The black eyes were vacant of
emotion now, but his faced sagged with suffering.

Gila straightened, steering Wee-People away
from the irritating tentacles of the jumping cholla
cactus. Dare she believe what her mind had
guessed . . . what Book's unusual emotional
display had revealed? Uncertain why, the fact
that Book had been in love with Kathryn Mc-
Candless disturbed her greatly.


They rode all morning and into the afternoon.
The blistering hours on horseback frazzled Gila's
nerves, but she resisted the urge to complain.
Only women complained. Finally Thorne called
a halt to the procession. He and the others
immediately sought sleep under the shade of a
paloverde when she told them she would stand
watch.

Gila's gaze scoured the countryside, wary of
any movement. No intelligent white man would
attempt travel at this time of day. It was just too
blamed hot! But the Indians were accustomed to

the scorching heat, in tune with the harshness of this raw environment. They would find midafternoon an ideal time to attack an unsuspecting white party.

She watched the distant horizon and found nothing amiss. Soon her attention was drawn to a brown tarantula as it moved away from the base of a spiny cholla toward a nearby saguaro cactus. As the fuzzy female reached its destination, a large black-and-orange wolf spider sprang from the saguaro. Gila stared in fascinated horror as the homesteader ate the intruder, then returned to the inner shade of the saguaro's accordian trunk.

Property. Gila wiped the sweat from her brow with the back of her hand. Even the smallest creature had to fight for its piece of earth, she thought. Everyone had to fight for it—the Irish, the Americans. Even the Mexicans were fighting for their land. And she understood why. In order to have any power or security, you had to have land. She sighed in disgust. And in my case, it's everything. Why did I have to be born a woman?

A single woman without property had few choices. She must either marry, teach school, or disgrace herself with the locals in one of the cantinas. Gila could never be a schoolmarm, she loved ranching her saguaros too much. And despite her forced engagement to Garrett O'Malley, she never dreamed she would really marry.

She'd never wanted to share more than a smoke and meaty conversation with menfolk.

Now, after her wedding night's wild abandon, she wondered if she were any better than the brazen trollops who entertained in the cantinas.

What possessed me last night? Gila wondered. She looked over at her spouse while he slept. For the first time since she sobered, she inspected him closely.

She appraised the dark thick locks that hung in shaggy strands about his face and shoulders. The shocking blue eyes were closed in slumber now, but she remembered the excitement she'd felt while they peered at her during lovemaking. That brief but soul-searching look had been a promise. What promise, she had no inkling. Yet one had been offered, and at that moment she had given herself to him completely, with no fear or regret.

Continuing her inspection, Gila condemned herself for such a womanly act. Pains of self-contempt knotted her stomach.

Just look at him! she thought. He hasn't had a bath since God knows when. Those eyebrows are bushy enough to be plowed. She passed by the aristocratic nose and allowed her gaze to linger at his lips. If she hadn't known differently, she would have thought his small, straight mouth was cold and unfeeling. His high cheekbones were chisel-sharp. He wasn't what anyone would call handsome, she decided, but there was something about his looks that made her want to keep looking. Too bad he was such an arrogant bastard! Just like a Mexican.

She turned and searched the sea of sand. What was that? Was she mistaken? No. There it was again. A flicker of light. Distant. Fleeting. She immediately swung around and knew her fear was fact. Another flicker. Yes, it was definitely a signal. Indians! They were surrounded!

"Thorne, wake up. We've got trouble."

If Gila hadn't seen Thorne's eye open, she would never have guessed he'd heard her. "Indians?"

"Yeah. Plenty of them."

Octavio sat up, wide awake. "How far off?"

Book yawned, then settled back into a comfortable position. "Close. The Chiricahua have followed us since morning."

The night wind felt good, brushing Gila's face with its cool strokes. The desert seemed tranquil. The stars hung low in a heavy sky, and the scent of primroses drifted on the breeze. Moonbeams guided Gila's progress and painted the pinkish sand a radiant silver-white. In the distance mountains crouched like sharp-eyed monsters.

As Gila guided Wee-People carefully, she searched the silhouetted night, wondering what would happen if Book were wrong. What if the Indians who followed were not Chiricahua? What if they were renegades? Please, God. Not again. "Are you sure they're Cochise's men?" she asked fearfully.

"Yes," Book answered without hesitation.

"Many pardons, Señor Book," Octavio interrupted. "But I pride myself on tracking. I saw no signs. How do you know this?"

"You have noticed the animal dung?"

"Yes, but that could be any horse."

Thorne cut in. "Not so, October. Apache horses eat different food than other horses. So 'tis natural that the leavings are different."

Gila glanced about nervously, wondering if the Apache were within earshot. "Why do you suppose they're following us? You and Cochise have a treaty."

" 'Tis fair bothered by the Mexican in our midst they are, I reckon," Thorne stated matter-of-factly.

Octavio burst out laughing.

Thankful for a reason to release some of her tension, Gila's ridiculing tongue rampaged, "You crazy Mexican! Don't you know Cochise'll scalp you if he catches you? Ever since Maximilian put out a bounty on Apache scalps, Cochise's been killing anything that even looks like it eats beans. Crazy fool!"

God! It would be just her luck to up and marry a worthless Mexican and have him killed off before she could "save" the family name. How could he laugh at such a thing?

Octavio chuckled louder. "I was just thinking, Gila, what a story you would have to tell when you returned home."

"Go ahead and laugh. Cochise has a way of taking the sass out of your saddle."

When Octavio laughed even harder, Gila couldn't decide whether she wanted him delivered into Cochise's hands or her own.

\*    \*    \*

It had been two days since Gila saw the signals, but the Indians had stayed their distance. Yet she knew they watched. Their voices spoke to her secretly. For one peculiar pulsating moment, she felt as if invisible fingers reached out and touched her, allowing a flow of life other than her own to surge through her. She condemned herself for such musings, blaming the night for her uneasiness.

Dawn broke as the weary foursome crested a rise in the untamed desert. Feathery green and yellow mesquite bushes colored the valley below. Wandlike, waving stems of red ocotillos were afire with the orange rays of sunrise. Gila looked toward the winking Santa Cruz and sighed. Reaching up to scratch her neck wound, she said, "I'd love to have a bath."

Thorne sat deep and easy in the saddle. "Go ahead, lassie. But you'll have quite an audience." He turned to Octavio, who reined in alongside him. " 'Tis the first time ever she's *asked* to bathe. Whatever you did to her, October, keep it up."

Gila flung out a white-sleeved arm in exasperation. "Men! One night in your arms and a woman is supposed to swoon every time you sway."

A slow smile spread across Octavio's lips. "Isn't that what happened, more or less, *dulce mia?*"

The curse words died in Gila's mouth. Indians appeared along the rise and swiftly encircled them. Fearsome warriors sat astride Chickasaw ponies. Slashes of yellow, white, and red paint indicated it was a war party.

Three Indians rode closer. Two were dressed in breechcloth and calf-length moccasins. Bloody scalps hung boldly from their waistbands, evidence of recent raids. The third wore some hapless soldier's jacket. He raised one palm. "Yha-ta-heh."

Thorne returned the greeting. The savage spoke again, this time in Spanish.

Gila glanced up, shuddering as one of the Apache met her gaze. A pungent odor drifted to her nostrils, an odor she remembered far too well. Without warning, the memory of her attacker returned. He seemed to be there beside her again. She began to tremble and was unaware she had swayed in her saddle until Book steadied her.

Thorne's voice boomed out in Spanish. "My daughter is weak as in the ways of all women. She carries a papoose."

Because of her hatred for Mexicans, Gila had never learned Spanish well. She had not understood everything Thorne said, but she heard enough to be insulted. "I told you, I *wasn't*—"

"Shut your mouth, lassie. You'll get us all killed."

Gila held her counsel, her back rigid with indignation. More words passed between Thorne and the interpreter, and the trio of Apache returned to the hillside.

Thankful but curious, Gila asked, "What did they say? How did you get them to leave?"

Thorne reined half-quarter. "Cochise is curious about you, October. He wants a parlay. These warriors are to escort us to him. Are you a brave man?''

''More than some; less than others.''

Approval shone in Thorne's hazel eyes. ''Good. You must show courage, but Apache detest conceit.'' He urged the roan into a canter. ''Let's move. There's a cave northeast of here. I've been there many times.''

They rode for several miles and Gila's thoughts weighed heavily on her mind. What would Cochise do with October? The Chiricahua's hatred for Mexicans was notorious.

She looked at her husband and marveled that he showed no sign of fear. He rode light in his saddle, calm and self-assured. Was it ignorance that steadied him or was he truly courageous? An unexpected rush of pride swelled Gila's bosom as she realized Octavio really wasn't afraid.

As they rode, the earth heightened into six mountains. As they traveled through a sea of saguaros, the land gave way to a large opening in the hillside.

Gila peered at it closely. ''Do they know we're here?''

Book's voice came from behind. ''They know. They have followed us.''

Gila turned abruptly and saw a line of warriors preventing any retreat. She turned back and discovered that two other braves guarded the cave's entrance. There was no route for escape.

A signal was given. Thorne moved forward. Gila and the others followed. Edging out of

bright sunlight, they found the darkness in the
cave blinding. Gila squinted, straining to see
into the black recesses. Apprehension tickled
her spine and began to bead upon her hairline.
Anyone could kill her, molest her, and she
wouldn't even see who he was. Gradually her
eyes adjusted to the shadows. She felt Wee-
People's muscles ease even as her own relaxed.

Small holes from surface breaks dimly lit the
colossal cavern. A chain of crystal-walled cham-
bers branched off into the mountainside. The
giant limestone teeth hanging from the roof of
the cave looked as if they were laughing at the
sun-baked desert beyond.

As Thorne led them deeper into the cave, Gila
marveled at the turquoise-colored underground
river that divided into an intricate network of
streams. Each rivulet filtered into one of the
corridors. Despite her fear, she was awed by the
beauty of the place.

The coolness of the cave was refreshing, yet
nervous moisture dampened her upper lip. She
and Thorne, Octavio, and Book were heading
for danger, possibly death.

"We wait here." Thorne's vibrant voice echoed throughout the passageway. He dismounted,
unbuckled·his holster, and laid his weapon on
the ground. Book, Octavio, and Gila did the
same.

Gila saw a flicker of indecision flash across the
interpreter's face, then just as quickly he ordered
the other braves to dismount.

A series of shrill signals resounded, and an

Apache voice called out in greeting, "Here he comes."

The sound of unshod hoofs against moist earth preceded the rider into the cavern. The Indian halted in front of Thorne. As he dismounted, Gila understood why the Chiricahua and all other Apache nations called this man "Chief of All Apache." Fine-toned muscles rippled with every move. Cochise was not a tall man, perhaps only three inches taller than she was. He was of medium build, his forehead high, the nose large and straight. A man reportedly in his forties, with dark, piercing eyes that bore through Gila's soul. She felt as if she'd been estimated and discarded, leaving no doubt as to who feared whom.

Cochise greeted Thorne in English, showing a respect he gave to few men. "So, my friend. You still paint hair with root of Spanish dagger?"

Thorne tilted back his red mass of hair and laughed. "Yes, great chief of the Apache, so that you will be sure not to mistake me for your desert foe."

The Apache leader voiced approval. "This is good. You speak as a man, a brave man." He turned to Book and nodded.

Book returned the acknowledgment.

Silent respect flowed among the three men. Gila wanted to scream at the preening trio, *What about October?* What would Cochise do with October? Yet she knew if she uttered one sound without permission, she would jeopardize all their lives. A man who could not control his woman was considered weak and not to be trusted by the Indians. It took all her willpower to restrain herself.

Cochise stood before Octavio. Octavio did not flinch. The chief touched the fingertips of his right hand to his forehead, then out toward Octavio. At precisely the same moment, both grabbed the other's right forearm and spoke a single word.

"Brother?" Thorne sounded as surprised as Gila felt.

The armshake strengthened. "Blood brother," Cochise proclaimed. "We will smoke the pipe of peace, my friend, and feast. Then we will talk. You will tell me why you ride with this flaming arrow." He spoke a few words of Apache and two warriors moved toward Gila. "Go. We will bring food and a blanket. It is not good for soft skin to hear the counsel of brave men."

Gila defiantly tossed back her hair, even as she swallowed back a lump of nervousness. "I'll go alone."

"This woman is of McCandless blood?" asked Cochise with no change in his expression.

"Aye, she's my daughter."

The chief regarded her a few seconds more. "She has much courage. You paint her hair as well—eh?" He pointed toward one passageway indicating all jest was laid aside.

Asking to stay was impossible and would make her lose what little respect she'd gained. Gila led Wee-People into the tunnel, moving deeper into the mountainside. Soon it opened into a small chamber with a turquoise pool.

She dismounted, realizing she couldn't have gone much farther as the slant of the cavern's roof was finally becoming too low to remain on horseback. She searched the dark corridor, checking to see if there were any movement. It didn't look as though anyone had followed her, but she was still nervous.

Fatigue lay heavily upon her shoulders, and the dirt and grime from three days' travel did little to help her temperament. She longed for the cleansing comfort of the pool, but could not bring herself to undress with so many Indians within spitting distance.

Gila bent closer to the water. Was the pool one of those bottomless pits she'd heard about? As she pondered the question, she wondered how October and Cochise had become blood brothers. No wonder he hadn't been afraid, she thought accusingly. Come to think of it, he'd been downright smug about it! She stood and irritably dusted the wet earth from her knees. She hoped he choked on the peace pipe.


Octavio passed the pipe to Book and inhaled the wilderness tobacco. He sat across from Cochise, his feet and ankles aching in the Indian position. The sumac and sage gripped his lungs, dulling the throb. The pipe passed until each man had tasted the aromatic leaves.

Then they ate a meal of long white shoots of

tule rushes, early wild onions, and horse flesh.
Cochise's eyes were sharp and missed nothing.
Octavio knew the leader had seen his revulsion
for the meat.

Cochise ate a healthy portion. "What do you
expect of government issue, my brother?"

Octavio nearly choked on his laughter as he
wiped his mouth on the back of his sleeve.

Cochise grunted his disapproval, wiping his
own mouth on his bare forearm. "You waste. It
is good for the skin. Great Spirit does not burn
his anger into the soul of those who use the
sweat of the horse."

Octavio nodded. "That is so, my brother. But
the woman does not invite me into the wigwam
if I soothe the Great Spirit."

A hint of playfulness twinkled in Cochise's
eyes. "This is so. I think my brother tells me the
Great Spirit rises in the west, not in the east. I
think the woman does not invite my brother into
the wigwam because his scalp smells too much
of painted badger."

Octavio reached up and felt the greasy locks
that remained coated with coal oil and mescal
salve. He'd forgotten! He laughed heartily. The
others joined him.

Cochise's voice grew calm. "Why does my
brother journey to the ranch of McCandless?
You have wounds."

Octavio related how Thorne had bargained
him out of prison. "I am a man of my word and
will hold to the agreement with McCandless. But
if you happen to be in contact with Juárez, tell
him I am alive and well. Tell him to strive and

prosper, that I will join him as soon as the bargain is met. And if you are able, contact my—"

Octavio was cut off by a bone-chilling scream echoing from one of the passageways. "Gila!"

The group reacted instantly, donning their weapons, traveling through the tunnel with lightning speed.

Book entered first, Cochise second, then the others. Gila struggled beside the pool, wrestling one of the warriors. Octavio started toward her but Book held him back. Before he could protest, Cochise made a command in Apache.

The brave released his hold and stood, arms folded across a broad chest. Yet the savage did not waver.

Cochise addressed the attacker. "White Bear of the Chiricahua. We have ridden many moons together. We have fought side by side, drunk tiswin, and called each other brother. Is this not true?"

White Bear nodded once. "This is true."

"Is it not also true that the law of the People protects all who enter the hospitality of our camp? That any warrior breaking the sacred law should meet the spirits of his fathers?"

"This too is true, but Geronimo speaks of—"

"Then, White Bear, self-chosen enemy of the Chiricahua, let this be witness to all Apache who walk the crooked path. To our brother, Geronimo." Cochise took an arrow from his quiver and armed the bow. "This is the way of the poisoned spirit." Cochise aimed, then let fly the arrow. The mark was swift and sure. White Bear fell dead, pierced through the heart.

Everything happened so fast, Gila stood in
mute horror. She could not believe Cochise had
killed the assailant without a moment's hesitation. And White Bear had shown no fear of
death. He accepted his fate unchallenged. Yet
*she* trembled. Like a woman, she thought.

The events of the last few days were almost
more than she could endure. First near-rape by
an Indian, then marriage to a Mexican, and now
another close call. Holy St. Patrick, what next?

She stared at the dead man, the stench of
blood and tallowed skin dizzying her in such
claustrophobic surroundings. Self-consciously
she wiped her mouth, then bent to the pool and
washed her hands and face, angry at the trembling that overtook her.

Long sculptured hands steadied her. She
looked up, saw the concern written in Octavio's
eyes, and thanked him silently. Yet her trembling would not cease. Hot tears burned her
cheeks as the realization of what could have
been bore deeply into her mind. She pulled
away from Octavio, unable to bear any man's
touch at that moment.

Somewhere beneath the terror of her
thoughts, an idea occurred. Hadn't she sensed
earlier that her attacker was near? White Bear
was one of the three who had approached the
party. She remembered the smell, the slash of
paint across his cheeks. How he must have
laughed! He thought he would be able to rape
her now as he had been unable to days ago.

Anger crept up and strengthened Gila. No one

would ever take her against her will as long as there was breath in her body.

Cochise looked at her and she felt as if he spoke a silent approval of this new anger seething within her. He turned and led his warriors back through the tunnel.

Gila looked at the dead man. "Do they expect us to bury him?"

Book held out his hand and she let him help her mount. "No, they will leave his bones to be scattered by animals. His soul must walk the earth endlessly for his shame."

"How long will we have to stay?" Gila asked, wanting to leave the place far behind her.

"Only Cochise can answer that," Book replied.

Gila was surprised when they returned to the meeting place inside the colossal chamber. Cochise and the war party were gone. Only the lingering odor of the peace offering remained. It was as if she and the others were the first people ever to enter the cavern.

"Where did he go?" she asked innocently.

Thorne muttered, "That's what the army's been trying to figure out for years, lassie."

# Chapter Seven

◆ ◆ ◆ ◆ ◆

"BEN'LL BE WAITING at the Shoo-Fly for us," Thorne informed them as the outline of Tucson came into view. "The others will be nursing whiskey bottles over at Congress Hall, you can bet."

Octavio grew wary, wondering what the ranch hands of the Circle-Shamrock would think of Gila's sudden marriage. Would they be as prejudiced as she? What if one of them had been her lover? He hadn't considered that until now. She was Cordoba in name only. Now that she had tasted the finer points of the marriage bed, would it be hard to keep her from a man's arms?

Octavio's memory swept back to the unspoken promise between them. No. That look was for me and only me. She might deny it with her words, but her eyes said yes.

Perhaps the term of his bargain with McCandless would not seem so long if Gila decided to spend her nights in his arms. Eight months was a very long time to be without a woman, and he had found the ecstasy prison had long denied him in Gila's wild abandon. Her inexperience and his abstinence had made him feel as if he were making love for the first time. The thought of more such nights was definitely worth pondering and might even be worth counting on, if he didn't have to consider Gila's prejudice and temper as well.

He stared at Gila as his horse trailed behind ̴ers. Her long auburn hair was pushed under

the crown of the sombrero to keep her neck cool.
The grime and perspiration of three days' travel
stained her white linen shirt. From this position
she looked as solid as a man, but the illusion
faded quickly when he noticed the seductive
way her ample hips moved with the paint's
canter.

Octavio's loins tightened, making him silently
condemn his physical reaction to her. How
could his desire be so abruptly triggered by this
well-endowed woman? Not only had he lost his
jungle sense, he had also lost his common sense.
This woman was nothing but trouble—vulgar,
insulting, prejudiced, and too robust. He had
always preferred a slim, petite figure, a waist he
could easily encompass with his hands. He liked
to feel protective, stronger, to make all the
decisions. With Gila, he never knew from one
moment to the next what she would do. There
was no reason for him to be attracted to her, yet
he was. And for the life of him, he was uncertain
why.

He remembered the fury that had overwhelmed him at the sight of his wife being
molested by the renegade. Gila was a Cordoba
now, and he would not allow *anyone* bearing the
Cordoba name to suffer abuse. But his reaction
had been more than a desire to save the family
honor. He had wanted to tear her attacker apart
limb by limb.

He would have gone to her defense, but Book
had stepped in. For which Octavio was grateful.
Cochise would not have appreciated any inter-
ference, even from a blood brother. Afterward

he had tried to comfort Gila, but she had shied away. Only Book could get close to her.

It was for the best. Gila had not welcomed his sympathy, he was certain. Yet his own reaction disturbed him. As they left the cave and traveled toward Tucson, he reasoned that the sight of a man forcing himself on a woman—any woman— could have brought on his frenzied emotion. A woman must be willing, not violently dominated. Lovemaking should be joyful and fulfilling, not dutiful, he thought. That was the very reason he had demanded that Gila beg him for the continued warmth of his arms.

A yapping dog interrupted his thoughts as they neared the presidio walls that surrounded Tucson. Octavio decided he would not allow the woman who now bore his name to cause him any more of these uncomfortable feelings. And the only way to do that was to make certain she remained in *his* bed.

The Sonora's northernmost outpost was not what Octavio had expected. Tucson's walls were made of the same adobe brick that guarded most of the settlements in the territory. Buildings lined the roadway near the fortress's southern gate. Animals grazed nearby. Crops were raised close to town—a reminder of frequent Apache raids.

He glanced up and saw movement in the Torreon, the two-story tower at the northeast corner of the encampment. A sentry was posted as lookout for possible dangers to and from all

incoming parties. From the distance between the
sentinel and himself, Octavio estimated the size
of the township. "Ten acres?" he asked aloud.

Gila cantered Wee-People alongside Octavio's
horse. "About that much, I guess."

He pointed to the edifice rising above the east
wall. "You have a church inside? I thought San
Xavier was large enough to administer to everyone in the territory." His attention drew away
momentarily to the old church outside the walls,
San Xavier, "The Dove of the Desert."

Gila wiped her sweaty brow. "No. At least,
not anymore. I'm afraid San Xavier has seen the
last of her glory, although we do hold our Easter
pageant there in mid-April. Too many Anglos
moving in, bringing new denominations." She
pointed to the east. "That steeple over there is
the military chapel, San Augustine, for our boys
at Fort Lowell."

"Fort Lowell?"

Gila leaned closer to Wee-People's neck and
picked burrs from her britches. "You might as
well say Tucson *is* Fort Lowell, the social center
of the Butterfield Overland Mail route. We've
got a school, a church, two newspapers, and a
theater. Oh, the soldiers are supposed to be out
to the south of town, but with the Chiricahua
siding with the Mimbres and the Navaho, the
bluecoats have been spending more time *inside*
the gates than out."

As they guided their horses down the Camino
Real, the main street of Tucson, the sound of
several dialects mingled with the yapping of a
dog. Children ran up to the tired foursome,

begging for pesos for their wares. Octavio was surprised that few of the other citizens paid their group any attention. An incoming party not attacked by Apache was—or should be—an oddity.

One soldier leaned against a post rolling a smoke, while another sat in a porch swing with a not-so-pretty señorita. Farther down the street, Octavio could hear the crooning of the Sonoran musicians playing fiddles and guitars. The ringing of iron against steel echoed from a blacksmith shop. The old saying is true, Octavio decided. Tucson *is* the melting pot of dialects and destinations.

The Tucsonians were preparing for evening, hanging lanterns at every doorway—an ancient custom also practiced in most Mexican towns. His countrymen were people of the night. Social life rarely started before sundown. The desert heat clings to midnight and stirs our molten passions, Octavio mused. He stole a glance at Gila, remembering the pleasure of her bed, yet unable to forget the sharpness of her tongue.

Heat lingered past sunset. The smell of the heavily populated area became increasingly repulsive. Garbage littered the edges of single-storied adobe structures. Mescal shops lined the roadways, reminding Octavio of livery stalls. To the west, another gate opened in the wall.

They passed the Tully and Ochoa Freight Company, but Octavio's attention was drawn across the road to San Augustine's chapel. In the cemetery, on the south side of the church, a mourner was bent over a newly marked grave.

"Apache," Gila said quietly.

"You know this for certain?"

Gila shrugged. "Happens every day. A party rides outta here. Only one person ever gets back. I think those bloody savages let one live just so the people back in town get to hear the gory details."

Octavio defended his blood brother. "That is not Cochise's way."

"Who but Cochise knows his way?" she countered, then rode ahead.

Octavio followed, silently taking in the character of the district. From the smell, he knew that the stables bordered the northern wall. He could hear the sounds of cantinas and houses of ill repute in the distance.

Another odor urged him to announce his hunger. "Where is that wondrous aroma coming from?"

"Oh, that's the stables," Gila mocked. "They're up closer to the north wall."

Octavio overlooked her gibe. "No, not that one, *dulce mia.* I smell lamb. Why don't we eat now? I'm starved."

Gila bristled in the saddle. "I am not your *sweet!* And why do you think you can tell us when we're going to eat and when we aren't?"

Thorne reined to a halt in front of the building that welcomed the travelers with its pleasing odor. The sign outside the entrance identified the place as THE SHOO-FLY RESTAURANT. "Man's right, lassie. I'm hungrier than a tick on a flea. Let's put your jawing to good use and eat a bite."

Octavio dismounted, resisting the pain that bit

into his moccasined feet as his soles touched the graveled roadway. After brushing off trail dust from his pants and waist-length jacket, he fluffed the white ruffles of his jabot. Thorne McCandless might be a great rancher, Octavio decided, but he does not choose well the apparel of a groom.

Back at the cave, his father-in-law had taken the garments Octavio wore from a saddlebag and said, "The men will expect the husband of my daughter to be dressed like a gentleman. I won't have you otherwise."

The moccasins had been a gift from Cochise. The chief had given them without comment. Later, Octavio learned from Thorne that the Indian leader had questioned the Irishman about his blood brother's injuries. Octavio was grateful for the pair of doeskins against his soles but did not think they complemented the rest of his festive clothing.

Octavio hitched his horse to the rail, then caught Gila by the waist as she dismounted. As her body finished the descent, his hands slipped upward, cupping the outlying edges of her breasts. He felt the tremor that shook her, then was pleased that the peaks contracted so eagerly to his touch.

"Not now, darling," Gila said sweetly as she turned to him. The smile did not match the anger that smoldered in her eyes. "You're embarrassing me."

Octavio released her, knowing they had an audience. A short cowpoke stood near Thorne, hand held out in greeting.

"How are you, Ben? Did you get full price for the horses?" Thorne shook the stranger's hand.

Ben thumbed back his hat over a balding head. "Yes, sir, sure did. Didn't lose a head. Cochise was good as his word. We got the usual guff off the new settlers when we got in town, but we settled 'em down. Guess it takes time for some fellers to learn that Cochise keeps his word to you. It's pretty hard to explain to 'em why you can get by them Apache and hardly no one else can."

Thorne slapped the drover on the back good-naturedly. "We've been through this before, ain't we, Ben?"

"Yes, sir. We have."

"By-the-by," Thorne said and turned to include Octavio into the conversation. "This is Gila's husband—October. He's got one of those fancy four-poster names, but October'll do just fine for us."

Octavio saw suspicion dart across the wrangler's face. Then he remembered his manners and offered Octavio his hand.

"*Gracias*, señor," Octavio said, noticing the handshake was firm, not half-hearted. "I am Don Octavio Diego Cordoba."

"Howdy," Ben replied, then moved quickly past him. The wrangler grabbed Gila by the shoulders and kissed her on the dimpled cheek. "Mrs. Cordoba, is it? Hell, I never would've believed it. Just wait till the boys hear about this. When did all this saddle-breaking take place, anyhow?"

Gila started to speak, but Octavio placed a

possessive arm about her waist. "You know our Gila, always making her lightning-quick decisions. Guess I just happened to be at the right place at the right time. Eh, my sweet?" He pinched her playfully. "Oww!" he cried. Pain gripped his instep and traveled up the back of his leg. Gila's boot had dug in with a vengeance.

She smiled sweetly and patted his rear. "Don't worry about October, Ben. He's just a little saddlesore."

Ben looked at Gila, than at Octavio. "Book, let's go get us something to drink. I think we ought to leave these two sweet-talkers alone for a while. Looks like they got some discussin' to do."

"No, that's all right," Gila protested and took a step toward Ben. "You and the boys and me can—"

"You go ahead," Ben said, waving her back. "Me and the fellas can wait till morning. Tell Miss Elizabeth your pa and Book are here. She's been keeping 'em a room ready. I guess you and your husband can make do in yours. Me and your pa and Book's gonna catch up on some drinking." The wrangler gave her an insinuating wink.

Gila secured Wee-People's reins. "Don't get any ideas, October," she said in a low voice, craning her neck to see if the others were out of listening range. "I'll play wife in front of the men so I can keep my property, but when we're alone you'd best keep your distance."

Octavio admired the curve of her hip as she bent to pick a burr off Wee-People's foreleg. He couldn't resist the urge to encircle her with his arms. She swung around, which was the wrong move to make, for it only reminded them both of how well their bodies molded together, how well each fit into the other's embrace. He lowered his lips to her own, tasting the soft, salty desire that had lain dormant for days and seemed to surface at his slightest request. The need to conquer and convince this woman who so blatantly hated his countrymen, so plainly elevated herself above his people, overcame Octavio. His kiss became more demanding, possessing, conquering her with the fiery passion he felt surging within his loins. The racing of her heartbeat mixed with his own as her resistance weakened. She leaned into him, pressing more firmly than before, her hands reaching to draw him nearer.

He had wanted to ridicule her, repay her for the snide remarks, make her want him. Instead she succeeded in making him want her. He'd acknowledged the spark of desire he'd felt when he helped her off the horse but decided those feelings were merely renewed lust, an enjoyment any woman would bring. Yet the kiss brought back the memory—a memory he would not long forget.

On the night of their marriage, she'd given herself completely, without restraint. Though physically she had been no longer a virgin, her passion was of no other kind. Octavio had felt a certain honor that he was the first to awaken the depths of her desire. That night he had been confused by her innocence, yet pleased. When he looked into her eyes a promise was made. He was to fulfill the need of her womanhood. But of her promise to him, he had no inkling.

Now, even as his loins ached for release, he pushed away. "Let us eat."

Her half-closed lashes opened wide. "W-what?"

"I said, let's eat," he repeated and motioned toward the restaurant's entrance. If only she knew how difficult it was to ignore the way her rapid breathing swelled her breasts. "I'm hungry."

Gila cursed as she fumbled to straighten her shirt. Running a hand through the rebellious strands at her temple, she tried to smooth them back and appear undaunted by his sudden practicality. She stomped through the swinging doors of The Shoo-Fly, her sombrero bobbing violently against her back.

Octavio followed behind her, smiling softly to himself, and whispered, "We shall see, *dulce mia*, if my will is greater than yours. I wonder which of us will be the beggar?"

The Shoo-Fly was a long, low-ceilinged room furnished with rows of piñon pine tables and benches. The place was crowded, living up to its reputation for serving the best food in Tucson. Because the establishment's owner, Elizabeth Dutton, did not permit liquor on the premises, the more respectable clientele of the township and neighboring Fort Lowell chose to dine there.

Gila sat at a table draped with a red-checkered

cloth. An elderly woman set a plate of lamb stew in front of her. Gila scooped a spoonful into her mouth, ate, then muttered, "Mighty tasty, Liz. How's business?"

The hefty woman slicked back her grayish blond hair, then placed both fists on her apron-clad hips. "Oh, about the same, I reckon. The place won't start crowdin' in for another week or so, I don't imagine. You coming back through?"

Gila noted the interest behind the question and knew it had nothing to do with whether she was coming. "Book'll be here. But don't put any store in him dancing, Lizzie. You know how he feels about it."

Elizabeth wiped her forehead with the corner of the blue gingham apron. "Oh, I know that, young 'un. But a body could have more pleasant things in mind." Her blue eyes twinkled with meaning.

"Pardon, señora. May I sit with you?"

Gila almost choked on her food as Octavio's hand rested on her shoulder. She hadn't heard his approach.

Elizabeth Dutton motioned to the adjoining tables. Though courteous, stern disapproval accented her voice and expression. "There are several other tables, señor. This lady is newly married. I'm sure her husband would not find your request . . . agreeable."

Gila could see the arrogance arching Octavio's brow and that undeniable look of resentment turning his sapphire gaze to ice-blue. He was about to say something ridiculous if she didn't let him sit. To save a scandal in front of Liz and her patrons, Gila waved him beside her. "It's all right, Lizzie," she assured her friend, "my husband will just have to restrain himself."

Octavio stifled a chuckle.

Elizabeth gave Octavio a look of reproval, then shot a glance at Gila. "Are you certain, Miss McCandless? I mean, Mrs.—"

"Cordoba. Señora Octavio Diego Cordoba," Octavio finished the title for her.

This time it was Elizabeth's eyebrows that curved upward. "You *know* this lady?"

Octavio put his fingers at the nape of Gila's neck and rubbed gently. "Well enough to know the pleasures of her bed."

Gila slapped him hard, putting all her frustration into the blow. "You son-of-a-coyote. I'll—"

Octavio grabbed her wrist, preventing her from repeating the impulse. He glanced about the room, then back at his angry-faced wife. "I'm afraid you have let all Tucson witness our first lover's quarrel." He stood, turned, and bowed, his hand sweeping grandly in front of him. "Forgive my bride, gentlemen. But she wishes for a second plate of stew, whereas I have need to satisfy another hunger."

Masculine chuckles brought Gila to her feet. She turned to the crowd and smiled. "I believe, darling, that you will need a bath first." She lifted her plate and poured the remaining stew over his head.

Laughter echoed from every corner.

\* \* \*

Elizabeth Dutton opened the door to an immaculate room. The fresh odor of soapweed indicated the effort the landlady made to keep her reputation of running the cleanest place in town. She stepped inside and motioned for Gila and Octavio to enter. "I expect you'll find this tolerable."

Gila thanked her. The four-poster bed looked inviting with its sheepskin coverlet and feather pillows. A lamp had been provided, as well as two reading chairs and a table.

As Elizabeth prepared to leave, she nodded at Octavio's clothes. "You take off your things and have your missus bring 'em to me. I'll see to it they get cleaned."

"*Gracias*, señorita."

Elizabeth motioned toward a room down the hall. "Your baths are ready, anytime you are."

Gila reached into her pocket, ready to give Lizzie extra money for the added luxury. Water was far too precious to use without payment. The Santa Cruz was just outside the fort, but there was always the threat of Apache ambush between the water source and Tucson. There was no telling what the woman had done to get enough to fill two baths.

Elizabeth pushed Gila's hand away, refusing the offered coins. "Keep your money this time. Let's call it a wedding present." She leaned closer, lowering her tone, trying not to let Octavio hear. "Let's hope some of that stuff on his skin will wash off." She shut the door soundly behind her.

Gila suppressed a giggle and eyed Octavio. His hair was matted with the chunks of meat and onions he'd been unable to brush away. The ruffled jabot was stained with sticky juice. "Maybe now you'll wash off that stinking stuff on your hair."

Octavio reached for her arm and caught it. "No, darling, *you* will wash it for me." He jerked open the door and pushed her out into the hallway.

Gila struggled to break free and clenched her teeth, eyes squinting from the rage that seethed inside. "Let go of me, October!" she demanded. "There's no way in hell I'm gonna bathe you. I won't and you can't—"

"Make you?" Octavio threatened in a quiet, deadly voice, edging her farther down the corridor. "Oh, yes I can, *dulce mia*. And you will do as I say or I'll tell every son-of-an-American-whore here that you are with child and it damn sure isn't mine. How will the mighty McCandlesses live down the scandal? How will you keep your precious property?"

Gila boiled with rage, yet she forced her voice into a low whisper. Sound and gossip carried in a place like this. "You made a bargain with Thorne. You promised."

"I did not say I would deny the truth. I merely said I would stay with you for one year. Of course, if I tell all, there is no need to stay, is there? You will lose your property. I stand to lose nothing; freedom is not yet mine."

Gila stopped struggling. "All right. All right! I'll give you a bath, but you won't like it."

Octavio caught her to him. With one finger he traced her cleavage and murmured, "You will do *all* I ask, *dulce mia*. I am a man of many moods." His smile widened at the tremor that instantly overtook her.

Though his hot fingertip sent a surge of warmth spreading through her limbs, she resisted the temptation to give in to the feeling that gripped her whenever her flesh contacted his. Her voice grew husky, but she willed contempt into her tone. "I will do anything but share your bed again. It will be a long time before I beg you for anything!"

"No need to worry, my sweet. You will beg me, I assure you. And I will not have you until you do." He pushed her through the doorway marked BATHS. Glancing at the tubs, he asked, "Are you afraid to undress or shall I turn my back?"

Gila bristled. "You said nothing about our sharing a bath. A bargain's a bargain. This is your bath . . . alone."

"Fine. Now, undress me."

Gila spun around and realized he meant what he said. Did he think the sight of him naked might make her swoon? She walked over and began to unfasten the buttons that held his neck ruffles in place. "Your hair smells horrible. What in St. Patrick do you use on it—coal oil?"

Octavio laughed. Gila wished the deep timbre of his voice didn't sound so pleasant. She was beginning to think she argued with him just so she could hear the vibrant tone again and again. Her fingers fumbled with the last button, then gathered the hem of the shirt and pulled the garment over his head. Her gaze took in wiry shoulders, broad chest, and finally the sallowness of his skin. For the second time since she'd met him, she became curious about his confinement. "What did you do to land in jail?" she asked as she unlaced his pants.

"I was a political prisoner, Gila. Does that distress you?"

"No," she muttered. *But taking off your britches sure does.* She tried to appear undaunted by her task at hand. Despite her earlier denial, his nakedness *did* bring on a certain weakness within her—weakness she was determined to fight.

She lowered the brown twilled linen and felt an instant, deep-seated fury rise at the sight of his scarred thighs. Once again she wanted to ask him how he obtained the scars but remembered his earlier refusal to speak of them. The look of pain in his brilliant blue gaze as she eased the cloth over his calves kept her silent. She yanked the garment to his ankles, forgetting that they were equally injured. Compassionately she looked up to see if she'd hurt him and was rewarded with a sight she hadn't expected.

"I have made you a brazen woman, my sweet," Octavio jeered.

Gila straightened, purposefully making her glance bolder and unashamed. "Just because I am a woman doesn't mean I can't appreciate the makings of a fine body. A man doesn't hesitate to look at a pretty lady. I was merely considering what you would look like with a little meat on your bones. Much as I hate to admit it, October, you could be a very handsome man."

Her dimple chose to indent as she fought off the blush that started to rush to her cheeks, revealing that she was not as bold as she pretended. A knowing sneer marked Octavio's expression as he became aware of her inner turmoil. She expected him to tease her, but he didn't. Instead, he stepped into and sat in the tub of water. Closing his eyes in comfort, he sighed. "Get the soap, wife. Scrub my back."

Gila hesitated, then pulled off her boots. A plan quickly formed and she had to prevent herself from laughing aloud. She reached for one of the bars of soapweed aloe that Elizabeth had made. After dipping the bar into the water, she lathered it vigorously, then gripped Octavio's scalp and began to rub as hard as she could.

"Ouch! *Madre Santísima!* Get my hair wet first!" Octavio grasped her hand.

Gila jerked free, the slickness of the soap on her hands making escape easy. She reached over, dipped her finger into the water in the smaller tub that remained on the burning coals, and drew her hand out quickly. She grabbed two towels and lifted the kettle. "You want wet. I'll give you wet." She poured the hot water over his hair.

Streams of curses and a searing scalp forced Octavio to his feet. As he grabbed his head, one foot slipped. He fell. Water splashed in all directions. Gila was drenched, but she could not contain her laughter. She might not speak fluent Spanish, but she understood every word October was saying now!

"Get the soap," he bellowed. "Wash me. Now!"

Gila stood her ground.

"The soap or your property. Choose."

She didn't trust that look in his eyes. It reminded her too much of how the desert sky looked just before it paled into one of those storms that spawned dust devils. Perhaps she shouldn't have been so ornery. Maybe if she could convince him she hadn't scalded him on purpose. "I'm sorry, October. How was I to know the water was so blamed hot? I was just doing what you told me to."

"So you say, *dulce mia*," he said evenly. "Now get the soap and let's get this over with."

Gila knew she could walk out now and there wasn't much he could do until he got dressed, but she didn't want a repeat performance. She relathered the soap and began to massage his hair. When she saw his pinkish scalp, she felt a twinge of regret. She must have really hurt him. "October, I—"

"It is of no consequence."

Gila completed washing his hair, gently cleansing and rinsing the dark locks as if they belonged to a baby. From there she began to scrub his shoulders with small circular strokes, then moved to include his chest and abdomen.

Octavio's eyes closed as the soothing strokes cleaned and comforted his sore, aching flesh.

Though his head still tingled from the shock of the scalding water, he felt himself drifting into a hazy peace. Gila's sudsy strokes and the heat from the steam rising from the water lured him into a state of utter relaxation. His hooded eyes opened and a curious thirst collected in the lower part of his throat. His attention seemed riveted on the perspiration that beaded across Gila's upper lip. Tangled strands of hair clung to her face as waves of heat from the water struck her.

Gila halted her circular motions and allowed Octavio to linger in his languid state. Realizing how wet her shirt had become, she wished she'd had time to grab another. She rinsed her hands thoroughly and removed the shirt, leaving herself naked to the waist.

Octavio stared at her, huskiness masking his question. "What are you doing?"

"I can't walk out of here in a soaking wet shirt. White shows everything, you know." She draped the garment across the towel nail.

Gila turned and was rewarded with his short intake of breath. Blue eyes stared boldly at her. Was it the water's steam or flames of desire she saw flickering in his eyes? she wondered.

Gila bent further into the tub, deliberately groping for the soap. After recovering it, she leaned coyly against his chest, holding one of his arms up to scrub, her breast lightly touching his chest. When she finished, she lifted his other arm and stretched more fully against him. She lathered his shoulders and neck. Slowly, seductively, she moved her hands down his body and massaged places she'd never touched before. Her own breath came in shallow gasps.

Her nipples grew taut with the want of him. His hands pulled her close, forging his molten lips to hers. She kissed him feverishly, wantonly. His arms encircled her, pulling her into the water with him. Gila laughed huskily, allowing another rapturous kiss. As his mouth moved to tweak a rosy nipple, Gila pulled away. "Not yet, darling," she whispered.

A moan gurgled deep within Octavio's throat. "When?"

Gila stood and stepped out of the tub. Jerking on her shirt, she held it closed with one hand and grabbed her boots with the other. "I'll tell you when . . . when *you* beg *me!*" She slammed the door and stalked out of the room, leaving a trail of steaming droplets.


Octavio woke. The aroma of fresh-baked bread urged his stomach to rumble with hunger. For a moment he forgot where he was.

Tucson. The Shoo-Fly. Gila's bed. He glanced about but knew she was not there. She had a way of filling a room with her presence, he thought. The room and bed seemed vacant without her.

After he rolled over and got out of bed, Octavio noticed his clothes lay cleaned and folded in one of the chairs. Pinned to the shirt was a note.

*October, Thorne's making final arrange-
ments with those Mounted Rifle fellas from
Texas. Book's over jawing with Mr. Oury, the
mayor. Me, I'm going to give Dublin a bath. Get
some grub. We'll be heading outta here soon.*

Octavio tossed the paper on the chair. "Who
the devil is Dublin?" He conjured up visions of
an Irishman as large as Thorne. Would this
Dublin fellow get the same sort of bath he'd been
given the previous night? Was he the father of
her baby? If so, why hadn't he married her?

Octavio slammed a fist into his palm. Thorne
had warned him he was not to trample the
McCandless name. His precious daughter
should be expected to do the same. Cordobas
were of equally fine stock!

Octavio dressed. When the comb touched his
tender scalp, he muttered an oath and slammed
it onto the vanity top. The moccasins he had
placed under the edge of the bed were gone. In
their place were heeled leather boots. How did
Gila expect him to wear them with his feet in
such bad condition? They were mending quickly
but would not hold up to the confinement of
boots. Was she trying to be thoughtful or vin-
dictive? Either way, she had managed to leave
him without proper footwear.

Boots would be better than being barefoot,
Octavio decided and managed to put them on.
But Gila had not guessed the correct size. They
were too big. His feet slid back and forth as he
walked, burning the already tender flesh. Deter-

mined to get the moccasins back, he swore, "Just wait until I find her!"

He shuffled down the hall, following the aroma that woke him. As he entered the kitchen, he was met with Elizabeth Dutton's polite, but reserved greeting. "Good morning," he returned and started for the dining area.

She offered him a plateful of steaming mesquite biscuits and gravy. "Your missus said for you to be sure and eat." She nodded toward his plate. "That's only water gravy, but worth eating. Them Injuns attack nearly ever' day lately. Not being able to get to them cows for days at a time has made their milk dry up. Milk is scarcer than a white man in Apache Pass."

After he finished his meal, Octavio strolled outside to view the town by daylight. He inhaled deeply, savoring the smell of freedom. Tucson was abustle. By sunlight, it was little more than a patch of desert encircled by an adobe wall. Sunbaked and sun-dried Mexicans lined the roadways and porches with their wares. Soldiers, teamsters, and miners filtered in and out of the various shops. Government wagons were being prepared for trips to Fort Yuma or the Rio Grande. The sounds of gaming at a monte table echoed from one of the nearby cantinas.

The buildings looked like boxes made of mud, and they were surrounded with broken pottery, garbage, and carcasses, accenting their crudeness. The settlement was parched and desolate from the glare of the desert sun, yet Octavio felt an undercurrent of vitality in its people. Each person seemed to know that the union of all had somehow defied the desert's death grip. He admired their courage.

Approaching the livery, Octavio heard a great commotion. People moved quickly in the direction of the corral.

"Saints and begorra, Dublin! Stop that! Do you hear! You toss that sand one more time, I'll chop that tail plum off you!" Gila's voice shrieked with anger.

A patch of sand instantly rose and fell just as quickly. Some in the crowd laughed. Others voiced their disgust while dusting themselves off. The group dispersed slowly, the entertainment having lost some of its appeal.

Octavio moved closer, eager to see this Dublin. Gila stood, wiping the dirt from her eyes and mouth. Sand soiled her hair and clothing. But Gila was not the spectacle that captured Octavio's attention.

In the corral stood the largest buffalo he'd ever seen. The hunched back stood as tall as himself. The horns, thick and curved, jutted out from the skull at right angles. The massive neck was covered with an unruly mane. The animal reminded him of El Diablo, the fiercest of his opponents in the bullring. But even Diablo was small compared to this American toro.

The buffalo's sightless pink eye only added to Octavio's curiosity. He broke the silence. "Does nothing grow normally in this territory?" he asked.

Gila turned and glared at him. "Dublin is a McCandless. McCandlesses do nothing, have nothing small."

"So, this is Señor Dublin?" Octavio chuckled at his sudden relief. "Is he yours? He'll bring a handsome price."

"I could get two thousand for him, but I won't sell. Ever." She stroked the animal's nose, then gave him an affectionate scratch. "I raised him from a calf."

"Why is he here?"

Gila explained the buffalo's presence. Octavio admired the ingenious plan of having the white bison ride herd with the horses. He might think little of her temper, but she was to be applauded for her master stroke.

Gila seemed momentarily pleased for the moment, then resumed her usual indifference. Was it because of his threat last night? he wondered. He'd never intended to break his word. His freedom was more dear than she could imagine. But he could not resist the chance to make her grovel for all her biased remarks. No one who ridiculed a Cordoba had ever lived to tell about it, but this cull of womanhood dared call him anything that came to mind.

She should never have poured stew on me, he thought, allowing his anger to renew itself. Why should I worry whether she was upset over last night? Does she forget that I am Don Octavio Diego Cordoba—great great grandnephew to the explorer Coronado!

As he recalled the insults Gila had poured on him since their meeting, Octavio's anger grew into a full-fledged fury. No more would she make a fool of him. She would continue to bathe the loins that stirred her dormant passions. Her breasts will ache with the need of these lips, but I will refuse to touch her. And when her eyes burn from the heat which rises from her thighs, I will not quench her! he vowed silently.

Octavio willfully controlled the rage that consumed him. At his lusty appraisal, Gila's disgust sharpened visibly. Had she guessed his thoughts or were they as obvious as they were painful?

She leaned forward and whispered something into Dublin's ear. The animal fell into step behind her as she headed toward the inner corral. Gila looked back over her shoulder and said, "Thorne said he'd be a little while yet, and Book's inside saddling the horses. You'd best get your look around now, if you're going to get one."

Octavio abruptly turned and muttered, "I've seen all that interests me."

## Chapter Eight

✦ ✦ ✦ ✦

THE SANTA CATALINA foothills lay far behind the McCandless party as sunset seduced the night riders with its lingering warmth. The light was failing but Thorne insisted on claiming a few more miles before calling a halt.

But traveling much further than that would be taking an unnecessary risk. When the party was in the desert flatlands, the moonbeams reflected off the white sand, making night-riding possible. Now that they were climbing into the juniper and oak forests of Mt. Lemmon, the treetops blocked the light. Thorne was too shrewd a rancher to continue much longer and risk injury to his valuable stock.

The days spent out in the open had stirred happiness within Octavio. Already he felt better than he had in several months. His skin had darkened to a healthier shade. The filth of imprisonment had been washed away.

He was glad that he had taken time to visit a barber and clothier before leaving Tucson. How good clothes could feel when they were the correct size and style! The moccasins, white shirt, and sturdy pants he wore now were more suitable for travel than the fancy clothes Thorne had given him. And the loose clothing and doeskins felt much better on his injuries.

A haircut and shave had raised his spirits considerably. He reached up and ran one hand through the dark wavy locks that stopped just below his collar. He felt as if a weight had been lifted from his head. At last, to feel like a human again! Last night's bath, despite all its complications, and this morning's grooming had restored him greatly.

He recalled the look that had darted across Gila's face at her first sight of his newly groomed person. In spite of his weakened condition, he knew he was strikingly handsome. Were he a braggart, he would have told her that few women had ever denied him their kisses. Many a señorita had voiced approval of his dark wavy hair and vivid blue eyes. Modesta often said the unique color of his eyes was caused by tilting his head so proudly.

Modesta. He had not thought of her in days. Octavio gave the horse his lead and tried to bring back her memory but could not. Instead a vision arose of auburn hair plunging heavily over ivory shoulders, then streaming seductively to the peaks of two well-rounded breasts. He remembered the taste of those lips that had so often ridiculed and accused, lips that his own passion had melted into bittersweet consent.

Octavio watched Gila's progress as she picked her way around a mulberry tree. He was surprised at the tenderness he felt toward her at this moment. She did not deserve this goodwill. He shrugged. Perhaps his sudden peace with the world and Gila was merely the result of being clean and shaven.

His mind roamed, and the angry words and actions that had passed between him and Gila receded. He remembered their wedding night and the way her flesh had softened beneath his gentle caresses, how her heart raced against his as each passion consumed the other. Her cheeks had flushed with the moment's headiness, her breath caught in rapturous pauses. For one mind-altering moment he'd forgotten he was man and she woman. They had become one. Just as the heavens and earth were one, the land and sea a continuous flow, so was the joining of Octavio to Gila. No more a single self. Forever half of complete.

The realization had shocked him that night. He'd been confused, disoriented; but somehow he knew these feelings were right. As if all questions had been answered, all doubts forever quelled by their perfect union. But how could that be? He did not know Gila. She was a stranger whom fate had chosen to share his destiny.

After their desires had melted into a sea of serenity, her eyes told him everything. The hazel pools searched his soul, questioning, pleading for an acknowledgment of all that had happened between them. He had wanted to soothe her with words but could not. No words could express the way he felt. Yet somewhere in the state of his uncertainty, she had found an answer. Her eyes softened into liquid rapture. She sealed the consummation with a kiss, a kiss that lingered and aroused Octavio's thirst even now.

Thorne called a halt to the proceedings, breaking Octavio's private thoughts. Octavio watched Gila more closely than before. He had not realized so many men would accompany the McCandlesses home. Thorne's herd had been larger than he expected. There were a good twenty wranglers riding back with the outfit.

Octavio dismounted, took his war bag and rifle, then draped them in the limbs of a piñon pine—a trick Gila had taught him on their first night outside of Nogales. Desert wolves were like the pack rats of Mexico. They dragged off anything that wasn't tied down.

While he was staking his pinto near heavy

grass, Gila handed Wee-People's reins to him. "The men will expect you to do this for me," she said, her voice low, almost a whisper. "Not that I can't take care of my own mount, but they'll expect it."

His fingers touched hers for only a moment, and he felt the same jolt that he saw flash instantly in her eyes. She jerked her hand away and mumbled, "I've got to get some grub."

Octavio smiled and reached to touch a rebellious strand of hair that had worked itself loose from the strip of rawhide holding back her auburn tresses. "So, *dulce mia*, you are a woman after all."

The flush on her cheeks was highlighted by the flickering of the newly lit campfire. "Don't you have any decency, October?" she whispered, yet he could hear the inner turmoil in her tone. "There are other people around."

Octavio chuckled. "Yes, there are. But I'm sure each of these men knows lust when he sees it."

Gila's eyes widened and she lunged at him, ready to strangle. A gopher hole foiled her attempt. She fell against him, and he caught her tight in his arms.

One of the wranglers guffawed. "Can't that wait till after supper, Gila?"

Gila started to right her position, then suddenly lay very still against Octavio's chest. She cocked her head toward him and muttered in low but precise words, "Put your arms around me, October. Kiss me and make it good."

Realizing her request was only to save her

further embarrassment, Octavio was tempted
not to comply with her wish. But the pressure
against his lower abdomen told him she was
poised to do him a painful injury. Well, he
wouldn't give her the satisfaction. She would
love to inflict such a wound to insure her freedom from his bed.

He would fulfill her wish. Perhaps she would
be more careful next time what she demanded of
him. "I'll make it look more than good," Octavio
promised. He pressed her closer, one hand
stroking the auburn tresses, the other caressing
her spine just above the buttocks. Softly he took
her lips, his tongue searching and finding its
mate. Moist shivers of pleasure shimmied down
to his own toes. But her own limp response
sparked his anger.

You'll not win this time, he swore silently. He
molded his lips to hers savagely, taking what
she tried desperately to withhold. A moan escaped her as she tried to push him away. Again
he demanded what was his. Octavio deepened
the kiss, fitting her struggling form into the hard
contours of his body. Still she struggled until the
kiss suddenly softened, sweetened in its taste,
and he felt her yield to the inevitable flame their
passions stoked. Then her hands ceased their
attack and delved into the ebony locks at his
temples. As she pressed closer, he felt her
trembling with desire, desire that warmed her
lips, flushed her cheeks.

Finally he needed breath of his own and
pulled gently away. She gasped, looking momentarily frightened by her own actions. Octa-

vio was surprised to feel not only elated but ashamed. Why did he feel as though he'd cheated them both in some unspeakable manner?

Gila took a moment to compose herself, then turned to the others. "You'll have to excuse my husband, fellas. He hasn't learned there's a time and place for such things."

Octavio faced the wranglers, prepared to accept their disapproval. But they were all busy, unconcerned with what had just happened. These were men of his kind. Men who did not interfere between a man and his woman. Perhaps the year would be less troublesome than he anticipated, or perhaps they merely wanted to see Gila corralled—a sight he doubted many of them had seen.

Thorne stepped up and handed Gila a skillet. "Why don't you get something to eat? I'll keep October busy. He and Henderson have first watch."

Octavio was stationed up the hill from the campsite. Leaning on one elbow, he searched the countryside for any movement other than from the people below. There was none.

His gaze returned to the campfire and he watched Gila moving from one wrangler to another, filling their tins. From her easy manner and the occasional laughter she returned when one of the men spoke to her, she appeared to be enjoying herself. There was a relaxed quality to her walk that wasn't evident when he was near her. Did he unnerve her in some manner? The thought both pleased and disturbed him.

One wrangler grabbed Gila by the waist and she fell into his lap. Octavio stood instantly, a hundred emotions surging through him. Was this man trying to solicit a response from Gila just as he himself had tried only moments ago?

Gila stood and pushed the wrangler to the ground. When the unfortunate cowpoke straightened and received an apparent tongue-lashing from her, Octavio felt an overwhelming commitment to brand every detail of the man's appearance into his memory. Sun-colored hair. Wide nose. Eyes too narrow to trust. A gnat's nest of a beard. Short neck. Compact shoulders. Probably an Austrian. Did McCandless hire any worthless bastard who strayed in and out of the desert?

Octavio's own hatred for the "emperor" Maximilian was so overpowering he found himself disliking anyone who was blond-haired and blue-eyed. A twinge of self-disgust soured his stomach as he realized how much like Gila he sounded. Prejudice should be reserved for an individual; it should not be a mark against an entire people, he reminded himself.

The men's laughter echoed up the mountain. Octavio relaxed and sat down. Why was he concerned? Gila could take care of herself. Yet her determination to deny she was a woman with a woman's yearnings had obviously never been tested to any degree or by any of these men . . . except one. Is one of these the father of her baby? Octavio wondered. If so, what must he be thinking, knowing the baby would be named Cordoba? Octavio knew the insult he would feel should another man ever seize the birthright of his own seed. Wasn't that the very reason he fought so hard for his beloved Mexico? He was determined to help Mexico's sons claim their birthright and not remain stepchildren to the world.

Though the McCandless hired hands had accepted him into the outfit with a wary welcome, Octavio knew their congratulations had been given more out of respect for their boss and his daughter than as any act of friendship toward him. These men lived hard, and he knew they would not take well to an outsider who didn't do his share of the work.

He stretched his legs, nestling into a more comfortable position amidst the pine's gnarled roots. He took off his moccasins and wiggled his toes, relieving the stiffness in his arches. He dug into one pocket and drew out the metal snuff can Gila had given him in Tucson, telling him he was lucky Liz had hoarded a single container of her famous salve. Opening the container, he inhaled the pleasant, healing odor of the gooey green substance that filled it. He dipped two fingers in, then wiped the ointment on his soles. A tingling warmth penetrated the wounds, making his feet feel as if a hundred tiny cactus needles were tickling them. The warm sensation subsided and gave in to a numbing effect.

Octavio pressed his feet against one of the tree roots, marveling that he felt no further pain. After replacing the lid, he put the can back into his pocket. Remembering the cigarros Thorne had given him, he searched through the war bag until he found one. He lit it and inhaled deeply, savoring the soothing nicotine. Contentedly, he blew out rings of smoke.

Today had not been a bad day. Gila had been decent to him, riding beside him for several miles, chatting amiably. He wondered if she were being social because of the other wranglers' presence or if she were just in a better frame of mind. Whatever the reason, he enjoyed the talk, noting her quick observations and obvious intelligence.

Octavio smiled and took another puff on the cigarro. Not so long ago he had thought a woman was good for nothing but a night of lovemaking and tending children. He had always respected a woman for the pleasure she could bring a man. Perhaps there was something he could learn from this American.

His gaze wandered back to the crackling campfire. Flames sparked and danced, sending a sliver of smoke curling upward. He marveled at the awesome hold the Irishman had over the territory and the Apache. Ever since Cochise and Mangas Coloradas had joined forces, Apache raids were more and more frequent. Yet the McCandless outfit camped as if there were no cause for alarm.

When Cochise gave his word that the McCandless outfit would not be attacked, Octavio knew no other tribe would dare disobey the order. Cochise and the other five Apache tribes

would stand against any renegade nation who
dared defy his orders.

Cochise. Memory of his once-dying blood
brother came vividly to Octavio's mind. It
seemed only yesterday, but it was more than
five years ago that Octavio had found Cochise
lying near Devil's Tank. Octavio had been running a message from Juárez to Hidalgo—one of
Juárez's chief officers—when he spotted an Indian near the deep water hole. The savage
appeared to be lying prone, drinking.

Octavio crept closer and watched for several
minutes. Realizing no one could drink for that
long and not come up for air, he wondered if
something were amiss. Was this a trick? Upon
closer inspection, he saw the reason for the Indian's immobility. A snake. Red, white, and black
bands encircled the head that had been severed.
A coral! The deadliest snake in the Sonora.

The savage might have killed a hundred white
men, but Octavio could not leave him to die if
there were a chance to save his life. Octavio
drew nearer and readied his gun when he saw
that the Indian's head was only at the edge of
the water. The snake trick had been used suc-
cessfully before, but this warrior gave no hint of
trickery as Octavio inched forward.

The Indian moaned in pain, and Octavio
crossed the remaining distance. He took the
knife from the savage's waistband. The Indian's
muscles quivered as if from somewhere deep
within his agony he fought to attack this new
enemy.

"I mean you no harm," Octavio assured him. "Hold still, compadre. I will have to cut the flesh and suck out the poison if you expect to live past sunset." Octavio cut an X over the swollen ankle where the snake had bitten. He lifted the heel, sucked the venom from the wound, and spit the deadly bile from his mouth. He repeated the process again and again until the blood ran a deep crimson.

Octavio tore a sleeve from his shirt and wrapped it around the calf muscle just above the injured ankle. He ripped the other sleeve and dipped it into the tank, then placed the cool cloth against the Indian's fevered forehead. For the next hour or so, Octavio wiped away the sweat as the Indian fought the snake's poison.

Had he reached the man in time? Had he taken enough poison out? Only time and luck would tell. Octavio rolled his blanket and placed it over the man, hoping the wool might help sweat out the poison and fever. The markings of lightning, hail, rain, snow, and sun painted on the victim's chest suggested much about the man. Red, white, and yellow paint across each cheek identified him as Chiricahua Apache, the fiercest of all six Apache nations. Other marks said this man was a chief. Since there was only one chief of the Chiricahua, this had to be Cochise!

Indecision washed over Octavio as he studied every detail of the legend's face. Considered the most aggressive of the Apache chiefs, already the warrior had established his name in the annals of Gadsden history. A moment of awe engulfed Octavio as he realized he might be the only white man other than Tom Jeffords who had ever been given the chance to inspect the features of the infamous Apache.

Octavio's mind warred. He should kill Cochise. Now, while he had the opportunity. Yet he couldn't force himself to commit the deed, despite the many lives Cochise had taken. To kill the chief now would be like trapping a bear as it lay dying. No, he would not kill him. Fate must choose to defeat a legend.

By morning, Cochise was better, and Octavio decided it was time to go before other Chiricahua came in search of their leader. He waited until Cochise regained consciousness and gave the chief a drink from his canteen. "I have to leave now, señor." Octavio spoke in Spanish, hoping the rumor that Cochise understood the language was true. "I left food and there's water in this canteen. Soon you'll have enough strength to reach the tank on your own. Your brothers will find you before the tank dries."

A question formed in the dark eyes.

Octavio replaced the flinted knife into the Indian's waistband. "I choose not to kill you. Adios, amigo."

Cochise extended an unsteady forearm. Octavio clasped it firmly. The voice was merely a whisper. *"Hermano de sangre."* Blood brother.

Awed by the honor a mere snakebite had allowed him, Octavio gripped Cochise's forearm with added pride and confirmed, *"Hermano de sangre."*

Memory of the day he became kin to the

fiercest Apache in the territory paled the minor nuisances of his life now. Gila was just another obstacle in his path to gain the throne for Juárez. Time. Time had a way of solving all problems. Just as it had with Cochise, so would it resolve his bargain with the McCandlesses.

All Octavio wanted to do now was to lie back and enjoy the crisp night air and the cigarro Thorne had given him. The fragrances of piñon and juniper swirled with the breeze while the stars overhead twinkled with a brightness he'd almost forgotten. The sky was an endless blanket encircling the earth with hidden warmth. Octavio felt at peace with the vastness, appreciating the freedom that previously had been denied him. Not yet true freedom, but freedom from the confinement of man-made walls.

No longer did he feel the fear of the vastness he had experienced on his first night on the trail with his new bride. Though he'd admitted it to no one, he'd been afraid. Afraid of the largeness of the world. The desert was so vast, so endless. He had seemed merely a grain in the sands of time, a grain miraculously surrendered from the confines of a prison hourglass. Still, a bit of sand that could be mixed with the oil of Juárez's inspiration to light the fire of Mexican independence from foreign rule.

As the days wore on, his fear subsided and he became more convinced of his destiny. He was, indeed, the grain by which Juárez would succeed. This Octavio knew with every drop of blood flowing in his veins. "This is my destiny and neither Cochise, Maximilian, nor Thorne

McCandless can prevent it!'' he announced to the wind.

He stared at the midnight sky, thinking each star seemed suddenly brighter, almost glistening in approval at his announcement. Filled with pride and respect for his destiny, he let a tear trickle down his cheek. His chest swelled with an emotion he could not name. Crossing himself, he silently thanked God for allowing him this new freedom and a chance to fulfill his fate.

# Chapter Nine

✦✦✦✦✦

GILA BARELY SLEPT that night. Home was near. She itched to get back to her cactus fields and tend her saguaros. With the pageant little more than two weeks away, she would have to farm her cacti and bottle her cures the moment she got home.

Shelly Kate will just have to see to October's settling in so I can get my work done, Gila decided.

Shelly Kate! What would her younger sister say once she found out about the marriage? She won't believe it. She'll suspect the reason for the hurried marriage. Will Thorne tell her the truth? How secret must the secret be?

As Octavio cantered his pinto alongside Wee-

People, the paint snorted. "I think Señor People does not like my company so much—eh?" he chuckled.

Gila shrugged. "Both of us enjoy our own company." She wanted to be left alone the remainder of the journey. "Did you need something in particular?" she relented at his pained look. Why did he have to look so distracting?

"I don't need anything, *dulce mia*," he replied. "I thought it would look more natural if I rode with you as we neared your home. If I were one of your father's men, I would expect you to be at your new husband's side, telling him all about his new home."

Gila wished she could find fault in what he said, but he was right. "Our ranch runs along the San Pedro Valley from the Galiuro Mountains up to Holy Joe Peak, and into the springs where the Aravaipa, Gila, and San Pedro rivers empty together. We're about ten miles south of the Kearney trail to California."

Octavio waved an arm in a sweeping gesture. "Does it all look as lovely as this?"

Gila breathed in the fragrance of the creosote bushes and paloverde trees that lined the banks of the San Pedro River. The flowered valley was a startling contrast to the land they had traveled the last few days. "No, it's not all this pretty. To the northeast of us is a terrible sandy wilderness."

She saw his surprise and laughed. "Arizona territory is like a lady, October. She changes her looks as fast as you can bat an eye. One minute you're in the saguaro desert, next in the pine

forests, and the next in a meadow full of wild-
flowers. Who knows what lies around the
bend?"

As they topped a rise, the land gave way to a
red-walled canyon. Turquoise mountains lined
the distant horizon. Book took the lead, guiding
them along the worn path to the canyon floor.
They traveled for several miles until the river
was joined by another.

"The Aravaipa," Gila informed Octavio.
"We're almost there."

A reddish brown cobbled wall of an ancient
pueblo spanned the bank of the new river.
Octavio reined abruptly and cried, "*Madre Santísima!* I have found it! I have found it!"

Gila turned Wee-People half-quarter. "You've
found what?"

Octavio spread his hands, encompassing all
his surroundings. "Your land! Your land was
once the discovery of my ancestor, Coronado.
This is the *Chichilticale.* That pueblo stained with
red ochre must have been the Red House of
which he wrote. And those mountains—"

"The Pinalenos?"

"Yes. They must be the turquoise peaks he
spoke of. The wilderness beyond your home is
the Great Despoblado. Taloned fingers of sand,
he called them. What a find! What a magnificent
find!" Octavio rode to Gila, grabbed her by the
shoulders and kissed her joyfully.

After the initial surprise of his kiss, Gila was
soon caught up in his enthusiasm. She knew the
kiss was not meant for her, but for his marvelous
discovery. Yet Gila had made one of her own.

When his lips released hers, she opened her
eyes to see his utter delight. October wasn't
aware of her disappointment and she was glad.
It was difficult enough to face the realization that
she wanted him to kiss her, much less to have to
feel the brunt of his possible ridicule.

Closing her lashes for only a moment, she
remembered the taste of his lips upon her own.
Ever since they had left Tucson, the sight of him
had been more than unsettling. The haircut,
shave, and bath made him devilishly attractive.
And now his nearness, blending with the smell
of leather, horseflesh, and aged tobacco, all but
unnerved her.

"Shall I kiss you again, my sweet? For the sake
of the men?" Octavio teased.

Gila's eyes opened in embarrassment. His
sarcasm sent a piercing arrow of anger through
her. "No!" was all she could manage. She
slapped the reins to Wee-People's flank and he
burst into a gallop. She rode past Thorne, her
words trailing behind her. "I'm scouting with
Book."

When she reached Book, she eased her mount
into an easy canter alongside his Appaloosa. The
Oriental offered no conversation, for which she
was grateful. She glanced back to see Octavio's
reaction and expected him to be laughing at her,
but he wasn't. Instead he was deep in conversation with Ben, as if nothing had happened
between them. Could he dismiss her feelings as
if they were childish whims? Perplexing tears
trickled down her cheeks. Saints and begorra,
had she lost her mind!

Determined October would not make a fool of her again in front of the men, she decided to ride beside Book the remainder of the journey and leave Thorne to acquaint her new husband with the Circle-Shamrock property.

Shimmering waves of heat rose above the ranch. Once again, the white buffalo's lead had announced their arrival. A group of wranglers waited on horseback at a boundary post.

Octavio knew the last leg of the journey would be well patrolled by Thorne's men. On a ranch the size of the Circle-Shamrock, the main house would be built several miles from the boundary posts, allowing plenty of time to warn the women and children in case of attack.

Thorne raised a massive hand in greeting. Each wrangler took off his hat as the Irishman passed by. When Octavio passed, he saw the wranglers eye him in curiosity and appraisal. He stared squarely at each one. He might be wearing the clothes of a Mexican peasant, but noble blood flowed in his veins.

After passing the wranglers, Octavio settled back from the group, taking in the beautiful countryside. Delicate pink sand verbenas, blue lupine, yellow brittlebush, and paloverde made the desert a rainbow of color. Flame-colored prickly pears blushed beneath the protective shade of the saguaros. In the distance, a waterfall invited him with its refreshing spill, making him eager to reach his destination. A swim would wash away the heat and dust of the road very well.

The party continued along the path that ran

adjacent to the canyon wall. His distance from
Book and Gila had shortened, and Octavio realized they had slowed their pace. They must be
nearing the ranch. A wave of relaxation washed
over the party and filled the procession with an
air of anticipation. Their journey had been successful. They were bringing home the herd.
Only Octavio felt like a stranger to their happiness and this curious land. How he envied
them, for he knew well the longing for home. He
spurred his horse into a gallop, halting when
he'd caught up to Gila. He wanted to be in her
company; she was the only home he would have
for the next year and it somehow made him feel
less lonesome to be near her.

Ahead, a large stand of pines was divided by
a gate. Above the arch an iron shamrock hung
boldly from two cross posts. As he rode through
the gate, Octavio noted the two lookouts stationed on either side. Soon his attention was
drawn to the house. A porch ran along its full
length and width. The entire west side extended
deep into the mountain, while the north jutted
out to form an L. Near the southern wall a
waterfall emptied into a blue-green pool and a
stream that wound its way back toward the San
Pedro. Beyond the northern wall, Octavio could
see the outline of several more adobe buildings.
Probably for the ranch hands, he decided. "It is
magnificent."

"It's real soul-soothing at times," Gila admitted. "Ma had to have something spectacular to
make up for leaving her beautiful home in
Ireland."

Ma? Octavio had given no thought to Gila's mother. A mother-in-law! *Madre Santísima!* What if she held the same prejudice as her daughter about his countrymen? Dread dried his throat, then knotted his stomach as he contemplated the image of an older Gila McCandless.

"Could we stop somewhere so that I might dress properly?" he asked. "I would not insult your mother with this peon clothing." Gila was quiet for so long he wondered if she'd heard him. He started to repeat the question.

"She's dead," Gila interrupted softly, her voice barely above a whisper. "She's been gone for almost seventeen years."

Octavio noted the determined barrier that held back the unshed tears in her hazel eyes. "I'm sorry."

A wave of tenderness washed over him, causing Octavio to reach for her hand. The movement was awkward, bringing the pinto and paint so close that his and Gila's legs brushed one another. Despite their clothing, his flesh jolted at the touch. His eyes met hers, and he knew instantly she experienced the same disturbance, for her hand tightened in his. She allowed her hand to remain there.

So! She was finally yielding to him. She was not the prickly pear she pretended to be. Now he might enjoy the pleasure of her bed for the rest of his stay. It disturbed him greatly to admit it, but he actually missed the enjoyment she'd given him on their wedding night. Last night he'd found it difficult to keep his hands from touching her when she bedded down beside

him. He supposed this unusual desire for her
was due to the many months away from female
comfort of any sort. Yet even now, as he glanced
at Gila, he felt stirred. Stirred by what, he was
uncertain. Gila was not beautiful in the normal
sense of the word, but her eyes beseeched him.
There he would not linger, knowing full well
what the hazel pools might extract.

And there was something almost daring in her
reckless disregard for her femininity. He had
never cared for stocky women, but he remembered the feel of her body as it softened with his
caresses. He had been surprised at the time, but
now he knew a full figure could be very enticing
and could offer warmth of many kinds on cold,
damp nights. "Tonight, *dulce mia?*" he asked,
squeezing her hand gently. She did not answer,
but her heightened color gave evidence that she
had at least considered his suggestion.

He halted at the hitching rail in front of the
ranch. From the center of the L-shaped house a
door opened and a small young woman glided
out like a ray of sunlight. Her hair was as pale as
the streams of yellow-white heat that glimmered
on the horizon. Her tiny nose was turned up
slightly, the delicate lips turned down in a pout.
The large, heavily lashed eyes were almond-
shaped and black. Her beauty alone was breath-
taking, but ebony eyes set against such fair skin
placed the woman above even the loveliest of
ladies.

Unconsciously Octavio brushed back his hair,
his appreciation of her beauty ending in an
unexpected "Uhh-hmmm!" Embarrassed by his

verbal approval, he was about to apologize to her, but to his chagrin realized she hadn't even noticed him amidst the group. Her full attention was upon Thorne McCandless.

Octavio stared at her intensely, wondering if he had been about to apologize to another female who held the same prejudice that Gila felt toward his people. Anger sharpened his inspection, and he left no pore undetected. An uncommon buzzing filled his ears as the roaring crowd of his bullfighting days unexpectedly echoed in his memory. Even the billowing dust and sweat of El Diablo's maniacal charge rushed back to vividly penetrate his nostrils. Sounds of unshod hoofs thundered closer and closer. The crowd drew its breath and waited. His chest tightened with anticipation of the bull's death thrust. He looked into its insane eyes and knew that he, too, must kill. The animal lunged. Octavio stepped aside. The crowd stood and cried, "Olé."

Wee-People snorted, shaking Octavio from his reverie. Was he going mad? Had too many days in the desert sun played havoc with his senses? His inspection of the young woman became even more intense, and he wondered if *she* might have evoked the memory in some way.

The long lashes over her ebony pools blinked back the blazing sunlight, causing a frown to wrinkle her forehead. "Really!" she complained. "Do hurry in from this dreadful heat or we'll be roasted." She turned abruptly and hastened into the house.

Octavio was amused as he glanced down to

find himself sitting straighter in the saddle. His body had not lost its senses! It definitely knew when a beautiful woman was in attendance.

The woman's lilting voice nagged at his memory. Where had he heard it before? Modesta's voice rushed back with its gaiety. For the first time in days, visions of his former love danced in his mind's eye while the echoes of the roaring crowd returned once more to disturb him.

Perhaps this woman stirred his memory of Modesta because, like his former fiancée, she was petite and beautiful. Yet how could a stranger provoke such a strong memory of Modesta, when he himself had been unable to conjure her image since having met Gila?

The party dismounted and tied their horses to the rail. Octavio followed Gila and Thorne toward the door the woman had entered. He noticed Book remained with his and the McCandlesses' horses, while the other men led their mounts past the northern wall and through a row of paloverdes.

Gila nodded in the same direction. "Through yonder are the bunkhouses and the corral. Most of the bunkhouses are built into the mountain like the main house."

Inside the house, Octavio's skin cooled rapidly. He took in his new surroundings. The large room was furnished with numerous chairs and several lengthy couches. A sideboard formed its own L in the corner of the room. The rawhide furniture was stained a bluish green. The wool rugs scattered about on the ochre-colored floor were Irish green. The room looked gaudy to

Octavio's aristocratic eyes, and he was reminded that the McCandless money was new money, far different from the wealth of his Castilian ancestors.

"Unusual colors," he commented, realizing Gila was waiting for his reaction.

"Yes, they are," she said stiffly, her back straightening as her chin tilted defiantly. She'd read him too easily. "Mother loved the colors of her homeland. She believed they would make the house seem cooler."

The bold tones of blue and green did add to the coolness, but Octavio wondered why the design had not been changed after all these years. There certainly was money enough.

As if she read his thoughts Gila explained, "Thorne won't change it. Says if the furnishings were good enough for Kathryn, then they're good enough for us lassies."

"Lassies?"

"You know, the little sunbeam who walked out and told Thorne to get off his saddle and get in here a few minutes ago. That's Shelly Kate, my sister."

"Did someone mention my name?" asked Shelly as she came through the doorway to the left of the sideboard.

Once again Octavio admired her beauty, taking in the slimness of her tiny hips, narrow waist, well-proportioned bosom, and enchanting face. A face vaguely familiar, yet unfamiliar. What had gone wrong with Gila?

Shelly Kate moved toward Octavio. "Why, Don Cordoba! What are you doing in this part of

the world? Last time I saw you, you were being
. . ." she paused delicately. "And how is
Modesta?" She held out her hand to him.

"Forgive me, señorita. Do we know each
other?" He kissed the back of her hand and
bowed.

Shelly Kate blushed as she curtsied. "You
shame me, sir. You are *the* Don Octavio Diego
Cordoba who accompanied Modesta Hidalgo to
Maximilian's ball last July, are you not? I rarely
forget such a handsome face."

So! This was the reason she brought back
memories of Modesta and the bullfight. A group
of Americans had attended the fight and the ball
that day. Since his duty was to slay Maximilian,
he had paid little attention to the visiting dele-
gation. But now, seeing Shelly Kate more
closely, he vaguely remembered being intro-
duced to her. She sat next to Modesta at the
bullfight, then accompanied her to the ball. She
was an old school friend of Modesta's, if he
remembered correctly.

"Who's Modesta Hidalgo?" Gila asked, her
hazel eyes hard and demanding.

"An acquaintance," Octavio stated arrogantly.
He didn't feel as if he owed her any explanation.
Still, it might be fun to see if Gila were suffering
any pains of possessiveness. "She was someone
I knew before Angelita."

"Angelita?" Gila tried to seem unconcerned
about his past, but there was a sharpness to her
tone. "Who's *she*?"

"Someone who saw me through some very

lonely times over the last eight months." Octavio could've choked on the laughter he was forcing back, but he didn't dare. Gila would not only kill him but all his living relatives if she knew she were fuming over a cockroach.

"Well, I don't know who this Angelita is," Shelly's fists balled against her hips, "but I certainly know Modesta Hidalgo. She was more than an acquaintance. Really, Don Cordoba! You slight yourself." Her eyes glinted with knowing as she looked first at Gila, then at Octavio. Her smile was slow, pleasant, and strangely satisfied. "Mo is the daughter of Benito Juárez's top generalissimo. Don Cordoba was engaged to her at the time he and I met."

Gila didn't give Shelly time to gloat. "You can wipe those eagle feathers off your mouth, Shelly Kate. Octavio's my *husband*."

# Chapter Ten

✦—✦—✦—✦

SHELLY KATE'S MOUTH gaped in surprise and a blush darkened her fair cheeks. "Your *husband?* I'm so sorry."

Octavio wasn't sure if she meant sorry that he was Gila's husband or sorry for telling Gila about Modesta. He decided to give her the benefit of the doubt. "There's no need, Señorita McCandless. Modesta is someone of the past, and you had no way of knowing about Gila and me."

Thorne stepped up to the sideboard and poured two glasses of liquor. "I believe tequila is your favorite, isn't it, October?"

Octavio thanked him, glad to have the drink. The recollection of old times was unsettling.

"Shelly, why don't you go fix us something to eat," Thorne commanded. "We've had a hard ride and could use a decent home-cooked meal."

"Then you'd best let me do it," Gila said. "Nothing she cooks is fit to eat." She stomped past Shelly Kate and through the door.

Shelly untied the apron that covered her yellow mutton-sleeved dress and threw it at Gila. "Here. You can have it. It wasn't *my* idea to cook for those heathens out back. If you hadn't gone gallivanting all over the countryside with those horses, I wouldn't have had to spend the last two weeks cooking in this heat for a bunch of starving no-goods."

Gila whirled. "If you had taken your turn, a lot of things wouldn't have happened."

The fierce expression on Gila's face made Octavio wonder about the undercurrent of words. Why were they so angry with each other? Had Gila been compelled to take this trip to keep her from her baby's father, only to be forced to marry a total stranger?

"Gila, go get supper started," Thorne ordered. After she left, he turned to his other daughter. "Shelly, get your bath before the rest of us. We'll all need one tonight." He motioned for Octavio to follow him.

Thorne led Octavio down a long corridor to the house's southernmost bedroom. The magnificent room had a four-poster bed and a massive dressing table made of mountain mahogany. A red sheepskin coverlet was spread across the bed, and matching rugs graced the floor. An ochre-colored davenport sat against the east wall beneath the room's only window. The window's shape was like no other he had ever seen.

"Shamrocks," Thorne told him. "All the windows of the Circle-Shamrock are shaped like shamrocks. Kathryn, my late wife, thought they were pretty, but they're practical, too. Easy to shoot out of in case of attack."

Octavio was impressed, but the lack of other windows could be dangerous. "What about a rear assault?"

"There can be none. The house is built deep into the mountain. For protection from raids and the heat. You could shinny down one of the smoke chimneys in the kitchen. But we keep a constant fire going now, so anyone trying to get in that way would either suffocate or get one hell of a hot saddle."

Thorne nodded toward the southeast corner of the room. "But just in case anyone's smarter than us, Book is stationed farther up the mountain. We'll get advance warning next time."

Next time? Octavio was about to ask if there had been an attack before when Thorne changed the subject.

"Well, make yourself at home. Gila will have supper ready in a little while, and Book will bring your bag. You might want to get the feel of the house. I always do when I'm somewhere new." He lifted his drink in salute. "And if you need another, feel free to pour your own. Just don't tax yourself with too many. I can't abide a man who can't hold his tonic."

Octavio thanked Thorne and closed the door after the big man. He finished off his drink and decided he would have another. About halfway down the corridor, he stopped at a door. After knocking and receiving no answer, he opened it. A nursery. A hand-carved swinging cradle hung in the corner. Wooden toys were piled inside a toy box. Dust, years thick, layered every corner of the room. This was not a new nursery for Gila's baby, but more than likely hers and Shelly Kate's. He stepped back into the hallway and walked on to the next room.

This must be Shelly Kate's, he decided when he noticed the dressing table full of jars and perfume bottles. Immediately he shut the door. He made a point of staying out of a woman's boudoir unless personally invited.

Sixteen years without a mistress was apparent in every room except the one that was now his and Gila's. The quality of furnishings was exceptional, but the years had taken their toll. Rugs were frayed, furniture scuffed. The interior design was useful, but not modern. His own mother would have insisted on refurbishing this hacienda every other year had it been her own.

Yet there was a quiet dignity to this house. He

felt welcome. He had found a stopping place from the heat. Whether it was from the heat of the desert or the heat of Maximilian's revenge, he was uncertain.

An appetizing smell drifted through the doorway Gila had entered earlier. Hunger steered him toward the kitchen.

Gila wiped her brow with one sleeve, then continued stirring the piñon batter. Though' the kitchen was relatively cool despite the constant fire in the chimneys, she always overworked herself whenever she beat the brown-spotted dough. She broke off a piece, patted it into a tortilla-sized cake, then placed it on the hot griddle. After repeating the process a dozen times, she poked the charcoal beneath the griddle, making certain the coals were well spaced for even cooking.

Satisfied, she opened the cupboard, knelt, and lifted a trapdoor. The odor of salted lamb rose, perfuming the air in the closet. She folded back the layers of protective covering and chose the finest meat. They had been without a good home-cooked meal for two weeks now, and she wanted to make this meal special. She refolded the coverlet and once again felt proud of herself.

The blanket protecting the McCandless horde of meat was made from the skin of a saguaro. One day while she was examining one of the giant cacti, she marveled at how well it retained its water, despite the heat. Since meat spoiled quickly, she decided to test the accordion skin and see if it would help preserve meat. She sewed a piece of cactus skin large enough to fill the storage pit and lap over the top. The combination of the waterproof cactus shell and the coolness of the underground larder allowed meat to stay fresh for weeks longer. Since food in the desert was precious, no matter how much money one had, Gila had been particularly pleased with her discovery. She had hastened to share the information with her neighbors.

"What is that wonderful smell, *dulce mia?*" Octavio asked, startling her from her thoughts.

Gila turned toward the door. How long had he been standing there with that ravenous look on his face? "Where's Shelly Kate?" she asked, expecting her sister to walk in behind him. "I thought you two would be knee-deep in memories by now."

As she placed strips of meat in the hot skillet, Octavio leaned over the stove, inhaling the aromatic smell. "Your father instructed her otherwise. Mmmmmm . . . I hope the food tastes as good as it smells." He opened his eyes and gave her a knowing look. "I am a man of *many* tastes."

"A man with such varied tastes knows better than to nibble from too many kettles," Gila said as she flipped the cakes. "His health might suffer in the end."

Octavio laughed and rubbed his buttocks in exaggerated defense. "I remember too well how one *suffers in the end.*"

Her laugh started as a low chuckle, then bubbled into a full guffaw. Instinctively, her palm moved to her mouth to hide her amusement, but the merriment in Octavio's eyes made Gila lower her hand to her side. He laughed along with her and she enjoyed his vibrant tone.

He fell silent, looking at her with such intensity she felt she would melt from the heat of his gaze. A smile lifted one corner of his mouth, and she wondered why the small of her back tingled with sudden warmth. Her hand trembled as she flipped the next cake.

Octavio watched. "What are those, my sweet? I've never seen such a thing."

Fighting off a momentary rise of anger, Gila wondered if she had misread his meaning. Perhaps it was curiosity, not sarcasm, she saw etched in his expression. "These are piñon cakes. They're made from the nuts of one of the local pines." She broke off a piece and offered it to him. "Try it."

Octavio took a bite. His look of approval pleased her. "It's my own recipe," she said.

He leaned against the wall, arms folded across his chest. "Tell me about the Circle-Shamrock, Gila. How did your father succeed when so many others haven't?"

Gila poured two cups of coffee and offered one to Octavio. She took a sip of her own. "Not much to tell, really. Thorne was—"

"Do you always call him by his given name?" Octavio asked. "Is this not disrespectful in America? In most of the countries where I have traveled, it is not customary."

Gila avoided his question. "Oh? You've traveled a lot?"

"I am a matador. I have fought the bull in many places." He looked at her earnestly. "You have not answered my question, *querida*. Why do you not call him *Father*?"

Gila lowered her lashes. "I just never have. I haven't felt like calling him Father." She couldn't tell October she saw no reason to give Thorne a name he hadn't earned. Irritation fueled her embarrassment. "Why must you always concern yourself with things that aren't your business!" She sat her cup down with a thud, spilling part of the hot liquid on her hand.

She swore, bringing the burned flesh to her lips. Octavio was at her side instantly, his fingers digging into the crock of lard near her stove. He rubbed it on the burn, and soon his soothing strokes eased the pain.

Gila studied his face as he doctored her hand. His concern filled her with tenderness. This was the second time he'd been kind to her. When he insisted on changing his clothes in order not to insult Kathryn, Gila had been pleased he cared what her mother would think of him. Mexican or not, he did have gentlemanly ways. And now, due to his quick thinking, he had saved her hand from blistering and kept her from losing several precious days in the saguaro fields. Slowly she pulled her hand away. "Thank you, I'll be all right. It's nothing, really."

Octavio gently kissed the flesh between her thumb and forefinger. "Forgive me, *dulce mia*. I did not mean to anger you. I'm afraid you are right. I do trouble myself with, as you say, things that are not my concern." He returned to his former position. "Now, about your father's success," he urged.

"Thorne came from Ireland, as you well know," Gila began. "He and mother came over just as the rebellion broke out."

"Which one? There have been so many in your father's homeland."

Gila ground prairie clover and wild buckwheat over the strips of lamb. "It was at the time of the Young Irelanders and Daniel O'Connell. The statesman and Thorne were thicker than quicksand, or so Thorne says. Which doesn't say much, by the way. Thorne stretches the truth to suit his needs. Still, he's mighty secretive about those years with O'Connell. Book, too. Whatever the reason may have been, the three of them chose to come to America—Thorne, my mother, and Book."

"But why the Gadsden?"

"Thorne heard there was plenty of territory waiting to be given away. No one bothered to tell him about the Indians. But even that didn't stop him.

"Mother chose this particular spot. The neighboring Aravaipa tribe were friendly, but the other Apache tribes gave Thorne a fair amount of trouble. He finally asked for a parlay with Cochise himself. That was about eighteen years ago."

"Many times on our journey here, I wondered how your father has managed peace with the Apache nation. May I ask how?"

Gila forked the meat onto one platter and placed the cakes on another. "The Irish rush into

situations head-on, never looking back. They
don't fear dying if they live by what they think is
right. Some folks think they're conceited, others
think they're just plain foolhardy. But they don't
dally around, living a coward's life. Like Thorne.
He let it be known he wanted to talk to the
*nantan* and would settle for no one else. A
Chiricahua brave rode right up to our front door
one day to tell Thorne Cochise had agreed to
meet him. How the brave got past all the lookouts, only St. Patrick knows.''

Gila opened the cupboard and storage door
again and reached for two accordion pouches.

''Why are you smiling?'' Octavio asked curi-
ously as she turned around and set the pouches
on the table.

Was her pride showing? she wondered in
embarrassment. The saguaro pouches were another of her inventions. They kept milk fresh for
several days. ''No reason,'' she said, not caring
to share her thoughts. ''I just felt like smiling.''
She hurriedly returned to her tale. ''The brave
took Thorne to Cochise's camp. Thorne made a
trade. He said he would allow the Apache leader
to choose ten of the best horses from each
remuda he was permitted to herd from Mexico.
Thorne would keep away from the Santa Cruz
River and not interfere in any of Cochise's raids.
If any of the McCandless wranglers did interfere,
they were to be handed over to Cochise.''

''I'm certain—'' began Octavio, then he became suddenly silent.

''You're certain of what?'' asked Gila, wondering what he had been about to say. Did he think

he could judge the right or wrong of Thorne's actions? So what if Thorne didn't interfere in Cochise's raids on the Mexicans? She might say anything she cared to about Thorne, but Gila refused to let anyone else do the same. He deserved respect as a man, whether or not he did as a father.

She lifted the platters of food. Her hands shook with anger, making her severely chastise herself. Who knew what October had started to say? Perhaps it had nothing to do with Thorne. Why was it that every time she was in her husband's company, she felt as if she were galloping uphill? He made her feel silly, clumsy, exasperated. And warm. No man had ever affected her this way.

Yet even as Gila pondered his attack upon her emotions, she reluctantly acknowledged the whispery voice reminding her of his scorching lips upon her own, the feel of those large sculptured hands tenderly caressing her, the strength of his sinewy muscles against her own yielding flesh. Gila's cheeks tightened with the blush that rose to reveal her thoughts. She wanted him, now, in the kitchen. Anywhere. But the memory of his goading voice mocked her. *The next time we make love, dulce mia, you will ask . . . beg me for it.*

"Why don't you go wash up," she said, desperately wanting him out of her sight. "Supper will be ready shortly."

Surprised yet thankful for his quick departure, she headed toward the supper table in the adjoining room. She set the platters down with little care, swearing as a piece of meat slid off and stained the tablecloth. Now she would have to change the blamed thing before supper. But why should she? For October? Certainly not for him, he who had told her she would have to beg him for love. Well, just let him beg for a new tablecloth!

# Chapter Eleven

✦✦✦✦✦

WHEN OCTAVIO ARRIVED in his room, the washing bowl had been filled with water. On the sheepskin coverlet lay a blue chambray shirt and matching trousers. His war bag sat undisturbed upon the ochre-colored couch. Whoever had provided the clean garments and wash water was considerate but not curious. His bag had not been searched, assuring him that Shelly Kate was not responsible. Gila had been in the kitchen. Thorne was above playing host. The rancher set the pace, and it was up to others to keep up.

That kind of man Octavio knew well. His father, grandfather, and all previous Cordobas, even Benito Juárez—men with whom his fate intertwined—were of that same breed. If he hadn't already, McCandless would soon learn that he, Don Octavio Diego Cordoba, was one of them too.

Octavio washed and dressed. The chambray felt good against his skin. His injuries were healing now and he felt renewed strength returning to his limbs. Gila's salve relieved the constant burning, and already the scars had lost the red-green tint of infection. Another week of the cactus medicine and his thighs would be completely healed.

Gila. What a strange woman she was. One moment cursing like a drunken *bandido*, the next as defenseless as a newborn calf. When he kissed her burned hand and she looked at him with eyes full of tenderness, he had almost taken her in his arms. The perspiration glistening on her forehead and neckline aroused his memory of that other night, when her skin had been moist from lovemaking.

He was surprised that he had thought her beautiful in the kitchen. Despite the nankeens and dirty blouse, the apron, the tangled strands of auburn hair clinging to her face and neck, he thought she looked the loveliest he had ever seen her.

Was it the smell of good cooking, which always aroused his appetites, that made her seem more beautiful than she was? No. It was her eyes. The hunger in them was not for food. The touch of flesh against flesh, lips against hand. *That* had awakened their appetites for each other.

Yes, for each other. Octavio was a man of truth. He would not deny he desired Gila. This large, very sturdy desert flower had somehow managed to lay claim to his loins. Disgust gnawed at his insides. She who had cursed his people. She who had kicked him like an animal. Yet he wanted her.

Octavio willed Modesta's image to come to him. He yearned for the soft petite contours of her waist and hips, the black silken hair, the small, round breasts. But the image wouldn't stay focused. Instead, auburn tresses swayed in the breeze, teasing the nipples of large, voluptuous breasts. Hazel eyes bore deeply into his mind, pleading. Gila stayed in his mind, softer, more fragile than ever before.

Octavio shook himself from the musing. He was more tired than he had thought. If Gila seemed fragile to him, it was most certainly due to his concern for her condition. That had to be it! Those tender moments were brought about because of her maternal glow. He turned the thought round and round in his mind, but his heart was not convinced of its truth.


Octavio entered the massive dining room that was adjacent to the kitchen. Four large tables and numerous chairs hinted at the actual size of the McCandless work party. For the moment, only one table was occupied.

Thorne waved Octavio to a chair. "I hope you found the place to your liking, October."

Noticing that Gila was already seated, Octavio chose the gray high-backed chair next to hers. "I did, indeed, Señor McCandless." He nodded once to Book, who sat at Thorne's left. "I would like to thank you, sir, for your consideration."

Fingering the blue chambray he added, "These fit well and are most comfortable."

Gila looked startled. "Your injuries aren't any better?"

"Do not concern yourself, querida," Octavio replied, wondering if she were truly worried about his wounds or merely the potency of her medicine. "I am well."

"Good," said Thorne. "Then you will be able to help roughsaddle this latest remuda. We'll need every available man since Gila will not join in the work this time."

"What!" Gila protested. "Who says I can't? Just because—"

"Do control yourself, Gila," Shelly Kate criticized. "You sound like a banshee."

All eyes turned to the parlor doorway. Shelly Kate was dressed in a resplendent gown of green silk. The skirt plunged to the floor in layers of ruffles. The heart-shaped bodice encased small, round breasts above a petite waist and hips. Turquoise-colored lace daintily ruffled around a long slender neck. The sleeves were puffed high above narrow shoulders, then gathered at each elbow. She looked like an emerald, freshly cut, a sharp contrast to her rocky surroundings.

Pale white-blond hair was piled high on her head, cascading in ringlets toward the nape of her neck. Smaller curls accented her temples, exaggerating her large black almond-shaped eyes.

Octavio rose and took a few steps before he realized he had moved. Since he was already standing, he knew it would be awkward not to continue. He pulled out the empty chair next to his. "Señorita McCandless, may I have the honor?"

Her black feathery lashes dipped slowly, a pink blush darkening her cheeks. "Why thank you, Don Cordoba," she said sweetly. She smiled and offered her hand.

Octavio bowed, brushing his lips against the soft flesh of her hand. Protocol was protocol, after all, he decided. She smelled wonderful. What was she wearing? Honeysuckle? Modesta's scent. Oh, but this one was clever. What was she planning? Was this for his benefit? If not, then whose?

Octavio seated Shelly, then himself. He turned toward Gila. Her cheeks were equally aflame, but not with embarrassment. Hers was the red of anger. Well, let her remain angry! He would continue to kiss as many hands as protocol and his mother's teachings dictated.

Shelly Kate leaned closer and giggled. "I do believe Gila is jealous, Don Cordoba." The black eyes twinkled mischievously.

Did this younger McCandless think he could not see through her ploy? What satisfaction did she derive from this?

The color of Gila's cheeks deepened. "You really should forget that ignorant custom, *darling*. No telling where someone's hands have been."

Shelly Kate's chin rose defiantly. "Father, really! Don Cordoba shouldn't have to listen to this kind of—"

"Please, señorita," Octavio interrupted. He

didn't need anyone to champion his honor. "Permit me to speak for myself."

"Of course."

Octavio turned to Gila, head high, shoulders squared. "As my wife, you will learn to hold your snake's tongue from this day forward. It is you who are ignorant of the grace and manners becoming to civilized people. To kiss another's hand is a supreme compliment. And a *true* lady never comes to the dining table unclean." He glared at her grease-splattered shirt, unkempt hair, and dirty fingernails. How could he have thought she was beautiful in such attire? "Any good cook washes her hands before joining her guests at the table."

Ignoring her further, he turned to the others. "Forgive my wife. She has not yet learned the customs of Mexican hospitality."

The warning from Thorne's deep-throated chuckle came too late. Milk spilled over Octavio's head and slid in sticky droplets down his chest under his shirt.

"How's that for hospitality, you . . . you . . . Mexican!" Gila shot up from her chair and stomped out of the room.

Octavio jumped to his feet, forcing back the words that raced to retaliate. He turned to Book, ready to defend himself against the Oriental's disapproval. His words to Gila had been harsh, but she deserved them. She had no right to insult his nation and his position as her husband.

Book forked a piece of the lamb, brought it to his lips, then halted. He stared squarely at Octavio. "One deserved the other."

* * *

Gila entered her room and swore. "Oh no you don't!" She jerked Octavio's war bag off the davenport. The soiled clothing that lay neatly folded on the bed was instantly crammed into the bag. "You aren't going to sleep here. Not now. Not ever!" She stalked to the doorway and tossed his belongings into the hall.

Back inside the room, she hurried to the chest and flung the drawers open one by one. "Where did he get all these? There weren't any—"

Book. This was Book's doing. He must have bought October all these clothes and accessories. So that was why Book looked more tired than usual. He had worn himself out hauling that darned Mexican's clothes around.

Book was stronger than a herd of buffalo and would never admit otherwise, but Gila had noticed he was suffering with his back more and more lately. His short breath when he carried her to Carlos's after the wedding, the deepening yellow under his eyes were signs of some inner sickness. He and Thorne were in their sixties and no longer young men. Yet every time she made a commotion about him taking it easy, slowing down, letting some of the younger men do the hard work, her hardheaded friend would work that much harder. He and that stupid Bushido he practiced. *Do not complain of pain. Pain is of the mind, not the body.* That might very well be for some people, Gila decided, but not for Book. If he grimaced, then something must be terribly wrong with him.

Gila thought of Book bringing in Octavio's war bag and arranging his clothes. "He's just going to have to stop toting for people. We're all adults and can take care of our own things, and I'll just go tell him so. Right now!"

Gila stopped midstride and chuckled. She could see herself marching up to Book, telling the old war-horse he could no longer oversee the loading and unloading, the actual care of his wards. Why, he'd think she'd lost her mind! He who practiced death before dishonor. Book would never admit to a sickness that would make him less than samurai.

What in St. Patrick was she thinking of? Her emotions of late reminded her of a tumbleweed on a windy day. She never knew where they would be. One minute happy, the next bawling her eyes out. All because of October. That Mexican had made her lose what little common sense she owned. Why did he have to go and say such a stupid thing at dinner?

Gila stared at her hands, turning them palms up, then down. How was he to know the piñon nuts stained her fingernails a dirty brown and that it took a few days for the stain to wear off? He would naturally think she hadn't washed.

She had deliberately not dressed for supper, wanting to make it clear to October that she would not change to the formal ways of his noble family. This was *her* home, and as long as they lived here, she would live as she pleased, dress as she pleased.

But her plan hadn't worked. Shelly Kate saw to that! Who did she think she was fooling, anyhow, with that stupid frilly-dilly dress? A one-eyed blind man would've noticed the stuffing that lifted and made Shelly's breasts look fuller. And October almost fell over himself trying to kiss her hand so he could get a better look. Stupid. Just plain stupid!

Gila lifted one of Octavio's shirts from the chest. It was white with multicolored embroidery along the neckline. So fancy, she thought. Fancy like October.

What a sight she must have been to him, especially after Shelly Kate's big entrance. Gila had always paled in comparison to her little sister. Thorne had never baby talked her when she was toddling, but he had cooed and spoken in nonsense words to her angel-faced, silken-haired sibling.

Until now, Gila had never given their differences much thought. After all, Shelly was the image of their mother, Kathryn. It was natural for Thorne to love Shelly mo—to love her in a special way.

But October was altogether a different situation. Like it or not, he belonged to her, and she wasn't about to let Shelly Kate charm him away. Besides, the man should have been smart enough to see through Shelly's flirting. For a man who pretended to be so worldly, he sure couldn't spot a smooth-talker when he saw one. Instead, he had strutted like a peacock for her.

Maybe she should have dressed for dinner. But if he hadn't been so all-fired in a hurry to compare her to Shelly, he would have seen her sister was merely using him to make her look silly.

Gila crammed the shirt back into the chest and slammed the drawer shut. "He deserved the milk over his head," she muttered, wondering if she should empty the remainder of his belongings on top of the war bag.

No. He could get them in the morning. He was smart enough to know that she wouldn't let him sleep in her room after the ruckus at the dinner table. If he wasn't, he was more ignorant than she thought. The sight of his bag in the hallway would be enough warning, if he were slow to get the message.

Now for a bath. She had even looked forward to her bath today, but Octavio's outburst had taken away the anticipation. He might think she bathed because of his ignorant remarks. If she didn't need one so badly, she would simply forgo the pleasure. But the sweltering days on horseback, preparing a meal for the ranch hands, then the family, had done its worst damage on her good humor and appearance. *Maybe I was a little too bullheaded,* she thought as she caught a glimpse of herself in the mirror. *I look like I've been hit by a tornado.*

Her auburn hair fell in tangled strands about her face. A smudge of flour dusted her lips. Grease splatters dirtied her once-white shirt, and the button that held the material together at her ample waist had come undone.

She stared at her too-round chin, her unaccented cheekbones, and finally her hazel eyes. She looked long and hard, critically surveying herself. She crossed her eyes and stuck out her tongue at the shabby image reflected back. A cry knotted in her throat and she flung herself on the sheepskin coverlet and wept until the racking sobs had long subsided and her heart was as empty as her dreams.

Octavio decided to excuse himself. He was tired, his injuries not completely healed, and now he was sticky with milk. What he needed was a bath and a dose of solitude. Which he was unlikely to get.

Book had said nothing more about his brusqueness with Gila, but when she'd left the room the conversation dwindled to mere politeness. He'd planned to ask Thorne's goals for the territory. He had not believed Gila's explanation of the treaty with Cochise.

Octavio lost all taste for food and conversation. Pride and good manners had provoked his sharpness with Gila. Being unable to contain his anger toward her left a bitter taste in his mouth. Why did he allow her to fuel his temper?

Octavio scooted back his chair and stood. "If you will excuse me, Señor McCandless, I am unusually tired. The meal was delicious and the liquor superb. I think I should like to walk the grounds for a while before I retire."

Shelly Kate started to protest, but Thorne's raised palm halted her words. "Certainly. The waterfall to the south of the house will do wonders on that milk, if you decide to take a swim." He took a drink of liquor, then added, "But don't be wandering too far. Ben and the boys might take you for an Apache, not being familiar with your ways yet."

"I understand." Octavio nodded to Shelly. "If you'll excuse me, Señorita McCandless, I bid you good-night."

"Shelly Kate," she added curtly, her irritation at her father apparent. "After all, we are relatives now."

"Yes. All this señor and señorita business is unnecessary," admonished Thorne. "From now on, we use only first names."

"Until morning then." Octavio half-bowed, turned, then left the dining room. Making his way through the house, he paused at the liquor counter in the parlor. Should he take a bottle with him? Getting good and drunk might settle him down. No. What he needed was a long walk. Time alone. A midnight swim to wash off the remnants of Gila's tantrum.

# Chapter Twelve

✦✦✦✦

THE NIGHT BREEZE felt good against Octavio's face. Locusts rattled their shivering love song from the rows of paloverdes that curved along the canyon wall. The desert moon rose high in the purplish black sky, sending silver slivers of light through the trees.

He peered into the darkness as a flicker of red pinpointed the lookout's position. *Never smoke on watch,* Juárez's commanding voice came back in drifts of memory. *One puff from your cigarro may be your last breath, for it assures the enemy of your location.* Octavio wondered if Thorne would appreciate the information or be insulted by it. Surely the rancher needed no one to tell him how to maintain safety.

The sound of the bubbling waterfall stirred Octavio from his thoughts and enticed him forward. Strolling past the southern edge of the hacienda, he noticed and took a path that skirted the paloverdes. The splashing soon became louder and louder, until finally the courting locusts were drowned out by the rumbling spill.

He rounded a wealth of trees and came to an abrupt halt. The moon was in full radiance now, its beams gliding to the water, sending sparkles like a million fireflies on the billowing surface. Liquid streams of silver slid down from somewhere high on the canyon wall, then cascaded into the effervescent pool.

Octavio breathed deeply as he moved closer to the water's edge, enjoying the moist spray that tickled his face. He looked back toward the trees, then searched the shadows high on the canyon wall, a habit he knew stemmed from the days he and Juárez had spent hidden in the Sierra Madres. No one was watching. Gila's mother had chosen wisely. This was an ideal location for a ranch. The moon lit the night, accenting the pinkish white sand. An enemy could be seen for miles.

Octavio took a cigarro from his breast pocket and lit it. He inhaled deeply and exhaled long, the smoke fading in lazy circles in front of him. Then he undressed. The breeze made him shiver but he paid it little mind.

After snuffing out the remainder of the cigarro, he waded into the water. His toes sank deeply into the moist sand, which shifted cool and smooth beneath his tender feet. He waded deeper and deeper, until the water struck him at chest level. The warmth of the afternoon sun still lingered, despite the cooling spray. Octavio bent backward and submerged himself.

How strange the waterfall sounded as it now pounded upon the pool's surface. It thundered like a thousand stampeding buffalo. Octavio swam beneath the billowing foam until his lungs were near bursting. He surfaced, making tiny moonlit circles ripple away to the shoreline.

The waterfall called to him again and he could not resist the urge to swim once more beneath the sparkling stream. Moving under it, the water pounding on his neck and shoulders, kneading the tense muscles of his back, he paddled further, then stopped.

Was that a light? Octavio surfaced, shielded his eyes from the spray and peered closer. A light behind the waterfall? There beyond the water, blocking a large opening in the canyon wall, stood a fence made of the same grayish wood that furnished most of the McCandless home.

Octavio swam closer. The fence seemed to have no entrance. Perhaps there was entry from somewhere in the mountain. Could he reach the other side by swimming underwater? Another thought troubled him. If *he* could, then an attacker might also.

He dove deep and swam toward the fence. His hands groped in front of him for contact with the wooden barricade. A current of cool water seemed to urge him backward to the spill, but a more insistent warmth beckoned him onward. His lungs felt heavy from the long moments underwater. But there! He found just enough room to squeeze through two protruding rocks. The warmth now rushed around him in a swirling tow, pulling him through the natural barriers and making him surface effortlessly.

Just as he had thought. This was the McCandless bathing chamber. The lantern hanging on its hook was the light he'd seen behind the fall. Its dying embers indicated someone had left just moments before. A blessing, indeed. He would have been hard-pressed to explain his presence.

What good fortune to have a place such as this, enclosed from prying eyes, a natural whirlpool fed by some hidden source of mountain springwater that soothed and eased tired muscles. A waterfall in which to frolic. No wonder the McCandlesses stayed so healthy-looking!

Octavio swam to the south bank, turned, and rested on a rocky ledge only a few feet below the surface. His gaze took in the cavern's inner sanctuary, noticing first a barred door on the opposite wall. Assuming it must be an entrance into the McCandless hacienda and estimating the position of the house and the waterfall, he decided the door led into Gila's room. But where? There was only one door in Gila's room and that led to the hallway. The southern wall was filled with rows and rows of shelves containing her cure-alls. Was the opening behind one of those shelves?

The door opened with surprisingly little sound and Gila came into view. Uncertain what to do, he lowered himself further into the swirling pool until only his nose and eyes were above water. What if she saw him? So what if she does? he decided on second thought. She is my wife. I have the right to be here. Yet why did he feel as if he were intruding?

Gila closed and bolted the door. She picked up the poker that lay beneath the lantern and stirred the coals until they lit the cavern with renewed light. Octavio watched as she unlaced the string of rawhide that bound her hair, letting the auburn tresses fall free to her shoulders. She slipped off her boots, then the nankeens.

The sight of soft white thighs as she bent to remove her pantaloons stirred Octavio's memory of another night when her flesh yielded to his own.

She laid the nankeens and pantaloons on top of her boots, then began to unbutton the dirty shirt. Octavio's gaze lingered at each button, his thoughts willing her hands to hurry to the next. His breath caught momentarily as she unfastened the last. She tossed the shirt to one side and stretched her arms high. "Oooh, that feels good," she sighed.

Gila didn't look too far along into her childbearing term. In fact, her body seemed firmer than on their wedding night. She looked as solid as Guadalupe Peak now. Octavio took in the fullness of her bosom, the ample hips made for childbearing. An unquenchable hunger coursed through his blood and raged deep within his loins.

Gila eased herself into the water, then lay back to float upon the water's surface. Octavio watched her drift lazily, taking in every inch of her glistening nudity. The rising heat from the pool flushed her skin, arousing a deeper warmth within him. Her low, steady breathing made her breasts rise and fall rhythmically, a sensuous accompaniment to the drums of desire that pounded at his temples. Octavio yearned to take her in his arms, to feel the beat of her heart against his own.

In an abrupt movement, she submerged. Did she see me? he wondered. If she had, he could not have denied his lusting glance. But after all the things he'd said to her at dinner, after her tantrum, how could he admit to her that he wanted her, above all reason, beyond all prejudice?

Fear overcame his worry. Hadn't she been under too long? He didn't know if she could swim, yet surely she wouldn't have gotten into the deeper part of the pool if she didn't know how. "Gila? Gila, are you all right?" he yelled and swam toward her.

Just as he was about to dive, she surfaced.

Relief washed over him. Gila flicked the water out of her hair and eyes, opening them to discover Octavio only inches away. She retreated toward the sandy bank, but he continued to close the distance between them.

Octavio expected her to object, curse, condemn, possibly even scream, yet she remained silent. She edged closer and closer to the bank until the water revealed the curve of her hips and all her glorious femininity above. In his mind he ravished every inch of her as liquid droplets pooled, then fell from her full, round breasts, her nipples eagerly erect for his touch.

The aching need deepened within him, the desire to mold her flesh to his own claiming him once again. He stared into the smoky green of her eyes and was engulfed with a sense of victory. She wanted him as much as he desired her!

He reached for her, forcing himself to control the insistent hunger raging within. Placing his fingers against the small of her back, he drew her to him. She shifted in his arms, an effort that positioned her precisely where she could feel his full intent. Her mouth opened in surprise and he did not let the moment pass.

His tongue met hers in a sensuous duel of thrust and yield, thrust and yield. Her lips were moist and urgent, equally seeking the same goal, the same satisfaction. Her arms slid around his neck, drawing him nearer. Her thighs strained to press closer to his own.

She relinquished his lips and moved backward

until she was only wading in the water. Lying back against the bank, she beckoned him to her with outstretched arms.

Octavio needed no further encouragement and made his way to the bank to lie beside her. Gila pressed her lips to his face, then she began to kiss his eyebrows and eyelashes, his cheeks, nibbling his ear, letting her tongue trace a long lazy circle of ecstasy from his neck to his well-corded shoulders. A low moan escaped from somewhere deep within him and he crushed her to him. Surely she must feel the fullness of his desire. She couldn't stop him now, even if she wanted to.

His breath came slow and uneven as her hands caressed his shoulders. Her fingers twined themselves in the dark curls of hair that spanned his chest, then playfully tugged until he muttered a pleasurable oath. Her fingers splayed, allowing her palms to fully knead the broad muscles. His flesh tingled in their wake. A chuckle escaped her as she bent her head and her tongue toyed with one of his nipples, making it peak to match her own. What glorious pain! Her hands encircled him, her fingers cupping his buttocks, kneading the rounded flesh as her breasts pressed wantonly against him. He shivered when her mouth claimed his, scorching him with a white-hot flame of eagerness.

She writhed against him, muttering incoherent words of want and need. Octavio knew her need, for it was as immeasurable as his own, and he could do naught but answer her persistent plea. Gently he eased his passion into the den of her welcoming desire, triumphant at the tremble that vibrated through her as he filled her. The quest was upon them and neither could turn from the compulsion that carried them. Her rhythm began to match his own, like the ebb and flow of a never-ending tide. Methodically he thrust, delving deeper and deeper into the fulfilling recess.

Octavio's mind whirled, just as the water eddied around them. He became lost in the throbbing course of his very lifeblood. Woman to man. Man to woman. Life in its entirety. There was only the rapturous movement of their bodies, one unto the other. One breath. One heartbeat. One soul.

The unquenchable yearned for quenching. His need rose, spiraling upward and upward, higher and higher, until, at last, it collided with her own questing climb. Together they burst into pure ecstasy. He called out his joy as she clung to him, falling, ever falling into the rapturous spill of love's ecstasy. A sigh started deep within Gila and escaped. Octavio too heaved a deep sigh. And in that moment their souls were united. No man, prejudice, or circumstance could ever part them again.

Octavio nipped Gila's lips playfully, then hungrily claimed them once more. As they kissed he moved her closer to the water, intent on seeing once again the droplets upon her voluptuous bosom and kissing the rosy peaks dry.

Unable to hide the huskiness in her voice, Gila warned, "We'll drown."

He traced a nipple with his thumb, causing it

to heighten once again. "Only in a sea of satisfaction, *dulce mia.*" He chuckled softly at his joke. She showered him with a smile, and he was surprised at how the sensuous tilt of her lips made his loins ache again with need.

"A poet as well, señor? You're a man of many notions."

"I've but one notion now," he said, reaching out to draw her to him.

She resisted and edged farther up the bank. "No, October. I'm not as warm-blooded as you. I'm not used to . . . well . . . don't expect me to keep up with you."

He followed her out of the pool and was pleased that her gaze turned to take in his full length. She blushed and grabbed the soiled shirt, holding it in front of herself as if for protection.

From him? She'd already given what he would never have taken from her. He gently took the shirt and dropped it to the earthen floor without taking his gaze from her. "So, *dulce mia,* I will have to help you learn to keep up with me." He bent and kissed her again, encircling her in the strength of his embrace. Her fingertips caressed his moist back, stinging his flesh with their burning warmth. She gasped, jolted by the intensity of their undeniable pleasure in one another. His mouth left her lips and smothered her neck in rapturous kisses.

How could he ever have thought her unwomanly? What a fool he had been to compare her to any other. He wanted to sweep her into his embrace and carry her back to the four-poster bed where they could linger with their lovemaking until dawn. He tried to lift her, but he could not. He was still weak from his months in prison. He smiled at her and chuckled. "You're more woman than I can handle, my sweet."

The grin that had settled onto his face quickly faded as Gila's anger was delayed by only a breath. "So! You think that's pretty funny, do you? Well, *I* don't! Why don't you just go get that Modesta gal and give *her* a bath!" She pulled away from him and stomped toward the door in her bare feet, not bothering to gather the remainder of her clothes. She removed the board that barricaded the door and jerked it open. "Find some skinny señorita to warm your bed!"

Octavio shook his head warily. What a predicament! Of all the women in the world to fall in love with, why did it have to be Gila McCandless? Even as he considered the women in his amorous past, he knew no other would be able to extinguish the frenzied flame that now burned for Gila's touch. No other woman at all.

Gila set the last bowl on the family table and surveyed the dining room. Everything was ready. Plenty of hot sourdough biscuits and steaming gravy awaited the first bunch of wranglers. More food was cooking for those already on duty. She counted the place settings, making certain there were thirty-seven. All there. Now for the bell.

She stepped into the parlor, opened the door, then suddenly changed her mind. Walking briskly down the hall, she came to a halt at her own door. What if he was awake?

So what if he was! She was still angry with him. Imagine, trying to pretend he couldn't lift her. She was a large woman and freely admitted it. But she liked her solid sturdiness. At least she wasn't one of those prancing little peacocks who wasn't good for anything but posing. Begorra, she wasn't so big that October needed to pretend he couldn't lift her! He probably laughed himself to sleep over that one.

Anger urged her into the room, her steps determined, her tongue ready to lash. As she looked at the sleeping form under the coverlet, she almost felt disappointed. She was ready for a good old cuss fight and now it would just have to wait.

Gila walked to the dressing table. She gave her auburn tresses a few harsh strokes, then replaced the brush. The reddish brown hair hung over her shoulders, ends still damp from the previous night's rendezvous.

She closed her eyes a moment, remembering his strong fingers caressing her shoulders as his burning mouth possessed hers with a fiery passion. The flames of desire he aroused deep within her scorched the very edge of her sanity. Resisting would have driven her out of her mind.

She willed her eyes to open and stared at her reflection. The warmth of his memory darkened her cheeks and caused her nipples to peak beneath her clean white shirt.

She looked once more at her husband, then back into the mirror. A sadness descended on her as she stared at her husky frame. Why had

he spoiled what they had shared in the whirlpool? His own need had been as great as hers,
hadn't it? That one moment of total possession
had been too beautiful, too natural to have been
merely carnal.

Had he felt the same? Had her soul touched
his as his had touched hers? No. He'd laughed.
Laughed at her size. He didn't care that he hurt
her. She was only there to satisfy his need. That
and nothing more.

Gila squared her shoulders, lifting her chin in
determination. Well, he would never discover
the truth. She would let him think she had used
him. She would laugh in his face if he said
otherwise. She turned quickly and left the room.

Outside, a steel triangle hung on the northeast
corner of the porch. "Too bad this isn't October,"
she muttered, lifting the bar from its hook. With
three full circular strokes, she clanged the signal
for mealtime. She hoped he choked on breakfast!

# Chapter Thirteen

✦✦✦✦

BREAKFAST SEEMED A century away, Gila thought as
she wrenched a pitahaya from the saguaro's
tallest branch. The spike at the end of the strong
pole that she held in her right hand did its work
efficiently, loosening the rind until the fruit fell

into the basket that was hooked to the leather belt around her waist. The basket prevented the easily bruised fruit from hitting the ground.

Carefully she placed the morning's harvest into saguaro wraps, then packed them snugly into baskets. With every movement she was thankful to Old One-Eye, the Papago Indian woman who had taught her how to preserve the cactus fruit.

Gila lifted her knife from its scabbard and made a small slit in one of the green pitahaya rinds. Gently she peeled back the layers and exposed its crimson pulp and tiny black seeds. Most folks didn't care for the seeds, but over the years she had acquired a taste for tem.

Gila ate the refreshing morsel ravenously. What in St. Patrick's name has come over me lately? she wondered. Her appetite had always been hearty, but now it was more than that. If she kept eating as much as she had in the ten days since she'd been home from Tucson, she would be as big as Dublin in no time flat.

She surveyed her harvest and shrugged. It wasn't nearly enough, but certainly all she had time to bottle. It would just have to do.

After everything had been loaded into the wagon, Gila hopped onto the buckboard and headed toward the house. The ride would take about an hour, so she propped her legs on the footboard and leaned her elbows on her knees. The position wasn't ladylike by any means, but it kept her buttocks from jerking back and forth on the wooden seat. A gentle wind brushed her cheeks as she grabbed the reins and giddyapped the horse. The power of pride at a day's work well done filled her and made her weariness seem only a necessary annoyance.

Halfway home she remembered the letter she had earlier stuffed into the pocket of her nankeens. Book had made one of his twice-weekly trips to the O'Malleys' that morning and brought the letter back with him. When the War Between the States broke out, the Butterfield Overland Mail Route folded. Now there were only scattered mail drops in the territory, one of which was the home of the O'Malleys.

Gila remembered the look of disapproval upon Book's face when he had handed her the letter from Garrett O'Malley. He made no effort to hide his dislike of the man. Not that she blamed Book. There was plenty to hate about Garrett, all right. Yet he seemed like a saint compared to Octavio Cordoba.

At least she knew how she felt about Garrett. Definite hate. With October . . . well, it was just so damned confusing!

Since their quarrel he had not shared her bed but had bedded down on the davenport in their room. He was usually gone when she woke up, and she rarely saw him except at mealtimes.

Despite the extreme hunger that had befallen her of late, she couldn't eat in front of him. She picked at her food and watched him out of the corner of her eye. She thought about him all the time, though she tried not to. A dozen times a day she asked herself what was wrong with her.

Unfolding Garrett's letter now, an answer came to her. "You're falling in love with your husband," she admitted.

There. The words were out. Finally speaking them aloud was a great relief. She *was* falling in love with Octavio, despite all their arguments, despite her hatred for his countrymen, despite her desperate attempt not to love him. *If only I didn't tremble when he touches me. If only our marriage wasn't based on a sham.*

"Well, I certainly can't live a life of *if onlys*," she told the horse. "Besides, he's barely speaking to me."

Stubborn pride settled in after a few moments, covering up her fragile new feelings. "Well, what do I care? I'm a McCandless. I don't need the likes of him or any other man!" She put away her thoughts of Octavio and concentrated on Garrett's letter.

*Dearest Gila,*

*Did you think you'd hear from me so soon? Fortunately I have been on personal assignment for J. D., so my letters get sent top priority.*

*Of course, I cannot tell you about my most recent assignment, but I can tell you that the D. forces may be on the verge of victory far greater than even J. realizes.*

*I will say this, my love. The deepest South plans a daring attempt. An attempt which will gain the attention of that evil abolitionist—L. Expect to hear of the death of a high official. Someone most dear to L.*

*Love to my adoring bride-to-be,*
*Garrett Sean O'Malley*

Gila briefly scanned the letter again. She hated guessing games as much as she hated Garrett's conceit. Why did he say the deepest South instead of just the South? Was that some clue? Why all this J. and D. nonsense? Even a fool would know he meant Jefferson Davis.

Though Gila didn't believe a government should tell its people how to live, she agreed with Abe Lincoln's position on slavery. Every man should be his own keeper. Freedom was a precious thing, but was it worth all the millions of lives that it cost to gain it? So many nations were fighting these days. The Mexicans against the French, Irish against British, Indians against white men, North against South. What would the warring prove? Had God in his great plan said that 1865 would decide who in the world would be free and who would not?

As Gila finally pulled into the yard of the McCandless stables, a ruckus over at the corral drew her attention. Immediately her gaze went to the wrangler who was riding out a bucking bronc.

October. In all his magnificent maleness. Naked to the waist. Muscles rippling with exertion, shiny with perspiration.

She watched the horse and rider in their battle of wills. Octavio's darkened skin blended with the horse's color, reminding her of a centaur. The two halves, man and horse, continued to fight, two wills fused into a singular movement. But there could be only one outcome. Each to become the master of the other. In this country, what good was a man without a horse and what horse would live long without man's help? A partnership was the only answer.

Why can't the world learn that, Gila wondered as she hooked her bootheel on the bottom rail of the corral post. She folded her hands across the top rail and rested her chin on her wrists. Why can't I learn that?

Octavio spoke calming words into the horse's ear. "That's it, señorita. That's it. You see. I didn't mean to hurt you, merely to tame you."

Ben held the newly broken bronc's reins while Octavio dismounted. "She's the only filly around here you've been able to tame."

The other wranglers laughed and Octavio joined them. There was no point arguing over a known fact. Ben couldn't have known he'd hit on Octavio's one sore spot.

Gila. Where was she? Octavio wondered. He hadn't seen her all day.

"Sorry, Gila," said Ben, looking genuinely embarrassed. "I didn't know you were standing there."

"It's all right, Ben. I took it as a compliment." She stared directly at Octavio.

That's what I like most about you, Octavio thought in silent approval. You always speak your mind. A man knows where he stands with you. He glanced over at the wagon. "Can I help you get those baskets into the house?"

She shrugged one shoulder. "If you want. I can handle it myself."

"I'm sure you can. If you'd rather I didn't—"

"No. I mean . . . I'd appreciate your help."

What? Gila was actually grateful for his help? Was she not feeling well? She hadn't eaten very much the last few days, and he'd worried that she might still be upset about their quarrel over her weight.

He had regretted laughing at her that night, knowing he had spoiled a special moment. At first he'd been angry with her, thinking that she'd reacted childishly. Then as the days wore on he knew that it had been he who had acted foolishly. He was surprised that such a strong-willed person as Gila would let such a thing bother her, but she was obviously sensitive on the subject of her weight.

Octavio lifted a basket and handed it to her. Perhaps if he had been given more time to get acquainted with his new bride, the two of them could have come to an easy companionship.

Easy companionship? he mused. Not with Gila McCandless. She demanded every ounce of a man's wit and ability. She was a woman to be respected. A woman to be feared. With her kind of woman, a man quickly forgot his freedom, his destiny.

"Is this the last batch?" he asked, balancing two baskets.

"It's going to have to be." Gila held open the door to the house with her boot and allowed him to enter ahead of herself. After they had left the baskets in the kitchen, she asked, "How about sharing some Irish whiskey with me before I get started with the bottling?"

Octavio liked the way her unruly hair clung to her face. It suited her personality. The dimple in her left cheek gave her an impish look when she smiled and made the sparkle in her eyes seem mischievous. "Thank you, I will."

He followed her to the sideboard in the parlor and sat on one of the rawhide stools near it. Gila poured two glasses of Thorne's best Irish whiskey.

"Thorne saves this for special occasions," she said.

"What is the occasion?" he asked, one brow arching in curiosity.

Gila smiled the naughty little smile he had thought about only moments before. "Let's just say it's a toast." She paused, then broke into a broader grin. "A toast to our next fight."

Octavio threw back his head and enjoyed a full, throaty laugh. "Better yet," he said, clicking his glass against hers, "a toast to our next fight and the reconciliation that I hope follows it."

The implication of Octavio's words reddened Gila's cheeks. Each took a drink. Their gazes locked as both lowered their glasses.

Octavio enjoyed the blush that graced Gila's cheeks. Beauty radiated from deep within her whenever she was being herself rather than Gila McCandless, the daughter who tried to be a son. "We can't go on like this," he murmured softly.

"I know."

"My, my. Isn't this cozy?" Shelly Kate

swished into the room in a rustle of pink ruffles. "Is this a farewell toast?"

"Farewell toast?" Gila's puzzled look warned Octavio that she knew nothing about his trip to the O'Malleys'.

The spell was broken. There was nothing he could do that could recapture the moment. He felt cheated. Shelly had interrupted at the wrong time, and from the smug look on her face she was obviously enjoying her handiwork.

He placed his palm on top of Gila's hand, but she quickly withdrew hers. He had known she would. She could be so obstinate at times!

"Your father has asked me to spend the remainder of the week, and possibly the next, at the O'Malleys'. There has been trouble with some of my countrymen. Señor O'Malley would like to settle the matter before he leaves for the festival of San Xavier. He's asked me to be interpreter."

"But if Cochise finds out there are Mexicans on the O'Malley spread, he'll go on a bloody rampage."

Octavio nodded. "Exactly. That's why I must be the interpreter. If Cochise gets involved, I will be very useful. Of course, I hope to settle the matter before that happens."

"Of course," Gila replied stiffly. "After all, we never settled anything before you came."

Why was she so quarrelsome? Could she be upset because he would be gone for a few days? No, her McCandless pride had been wounded. That and nothing more.

"I'll ignore your sarcasm because you are obviously upset," he declared.

"Damned right I'm upset." Gila's eyes flashed with the anger that sharpened her tongue.

"Oh, my goodness. I certainly didn't mean to start a lovers' quarrel," Shelly Kate purred in obvious delight.

"The hell you didn't," Gila and Octavio exclaimed simultaneously. Both broke into a laugh as Shelly Kate gathered her skirts and huffed out of the room.

"A toast!" Octavio offered, lifting his glass in salute.

"A toast," Gila agreed.

The crystal glasses clinked with a sound as fragile as their new truce.

# Chapter Fourteen

✦✦✦✦

GILA PATTED WEE-PEOPLE'S neck and straightened as Thorne struck four rounds on the triangle. He replaced the bar on the hook and hailed the men who were gathered on horseback in a semicircle in front of the house.

"All right. Listen well! I want every man jack of you on your best behavior."

Grumbles rippled through the wranglers. Gila

understood why they were complaining. During the Easter celebration in Tucson, Thorne expected the McCandless ranch hands to drink the most liquor, win the most races, and do the most damage in any fight. The tradition was almost twenty years old. Thorne was not about to let the men slack off now.

Most of Gila's time at the San Xavier pageant would be spent selling her remedies. The boys would just have to make do without her. Thorne had insisted on keeping her out of the proceedings, in the event she was truly pregnant. What snake fodder! Ben could rope just as fast as she could. He would take the roping contest for sure. Billy Puckett was the best wrestler on the ranch. He might be fortunate enough to win the Buffalo-Wallow if he drew a late number. Book was the most skilled horseman in the whole bunch, but he was staying home to mind the ranch. That left her to win the riding contest. Sisneros, one of Pete Kitchen's men, would take first prize if she didn't enter, and Thorne wouldn't settle for that.

Gila studied Book, noting the pallor around his lips and the pain-filled set of his jaw. He was definitely sick, but he was certain no one else noticed. The fact that he was staying home, however, was enough to confirm her suspicions.

Once, a long time ago, she had asked Book what was so special about the San Xavier Easter gathering. He never attended other community socials but never missed the pageant.

"Where many people raise dust, so gather the

sands of truth," he'd told her. When she'd asked what he meant, he assured her that she would one day understand.

Finally she had understood. She watched Book study the people at the pageant. He noted their habits, their pride, their failings, their successes. She began to observe people, too, and it was not long before she learned many things.

She learned to trust her first impressions and to weigh people's strengths and weaknesses. This helped in her business dealings and gave her the assurance that so many of her male friends admired. Above all, she earned men's respect by learning to control her emotions and conduct herself logically.

Until October came along! When he showed up she had lost all manner of good judgment. She knew she had fallen in love with him, but she could not make herself tell him the truth. Her nights were too long without him, yet her days were full of the icy disillusionment of her prejudice against his people. Why did her mind and body continue to war? What strange hold did this Mexican have upon her?

Gila studied him as he sat deep in his pinto's saddle. His absence had given her a hunger for the sight of him. He had lost his gaunt look and his mouth was no longer a grim, straight line but had relaxed into a sensuous smile. Why hadn't she realized before that the sneer was merely a ploy to hide his pain? Like a McCandless, he too was proud and seldom discussed his injuries.

And Shelly Kate! Her choice of riding apparel was ridiculous! If she'd had anything to say about it, her sister would have changed that bit of pink fluff-and-ruffles she called a dress for something more sensible. But Shelly Kate insisted that if they were to meet any neighbors on the way to Tucson, she would just die if she weren't dressed properly. Well, what would her dear sister do if one of those "neighbors" happened to be wearing feathers and toting a tomahawk? She might just die anyway!

Whoa! Why are you so riled at Shelly Kate? Gila silently reprimanded herself. She's been this way her whole life. She might be an arrogant little cuss, but she's still your sister.

All Shelly's oohing and ahhing over October at least had kept him out of Gila's way. And he hadn't minded at all. Seemed to enjoy Shelly flitting over him like a fly around a sweaty horse. Everywhere he went, Shelly'd been one petticoat behind him. Not that I minded either, thought Gila.

She rode toward the wagon, critically surveying the wood boxes filled with bottles, snuff cans, any container she could find in which to put her cures. She had been lucky this year. The saguaro pulp was exceptionally juicy, the color a deep red—almost purple. Next to her cures, eight jugs took up one corner of the wagon. This year's Blarney-Brew was the best she'd ever made. She couldn't wait to share it with the boys. Too bad Book wasn't going. This batch deserved the same recognition he'd given the original.

She glanced once more at the Oriental. Suddenly an ice-cold tremor crawled like a centipede up Gila's spine. Even as her mind whispered the unspeakable, her heart denied it with every beat.

"No," she whispered softly, as if speaking it aloud would make her words true. "He'll be here."

"Did you say something, *dulce mia?*" Octavio asked.

"No. You're hearing things," replied Gila, irritated at October, yet uncertain why.

An expression of curiosity passed over his features, but Gila's cold stare brought an abrupt halt to any question he might have asked. He turned back to continue his conversation with Shelly Kate.

Overcome by sudden emotion, Gila dismounted and ran to Book. She gave him a fierce hug, for once disregarding his aversion to displays of affection. His powerful arms returned the embrace, and she felt somewhat reassured. Still she did not like the almost inaudible sigh of pain that escaped him when she tightened her arms around him.

"Watch out, Book old boy, you know how Mexican tempers can get," one of the riders chided the pair.

Gila gave the men her haughtiest McCandless stare, making the ensuing chuckles die immediately. Turning to inspect Book's face more closely, she asked, "You want me to stay with you?"

"Sell your cures," he replied stoically. "There will be much distress if you do not." A smile edged one corner of his mouth. "I am anxious to hear of your success."

The twinkle in his eyes reassured her. She hurried to Wee-People, lifted one boot into the stirrup, then straddled the paint. A sharp pain knifed her abdomen as she settled into the saddle, making her clutch her stomach.

"The baby?" Octavio asked, his expression one of deep concern. Had she uttered some sound or was the pain as evident on her face as it was in her stomach?

"Baby!" Shelly Kate cried, unable to hide her astonishment. "You're having a baby?"

Shelly's look of disgust was so irritating, Gila decided to confirm what she herself merely suspected. "Yes, dear sister. You are going to be an aunt." For once, Shelly Kate was speechless.

Thorne mounted the roan and waved his hat in four full circles. "Move 'em out!"

Each rider fell into line behind him as the outfit moved out. Shelly Kate had caught up with her father, leaving Octavio to ride alongside Gila. From the exaggerated hand gestures and tossing of her blond hair, Gila could tell that Shelly was in a heated discussion with her father, no doubt demanding from him all the details of her sudden marriage. Would Thorne refuse to give them? If he did, it would be the first time he chose to consider her over Shelly.

The ache in Gila's stomach lessened, subsiding into the fullness that had worried her the last few days. It was a week past her schedule, which was very unusual. The monthly flow had always been a nuisance to Gila, coming every twenty-eight days, right on time. A cruel reminder that she was, after all, a woman. Now she prayed diligently that it would come again, especially this time.

She urged Wee-People into a fast trot, riding ahead of Thorne, Shelly, and the others. She needed time alone to think. To pray.


The serenading of a lovesick caballero greeted the McCandless outfit as they rode into Tucson. The ever-present odor of confined civilization littered the air. As Shelly Kate rode past, the singer forgot his courting momentarily to gawk at the beautiful blond.

Shelly Kate was dressed in silk the color of delicate pink sand verbenas, and her long flowing curls were tied at the crown with a matching ribbon. Blond locks fell to her bare white shoulders, nudging the ruffles that covered just enough bosom to be discreet. Well, she certainly knows how to make an entrance, Gila scoffed to herself.

Octavio's voice interrupted her thoughts.

"What?" she asked. "Did you say something?"

"It's a beautiful night for love, *dulce mia*," he replied. The slow seductive words sent an unexpected thrill down Gila's spine that ended in a pleasant quiver near her thighs.

It *was* a beautiful night. The sky formed a blanket of purest black with echoes of sunlight glittering the heavens. She wished for a moment that her feelings for October were as clear as the stars were bright. But they were as cloudy and murky as the night before a big storm. And, oh what a storm. Could she conquer her conflicting feelings for him? And if not, would the child of their passion also be a stranger to her love?

Why did she need October, want him so much? she wondered. Had he lain awake wondering if she thought about the hours of their mutual satisfaction? Or did he prefer the silence between them, not caring that their souls had been scorched by their lovemaking?

Was it possible for two people to love and hate each other at the same time? She had no answers. Yet she knew she wanted to share his bed this night. She offered her hand to him. "Perhaps it *is* a night for love," she whispered and stared deeply into his questioning eyes.

The mockery she expected in the depths of those sapphire pools did not appear. Instead October raised her hand to his lips, searing her flesh with the flame of his intention.

Thorne turned half-circle at that moment. "Let's stop at Congress Hall before we go to the Shoo-Fly. Elizabeth will keep the lights burning for us. I need a tonic. In fact, a couple of tonics." He looked from Octavio to Gila. "I think we all do."

# Chapter Fifteen

✦✦✦✦✦

GILA WOKE TO the rattling of pots and pans in Elizabeth Dutton's kitchen. The landlady was always up before dawn, though she went to bed long after midnight.

Twirling one of Octavio's long dark locks around her finger, Gila nestled comfortably against him. The previous night was too wonderful ever to forget. Gila had surprised everyone by saying she didn't want anything to drink and wanted to get to bed early. After several drinks with Thorne, Octavio had excused himself and hurried back to the Shoo-Fly.

In the meantime, Gila had paid Elizabeth dearly for some of the lady's special prickly pear soap. Elizabeth usually kept it for herself, bathing in it for her special man. But Book hadn't come along with them this year.

Gila took a long, lingering bath and scrubbed her hair with the special soap. Naked, she settled into the starched white linen sheets. She hated her burning desire for her husband with every beat of her pulse. Yet when he stepped into their room, she eagerly opened her arms and beckoned him to her.

They had made love gently, slowly, carefully possessing each other. The moment of oneness came, and a joy deep as the San Pedro Valley filled her heart and overflowed into tears of ecstasy. How she had trembled in his arms when she realized the tears of fulfillment were his as well as her own.

Gila held him against her, caressing him, cooing endearments until his breathing took on the slow, rhythmic tide of sleep. She lay awake until the wee hours of the morning, marveling at the incredible completeness they gave each other.

The smell of sizzling meat reminded Gila that morning had come. Truth came, too, with the break of day. Now she must get up and become Gila McCandless—hater of Mexicans, hater of womanhood, but more important, the best trader in the territory.

She rose with a bounce. "Get up, October. We're scorching daylight." She flicked his buttocks playfully with the white shirt.

He rolled over and groaned. "*Madre Santísima,* wife. Are you trying to dismember me? A little closer—"

Her chuckle stopped him as she finished buttoning her blouse. She tucked the tail into a clean pair of nankeens, gave her hair a few quick strokes of the brush, then headed for the door.

"We McCandlesses are the best ropers in the territory. We know *exactly* where we aim."

Gila shut the door behind her, not allowing him time to answer. His deep, vibrant laughter followed her down the hallway, widening the smile that already caressed her lips.

\* \* \*

Gila worked hard most of the day, setting up the stall where she would sell her cures the next day. On her way back to the Shoo-Fly, she noticed that all was in readiness for the pageant. Lanterns outlined the roadway leading from Tucson out to San Xavier. The gleaming walls of the White Dove of the Desert towered majestically, accented by the glowing decorations. Desert flowers colored every rampart. It was as if the townspeople had dressed a bride for her wedding. There was a merging of faith and hope that defied the infinite desolation and dangers of the desert.

There was one danger the people of Tucson would not have to worry about tomorrow. Cochise. He could easily have attacked during the annual festival, but the Chiricahua leader never chose to do so. Never in all the years of her life, Gila remembered.

Once when she and Book had been studying the crowd, she'd glanced to the mountains bordering Tucson to the east. Across a ridge, Cochise and his warriors intently watched the festival.

"Why doesn't he attack?" she'd asked. "We could never make it back to the fort. Not all of us."

Book stared at the scouting party. After a long silence, he informed her, "Cochise is a man of religion. Though he may not believe in your God, he respects any tribe's rituals. White man or Indian, it does not matter. Chiricahua believe it is bad medicine to anger any god, so they will not interfere."

"You mean he thinks all this hollering,

whooping, and yelling is a *religious* celebration?"

Book waved one arm at the crowd. "The original festival was to give thanks for the arrival of Christianity among the heathen. This is white man's way of saying life is good."

"They must think we're plum loco."

"They are very much like your people. After their own ceremonies, Chiricahua drink and dance and make as much noise as you do."

Gila did not understand how Cochise could lead a fierce attack one day and allow his enemies to celebrate the next, but she had to respect him for it. No wonder Cochise was a legend.

Tired and ready for a bath after spending several hours decorating the church, Gila headed toward Ocha and Tulley streets. Her booth was near the freight company. Close to the main street, yet out of the roadway. She had seen many a booth and its wares destroyed by thundering horse hooves during the races or torn apart by a bad-tempered buffalo during the Wallow.

At the Shoo-Fly, the smell of baked bread greeted her as she hitched Wee-People to the post outside the inn. Suddenly her throat became dry, her nose and mouth tightened. Nausea swept up like a windblown tumbleweed. She steadied herself against Wee-People's flank, blinking back the speckles of starlight that swirled in front of her. She reached for the saddlehorn, but it was too late. Desert sand rushed up to engulf her.

Gila woke with a deep throbbing in her head. How did she get back to her room at the Shoo-

Fly? Why was she in bed? What was that horrible taste in her mouth? She blinked several times, trying to make out the blurry image in front of her.

A vaguely familiar man held a ghastly smelling object under her nose. "Mrs. Cordoba? Gila? Are you all right?"

"I will be when you get that stuff away from me." She pushed at the offensive container, surprised at how much effort it took to move.

The man laughed and took the jar away from her nose. "I know you're going to be just fine. Do you remember me, Gila? Dr. Williams from Nogales."

The heavyset doctor opened the door and beckoned to Thorne and Octavio. "You can see her now. She's had a hard time, but she's going to be all right."

Octavio edged past the physician as though he didn't want to get anywhere near him. Gila wondered why he was acting so strangely.

"The baby?" Octavio asked the doctor as he drew near the bed.

"She's a healthy woman. Still, she's not so far along that she couldn't miscarry. You'll need to make sure she doesn't try to ride rough herd over the proceedings as she usually does." He turned back to Gila and gathered his black bag and tools. "That means no Buffalo-Wallow for you this year, young lady."

Thorne thanked the doctor and handed him several bills. Octavio looked disgruntled about the transaction. Was he upset because Thorne was paying rather than himself?

The doctor bid Gila farewell, reminding her to take care of herself. "That is, if you really want that baby."

Gila turned away, hoping Octavio and Thorne would also go before they saw the flood of tears threatening her eyes.

So, it was as she feared. She was pregnant! She glanced at Octavio. His face registered an expression she was certain was disappointment, then became blank. "You're not fooling me," she said bitterly. "You can't be any more sorry than I am. You came that close." She snapped her fingers for emphasis. "That close to your freedom." Gila glanced at Octavio, then back at Thorne. "I almost saved the precious name, didn't I? But this baby has the luck of the Irish, it does. The wee one is half McCandless—a survivor. No such luck for you, October. Now you'll have to wait out the full term. No such luck for you *or* me." He'd made it clear that no child would keep him from his freedom and she'd be damned before she told him the child was his. The tears came now, slow and soul-wrenching, yet she refused to allow a sob to escape her lips.

Octavio beckoned to Thorne. "Would you leave us, Señor McCandless? I must speak to Gila alone."

Thorne hesitated, then finally agreed. "I'll be over at Congress Hall if you need me." He left, shutting the door behind him.

Octavio sat on the edge of the bed and cupped one of Gila's hands in his own. Something about the gentleness of his touch ignited her deep need for him, and she was unwilling to remove her hand from his. If only things could be different.

He stared at her for several moments, almost as if he were not sure where to begin. She wondered why he took so long to speak. She knew exactly what he was going to say. Certainly you can find a way to lose the baby. Maybe tomorrow at the horse race or the Wallow. It would be a sure way out of their marriage. But he didn't say that at all.

"Gila, what kind of man do you take me for?" He studied her so intently she became uncomfortable. "Look beyond your hatred for my people and tell me what you see."

Why did he have to bring her prejudice into the conversation? This was no time to argue about his nationality. Stop, October, she pleaded silently.

"You can't, can you?" Octavio said quietly, almost accusingly. "You can't see beyond your hatred because you've never tried. Why? Am I so repulsive that you cannot?"

Gila turned away from him, but he brought her gaze back to his with a gentle nudge to her chin.

"I am not so repulsive that I cannot share your bed, mold my flesh to your own." His clouded blue eyes seemed to search her soul to its very depths; they were a mirror to the desire hidden deep within her thoughts, her dreams, her being. "Why are you afraid someone will discover that you are a woman of passion? It is becoming to you." He traced a fingertip across her lips. "I am a proud man, *dulce mia*. Proud enough to want my woman to claim me in the light of day as well as the night. But until that day comes, you will never possess my heart. Our desire for each other is undeniable, but until you can call me husband—no matter who is listening—you will never know what it is to be a true wife."

"A true wife!" Gila shouted and sat upright. Her head and stomach became dizzy and nauseated with the movement. "I never wanted to be a wife. Never! And I don't want this baby!"

"Then perhaps you should not have the baby," Octavio said, his jaw tensing with anger. "You behave little more than a child yourself. As you have said, the babe is half McCandless. Half you. Does that make no difference to you at all? I know nothing of the father, but what if it were mine? Would you prejudice yourself against your own flesh?"

The truth of October's words echoed through Gila's mind. The child *would* be half-breed. Mc-Candless and Mexican.

"I'll leave you to your thoughts, señora." Octavio rose. "Your father is good company. He judges a man by his worth, not by his country."

As he turned to leave, Gila was reminded of how very Mexican he was in his waist-length green jacket and matching trousers with silver conchas sewn down each side fitting snugly over his lean physique. A matador's body. So handsome. So arrogant. So Mexican.

She stared at the door for several moments

after he had left. Her eyes closed with the memory of his touch and she reached up and pressed her lips with unsteady fingers.

She wished she could call out to him to return to her, but the act would be wasted. He would never believe how sorry she was for all the hurtful things she'd said to him or that she truly meant the five words that escaped her lips. "I love you . . . you . . . *Mexican.*"


# Chapter Sixteen

✦✦✦✦✦


OCTAVIO STOLE A glance at the congregation that filled San Xavier chapel for the holiday mass. He was surprised to see even the most foulmouthed wranglers in attendance. Obviously this Easter mass was of great importance to the community.

He looked at Gila, who sat to his left. The fact that he wanted her to love him pierced him like one of El Diablo's unexpected thrusts. The ache in his heart was as severe as if he had been horned by his notorious adversary.

Gila's head was bent in diligent prayer. Octavio was certain it had something to do with the child. He'd noticed the pale, taut lips and dark circles under her eyes when he offered to escort her to the mass. She had not rested well.

A gentle nudge in his left ribs embarrassed him into attention. Gila gave him a sharp, demanding look, making him sit still straighter on the planked pew. The padre's chanting distracted him momentarily, but soon his thoughts returned to the frightening discovery of his love for her.

How much easier it would be to nurse an injury from El Diablo than to survive Gila's deep knifing of his soul. Love for her punctured his pride, twisting all his reason, whittling away at his sanity.

The previous night when he had accused her of prejudice toward him, he had realized he was just as guilty as she. He relished their nights together, yet he too failed to acknowledge her as his lover during the day. No flowers. No serenading. No discreet hand-holding or long, lingering looks.

Why?

Another fear rose and announced its presence. What would happen on the day he was free to help Juárez if his desire to stay with Gila were stronger than his determination to free Mexico?

No! His destiny called him. Love was nothing compared to duty. Until Mexico was free from foreign rule, love for Gila could be only a distant thing, a far horizon yet to be completely explored.

Octavio could imagine her reaction if he professed his love. The pain of her ridiculing tongue would slice deep, wound him more severely than any of her previous slurs.

Again a nudge in his side. Octavio raised his
head to discover the others standing, preparing
to leave.

"I didn't know you were such a praying
man," Gila taunted as she urged him into the
aisle.

Frustration gave rise to unthinking. "I thought
one of us should ask for the child's safety."

Gila brushed past him and through the chapel's ornately carved doors, her stricken look
making him regret his cruel words. A deep
sadness washed over him as he turned and
studied the ceilings and walls of the famous old
church. How had his forefathers ever tamed the
heathens of this sun-scorched wilderness? How
could he ever tame Gila . . . or his love for her?

Gila counted the silver and placed it into the
already bulging money bag. She looked over the
goods traded for her wares and was pleased.
Most would come in handy sooner or later. It
had been a very good morning; almost all of the
pies and cactus jam were sold before noon. She
had only some saguaro salve and Blarney-Brew
left. Traditionally, the salve never ran out until
after the Buffalo-Wallow. The injuries the wranglers suffered while wrestling giant bisons usually required more than a little of her medicine.
She affectionately called her cure "a dab of salve
and mug or two of Blarney-Brew."

She squirmed, tugging at the tight-fitting
waistband of her black skirt. The frilly white
blouse was uncomfortable too, but the ruffles

conveniently covered her neck wound. She couldn't wait to get out of these gut-clutchers, but until she sold all of the jams and pies she'd have to remain in feminine attire.

The people who bought her wares were a mixed lot. They would never accept a woman conducting business in nankeens and a shirt, not when the celebrations brought in outsiders from far settlements. This code of respectability allowed the people of Tucson to consider themselves "civilized."

Gila might have laughed at their airs and worn what she pleased, but then no one would buy her wares. She would be dependent on Thorne for everything, and she would never allow that to happen.

She brushed back the auburn ringlets that accented her forehead and cheeks. How silly she'd been to add the vain touches. But she'd felt frivolous and softened her usual boyish look with a black silk ribbon and a frame of ringlets around her face.

The afternoon wind was blowing steadily now, a brief yet welcome relief from the desert heat. How did Shelly Kate and the other ladies manage to keep their hair out of their eyes? Gila looked at several women in the crowd. Most of them held multicolored parasols to block the sun and wind. She would rather her hair blow wild than hold one of those sissy sticks over her head.

A swarm of people lined Tulley Street. She guessed nearly five hundred people had come to view the Buffalo-Wallow. It was almost everyone's favorite.

Gila pushed toward the front row of the crowd. Several men stepped aside, murmuring pleasantries meant for any lady who might be close at hand. There were fifty men to every woman in Tucson, so Gila never took their compliments seriously. But for getting a good view of the Buffalo-Wallow, she had to admit being female had its advantages.

A square wooden pen stood in the middle of the street. The crowd parted as Thorne led Dublin into the hastily made arena. As always, appreciation for the white buffalo shuffled through the spectators like cards from a fast-handed dealer.

Gila's chin lifted with pride as the majestic animal moved toward the center of the pen. Dublin's muscles rippled with strength, both nostrils flared with purpose. She had scrubbed him vigorously that morning, waxing his horns to shiny peaks. His fur was as white as the salt pits in Silver Canyon. The silver nugget hung around his neck like a king's medal of order. Dublin was the embodiment of his breed—awesome, fierce, regal.

His kind is almost extinct, she thought. Sightings of great whites were fewer than ever before. Even the normal herds were dwindling to nothing.

Gila had tried on several occasions to provide a mate for Dublin, but he never seemed interested in any of the females she borrowed from the neighboring ranchers. Dublin was as confirmed a bachelor as was Book. She had thought the three of them—she, Book, and Dublin—

would all stay single, but fate had chosen otherwise. Here she was, married and pregnant.

Where was October now? Would he come to watch the Wallow or was he visiting some pretty señorita?

The starting gunshot startled her. She turned quickly and saw the first contestant was already in the ring. Billy Puckett, the Circle-Shamrock's best wrestler, had the misfortune to have drawn the first number. She was disappointed at the stroke of bad luck. Dublin wouldn't even begin to tire until the fourth or fifth man. Billy had his work cut out for him.

Billy, like the other contestants, had ten minutes to snatch the silver nugget from around Dublin's neck. If the rawhide string that held the nugget broke, Billy's efforts would be in vain. The necklace had to be intact. The contestants couldn't just grab the pendant and jerk it away. Few ever succeeded. Some years there was no winner. But if there was, he was usually a Circle-Shamrock man. This year, however, the Circle-Shamrock seemed to have little chance to win the Wallow or the horse race. That was certain to wreak havoc on Thorne's temper.

Billy failed. Sisneros, from Pete Kitchen's place, failed also. Gila was proud of Dublin. Her only regret was that none of the Shamrock's boys would be the one to defeat him.

She caught the flash of medals on a gray uniform as a rebel soldier moved up beside her. She chose to ignore him and kept her eyes on the pen. If she acknowledged him, he would no doubt turn on his Southern charm. Whether she wore a wedding ring or not, a lady was safer to ignore a graycoat.

There was a stir in the crowd. Gila strained to see the object of their interest. A figure in a bright yellow outfit edged his way toward the gate. Across his arm was draped a large piece of red cloth. It was October! Why in St. Patrick was he dressed like that?

"Contestant number three," Thorne announced. "Don Octavio Diego Cordoba of the Circle-Shamrock." Octavio bowed low to the spectators.

Even as she admired the man she loved, Gila could not control the smirk that lifted one corner of her mouth. He looked like a dandy in those knee-length britches.

"Isn't he that famous matador—Don Cordoba? The one who defeated El Diablo?" a lady near her asked.

"*Sí,*" a Mexican man replied. "I wonder what he's doing here. He disappeared almost a year ago and has not been seen until today. Some say he tried to kill Maximilian. I wonder if the emperor would be interested in Cordoba's whereabouts?"

Gila turned and unsheathed the knife she'd strapped to her thigh. "I would not count on your whereabouts for very much longer, compadre, if you so much as open your mouth to anyone about Don Cordoba."

"That's Thorne McCandless's daughter," she heard someone tell the Mexican. "You better listen to what she says or you'll be sorry."

Being a McCandless had its uses, she thought

as she directed her attention back to the pen. But could October really be in danger. Had he tried to kill Maximilian?

At least the peasant's outburst had confirmed one thing. Octavio's regal bearing, his courtliness, was not an act. He was a true nobleman.

Octavio strutted into the arena and undraped the red cape. He held it to his left side and shook it at Dublin. Dublin's shoulder muscles contracted, his head lifted slightly. The lid over his one good eye lowered, while his nostrils grew wide with anger.

Uh-oh, Gila whispered to herself. She watched intently as Dublin's humped shoulders drew back like a bow. He flung himself toward the red cape. The cloth swirled high above Octavio's head and came back down to the right side just in time to take the buffalo's next charge. On and on the matador teased and whirled, wearing the bison into a frenzied rage. Her heart beat rapidly as she noted Octavio's own tense muscles, the firm set of his jaw, the deep concentration in his blue eyes.

The Mexicans in the crowd began to shout, "Olé!" Caught up in the emotion of the moment, she shouted along with them, her blood racing with each thrust and swirl.

Dublin's steps began to falter. His shoulders heaved with the strain of the constant whirling.

"Two minutes," Thorne warned, pistol raised to signal the time limit. "Two minutes."

Octavio positioned the cape once again. Dublin bent his head and thundered toward him. Octavio let go of the cape and leapt onto Dublin's back. One hand gripped a horn, the other grabbed the necklace. Dublin shook his head violently, almost unseating his unwelcome rider.

Octavio bent forward and slid the necklace over the animal's massive neck, holding it high for the crowd to see. A roar of approval met with the matador's retreat from Dublin's shoulders and followed him through the gate.

The spectators went wild with excitement, jumping up and down, clapping their hands. Strangers shook hands, even hugged one another. As she applauded, Gila accidentally bumped into the rebel soldier she had noticed before Octavio entered the arena. He grabbed her by the shoulders and crushed her to him. She pushed him away, looking up to deliver a tirade. But no words came out.

The rebel was Garrett O'Malley!

His sandy brown hair still tumbled boyishly over his wide forehead. Fawn-brown eyes ravished her from head to toe, then returned to linger on her breasts. A slow, seductive smile lined the lips he lowered toward her own. "Gila, my love."

Her protest was broken by his hungry kiss. His hands pressed her closer, holding her fast against him.

"Is this someone I should know, *dulce mia?*" Octavio demanded.

Gila took the opportunity of Garrett's surprise to escape from him. Brushing back the wisps of hair that nudged her flaming cheeks, she said, "This is Garrett O'Malley, my neighbor and an old friend." She turned back to Garrett. "This is my husband, Don Octavio Diego Cordoba." The look on Garrett's face was worth acknowledging Octavio publicly.

"*Husband?*" He took a moment to recover, then offered his hand to Octavio. Octavio refused the handshake and merely nodded in acknowledgment.

Garrett's hand settled slowly to his side. "You must forgive me, sir. When I left for the war, Gila was to be *my* bride."

Gila looked from her former beau to her husband. Snake fodder! What was she supposed to do now? Garrett was taking this much better than she'd expected. Yet he'd purposely let Octavio notice him wiping his hand before offering it. Did he have some personal distaste for October? Or could Garrett actually be jealous? Did he really care for her and not just for her father's money and land?

From the looks of October, he wasn't happy with Garrett either. He probably thinks Garrett is the baby's father! But she had the feeling something else was going on, too. She couldn't resist the impulse to ask, "Do you two know each other?"

Octavio gave a brief shake of his head. "I don't believe I've had the pleasure." The last word dripped icily off his tongue.

"I've seen so many faces, I can't recall," Garrett replied, but something in his manner convinced Gila he was lying.

Whether they had known each other before seemed unimportant at the moment. She had more vital things to worry about. She'd forgotten

all about Garrett's and Thorne's promise to
Garrett's father. How would Thorne honor that
deal now that she was married to October? A
terrible fear rose and lodged itself in her mind.
No! He wouldn't do that, would he? Not to
Shelly!

Gila's head ached with the uncertainty of her
thoughts. Maybe a drink would help her decide
what to do.

"Isn't it hot?" she asked, fanning herself elaborately with her palm. "Let's go have a drink.
The next contest isn't for another half hour. I
need a drink real bad and can't wait to get out of
this dress. Don't you want to get out of this
heat?" She realized she was just prattling and
giggled self-consciously.

Garrett and Octavio offered an elbow at exactly
the same moment. Feeling slightly wicked, but
rather pleased at Octavio's jealousy, she accepted both. Each man eyed the other, making
Gila smile. Finally she understood why some
women hankered after male attention. She had
never realized how much fun it could be. With a
newfound gusto, Gila gave both men her most
earnest attention.

# Chapter Seventeen

✦✦✦✦✦

GILA THOUGHT THE pageant had been successful, but Thorne did not share her view. Although October had won the Wallow and the Shamrock wranglers placed first in five other events, Thorne was livid about losing the horse race. The ranting and raving had started this morning as soon as they rode out of Tucson and Gila could only hope it would end by the time they camped. She was certain everyone else in the outfit was as tired of hearing her father's complaints as she was.

It was late before Thorne called a halt to the daylong journey. Gila was more than happy to dismount. The hours on horseback had brought a soreness to her back and thighs. She realized these new aches and pains were from the baby, and this both disturbed and pleased her.

Doubt had crept into her thoughts since the doctor's visit. She'd argued a blue norther with Thorne, denying that the Indian had raped her. And yet . . . could she be so certain? She might have lost consciousness before Dublin arrived. And if she had, the Indian could have taken her before she revived. But how could that be? Wouldn't she have felt something?

No. I refuse to believe it! she thought stubbornly. I *won't* believe it. The baby is October's and it's no time to start doubting my own memory now.

The sight of her sister still astride her horse

drew Gila out of her thoughts. Why was Shelly just sitting there? Her gaze followed the direction her sister's had taken. Garrett, of course!

Garrett O'Malley had hobbled his own mount and was walking toward Shelly Kate. "May I help you down?" he drawled seductively. Shelly's blond frailty, her creamy white skin, seemed even more delicate after long hours in the sun. The blue ruffled parasol she carried had helped little. Her face and neck were flushed, and she looked as if she might wilt any moment.

Gila compared her own clothes to Shelly's. Of course the nankeens were more practical than the blue cotton dress her sister wore. More practical, more logical, but definitely unfeminine.

Garrett took Shelly Kate by the waist and gently lowered her to the ground. The act took longer than it should have, with both parties acting as if they didn't want to release each other.

Gila felt a twinge of jealousy and it surprised her. Garrett was enjoying her sister's company more than he had ever enjoyed her own. Why should she be jealous of a man who had made such a fool of her? A man she despised. She turned away and bumped face-to-shoulder with Octavio.

"Is he the one?" Octavio asked. "Is he the father?"

Gila gazed into the narrowing blue eyes and shivered. What lay hidden in October's look? Was it envy of Garrett? No. More likely, male pride forced him to look at her that way. "How could that be?" Gila asked in a scathing tone. "Garrett's been fighting with the Confederacy the last three years. He couldn't be the father."

"Then you wish it were so. I see it in your eyes."

Gila shivered under Octavio's unrelenting gaze and turned away. He had seen fear in her eyes, not wishful thinking. What would October do if he ever found out Garrett had taken her virginity?

Octavio grabbed her by the shoulder and pulled her roughly to him, turning her around and forcing his lips upon hers. She struggled to break free, furious at his brusque possession. Just as quickly, the kiss softened. The grip of his fingers slackened into a caressing embrace. She could have broken away without much effort, but something in his manner confused her, begged her to remain in his arms.

Finally, Octavio relinquished his hold, his own confusion evident. "Do not tease me, woman. Desire runs deep in the Cordoba blood," he warned huskily.

The warm flush that raced up her back and down to her fingertips assured Gila that Mc-Candless passions were the equal to any Mexican family's, no matter how noble its origins. "I don't tease or make false promises," she said haughtily.

"Really, you two," Shelly Kate interrupted as she and Garrett walked toward them. "There is a time and place for such things, and it's certainly not on a trip with so many men around, don't you think?"

Gila moved deliberately into Octavio's arms. "Those men, as you call them, mind their own business. Unlike some people I know."

Garrett drew Shelly closer. "Then we mustn't let one sister get the better of the other, must we?" He kissed Shelly fully on the lips.

Gila's cheeks grew hot with anger. What was Garrett trying to prove? A hard grip on her elbow stopped the rebuking words that were ready to spill from her tongue.

"It is none of your concern as well, *dulce mia*," Octavio warned. At her stiff reaction to his words, he added, "Or is it?"

The grip loosened before Gila could answer. She felt as if she had lost more than any battle of words.

Later, as she was cleaning up after supper, Gila watched her husband head up the mountainside for his turn on watch. He'd been extremely tense during the meal, speaking only when asked a direct question. Now she saw his body loosen with every step he took away from the camp.

He probably couldn't wait to get away from me, she thought. He prefers being alone to enduring my company. Not that she could blame him. He had tolerated a lot from her since they'd met.

She bent to clean another plate. Suddenly a pain wrenched through her back, making her catch her breath. She straightened and silently spoke to her unborn child. I would bet a field of saguaros, if I was a betting woman, that you're a boy with a temper just like your father's. Every time I think of him, you give me a pain. You Mexicans are an emotional lot.

"A smile becomes you, Gila," Garrett crooned as he sat beside her. "Why don't we take a little walk? I want to talk to you."

"Won't Shelly Kate get mad?" she asked curtly. "Besides, I don't think we have anything to discuss."

"You're wrong. We do." Garrett's hand on her elbow and the tone of his voice warned Gila that he would make a scene if she didn't comply with his wishes. But she didn't want a ruckus with October as well. If he saw her and Garrett together, he would only assume the worst.

Knowing October would not desert his watch, Gila finally agreed to Garrett's request. Her curiosity overruled her better judgment. She motioned to a well-lit spot just on the border of the campsite. Shelly Kate had bedded down for the night, so there would be no argument from her. Gila propped her aching back against a juniper tree and waited until Garrett sat down beside her. "Now what's so damned important?"

"You and me," he said, placing a hand upon her knee.

She shoved his hand away immediately. "There is no you and me," she insisted. "Come to think of it," she added, "there never was a you and me." Any jealousy she'd felt earlier was only a holdover. After all, much as she hadn't liked it, she had been engaged to him.

Garrett laughed, a deep, resonant laugh, drawing a few curious stares from the wranglers.

Gila's cheeks grew hot with embarrassment. Surely they didn't think she was being coy with him, did they?

Octavio had won their respect by pulling his share of the work at the ranch. He roughsaddled the broncs and enjoyed rather than resented the long, grueling hours. Gila knew she would lose much of the wranglers' respect if they thought she was trifling with Garrett while her husband was on watch for their safety.

"I see you haven't lost any of your sass," Garrett complimented. "It becomes you. But there's something different about you. You're almost beautiful." He nodded. "Yes, that's it. You've become prettier since the last time I saw you."

"Why you conceited—should I bow now and kiss your feet or wait until you consider me fairly decent!" Gila held her name-calling in check. Deliberately lowering her voice so the others wouldn't hear, she added, "If Thorne hadn't personally invited you to ride with us, I'd send you hightailing out of here quicker than a brush fire." Her voice trembled with the anger erupting within her. "My husband is extremely jealous and won't hesitate to put you and that so-called southern charm of yours in its place."

"Gila, you don't understand," Garrett said, his tone taking on a serious quality. She looked and saw a curious expression on his face, one that she'd never seen before on Garrett, yet one she recognized, for she had seen it many times in a different pair of eyes, eyes as blue as sapphires. She should pull away now, before he mistook her inaction as consent. Yet something in the way he took her hand in his made her wait.

"In the war," he began slowly, almost whispering, "lying in the battlefield trenches, listening to the cannon fire, smelling gunpowder and the stench of dying flesh, I'd hear the moans of men around me. Confederate or Yankee, a moan sounds the same. I never knew whether to help the next man or stay where I was. The few times I did try, I regretted it. The friend was always too far gone to save, and the other times I nearly got my head blown off my shoulders."

"Why are you telling me this?" Gila asked, shifting uncomfortably against the juniper. "What does this have to do with me?"

"I saw death every day for three years, and it made me realize what life meant to me. What *you* mean to me. Our fathers may have made the choice for us to marry, but with your business knowledge and my powers of persuasion, we could make one hell of a successful team."

Gila withdrew her hand as she finally and completely let go of the past and what might have once been between her and Garrett. "I'm sorry the war was so cruel to you, Garrett. Honestly I am. But I'm not sorry that I can no longer marry you." She motioned up the hillside to where Cordoba was positioned. "Octavio is my husband. I belong to him now."

Garrett pulled her roughly to him, catching Gila awkwardly off-balance, and kissed her. She could think only of October's lips on hers and began to tremble. Obviously misreading the reason for her shiver, Garrett let her go.

"So, you still care for me more than you want to admit. Annul this marriage, Gila. Let me give you children for the O'Malley-McCandless empire."

Gila slowly stood, a sadness enveloping her. "You really don't understand, do you? All you can think of is having your own empire. It doesn't have anything to do with me. Or Shelly Kate for that matter." He started to protest, but she refused to let him interrupt her, placing a warning palm out to stop his words. "Don't think I haven't noticed you bellying up to her. Sixteen may be young for a man, but for a female, sixteen is the beginning of womanhood. Shelly Kate is primed for falling in love, so don't take advantage of the infatuation she's had for you all these years." She moved out of his reach. "One of these days you're going to need a woman like her. One who will love you too much to see your conniving nature."

He grabbed her by the shoulders and tried to hold her against his chest. "Is he so much better than I was? I'm no longer a boy, Gila. There are many things I can teach you now."

"Don't touch me," she cautioned, jerking away from his viselike grip. "You never wanted me. You only took me to win a bet. I doubt you really want Shelly Kate. We're simply an end to a means. Nothing more. A way for you to get the precious north section." Reading the guilty expression on his face, she added, "I suspected as much. But I'm not surprised. One day, if you're really lucky, you'll get both Shelly and the land. Pretty darned good bargain, if you ask me. But in order to get Shelly, you're going to have to prove to me you love her. And so far, buster, you aren't doing a good job."

"You love him, don't you?" Garrett asked incredulously. "You actually love that Mexican. A *Mexican*, Gila. Mexicans killed your mother and almost did the same to you and Shelly Kate."

"It doesn't matter," Gila went on, "I have no right to blame him for something that happened long ago. Nobody has a right to blame a nation for something done by a handful of evil people." A weight seemed to lift from her. A weight she hadn't known was burdening her.

"Where did you meet this Mexican of yours?" Garrett asked in contempt, sarcasm curling his upper lip.

Where was this question leading? How much had Garrett been told and by whom? Her earlier suspicion that October and Garrett knew each other crept into her thoughts. "I met him on the last roundup," she said evasively, yet truthfully. If she shied away from answering, he would suspect that she was trying to hide something from him. If she said it was none of his concern, Garrett would hound her and everyone else until he found out the truth. The best thing to do was to settle his suspicions now.

"You know," she suppressed a giggle as she made up her story. "It was love at first glance." The thought that she'd been drunk, wearing yellow ruffles, her dusty red bandanna, and boots, not to mention October's malnourished, pallid face was enough to make anyone laugh. Love at first glance? It was all she could do to keep a straight face.

"Let's see. You've only been married a matter of weeks, then," Garrett estimated. "Surely you received my letter telling you I was on my way home. No?" He took a long, lingering look at her bosom, raking his eyes over her in a look of blatant lust. "I can see why the Mexican wanted you. You're quite a woman, Gila." Garrett's finger shot to her neck and purposefully plunged to her breast. "A woman like you needs a man. Did you tell your lover that I was the first to touch you?"

Gila slapped him hard and the sound echoed across the camp. "You keep your hands off me, Garrett O'Malley," she said coldly, fury making her words low and precise. "Keep your thoughts, your plans, and your empire as well! Touch me again and I swear, I'll have October thrash you."

A noise alerted them and they saw Ben approach. The wrangler didn't look at Gila as he delivered his message. "Octavio says he wants another man on watch. There's a scouting party camped on the next rise to the northeast, and he doesn't recognize any of their markings. Says you should go up and join him, Garrett."

Gila's heart seemed to drop into her stomach. Had October seen the kiss from his post up the mountain? Or the slap? The thought of her husband and Garrett spending the next four hours together wasn't one she welcomed. A soft curse was all she could muster as Garrett and Ben left.

Gila smoothed back a wisp of auburn hair that blew across her mouth, reprimanding herself for having worn it down this morning. Between the wind and Wee-People's jogging up and down, it was impossible to keep her hair from becoming a nuisance. Why hadn't she tied it back this morning as she usually did? How in St. Patrick's name did Shelly Kate manage to keep control of her hair. And her temper, Gila wondered as she tried to stuff the auburn tresses under her sombrero.

Her own temper was getting the best of her today. She had tossed and turned during the short time she'd slept. Thoughts of Garrett's and October's conversation while they were on watch gave her no rest and plenty to worry about.

What if October told Garrett the truth behind the marriage? Garrett had every right to demand justice or repayment of some kind from Thorne. He wouldn't take lightly the loss of the property he'd been promised in her dowry and the prestige that would have been his had he married a McCandless.

What about October's curiosity? He'd been so certain Garrett was the baby's father. Now that he knew that was impossible, he might have persuaded Garrett into finding out who was responsible. That could lead to all sorts of eyebrow raising.

Gila warily eyed Octavio and Garrett, who were riding point. What had passed between them while they were on watch? She hadn't seen them say anything to each other today. It was enough to make her scream.

Shelly Kate reined alongside her, interrupting her troublesome thoughts. "Your hair looks so lovely," she chided.

Gila glared at her sister, hating the heat rising to her cheeks. This was the last time she would wear her hair down, trying to compete with Shelly's uncommon beauty. She was tired of seeing the look of appreciation in October's eyes whenever he glanced at her sister.

"I doubt your husband even noticed your efforts," Shelly said acidly. "He's been so preoccupied. I haven't seen him talk to anyone but Father."

October had spoken to Thorne? When and for what reason? "Maybe he's tired from last night's watch. There was chance of trouble for a while, but Garrett said the scouting party left at dawn."

"Did Garrett talk to you this morning?" asked Shelly Kate, a frown furrowing her brow.

"Yes, for a moment."

"Now I see." With a slow smile Shelly eyed Gila's hair.

Gila slowed Wee-People to a walk as she turned toward her sister. They could catch up with the rest of the outfit in a matter of minutes. Right now, she needed to set things straight. "If you think I wore my hair down for Garrett O'Malley, you're sorely mistaken. I never gave a hang for him."

Shelly tossed back her mass of ivory-colored hair. "You mean he never gave a hang for you."

Gila wanted to slap the sass out of Shelly but decided it wouldn't do either of them any good. Shelly was a McCandless and McCandlesses seemed to learn their lessons the hard way. "Okay, so I'm not beautiful. I've never tried to be. That's always been your sock to darn. All I'm saying is, watch out for Garrett. Don't fall in love with him too quickly. Be sure you love him."

"Heed your own warnings, sister darling," Shelly retorted, her ebony gaze narrowing toward the subject of their conversation. "I've loved him for as long as I can remember. But you were always the one who got to walk with him or go to socials with him. I've waited a long time for Garrett to come home from the war, a long time to persuade him not to marry you. Fortunately, you took care of that by marrying Octavio."

Determination straightened her back and sharply set her petite shoulders. "I'm sixteen now, fully grown," Shelly insisted. "Neither you nor anyone else can stop me from having him. And if you do try—" She gave Gila a fierce glance. "Then I'll tell your secret."

The cloud of dust that trailed Shelly Kate as she galloped toward the point riders muffled Gila's cry of dismay. Was it possible Shelly knew of the attempted rape? What had Thorne told her? Worse, did October know?

Perhaps Shelly was merely guessing. Her sister was clever, even devious at times. She might have overheard Thorne and Book talking and put two and two together.

What should I do? Gila wondered. Do I keep Thorne's suspicions secret and save the McCandless name or take the chance that Shelly was only guessing?

Her stomach fluttered and she suspected the baby stirred within her, even though it was far too soon to feel any real movement. She smoothed the material covering her abdomen, stroking the tiny life growing inside. "I don't have a choice, do I, wee one?" she whispered. "If I don't try to stop Shelly, she'll be hurt and her life will be ruined. One ruined McCandless is enough."

Though Gila's mind was set, she wondered if it were already too late to help her sister. Garrett knew Shelly was the last and only road to McCandless wealth now that Gila was married to October. Shelly would be easy prey because of her misguided love for him.

"No," Gila said with conviction. "It's up to me to stop him." She pondered the problem for several moments. The solution came bright and clear. Somehow she had to convince Garrett that she still cared for him. She could tell him that when October left her later in the year, she would be free to marry him. Shelly Kate would see Garrett bellying up to the McCandless fortune rather than loving any one sister for herself. Hopefully she would turn away.

But what of October? Already he believed that

she loved the rebel. He would never go along with her plan if she told him the truth. Yet her sister's happiness was at stake. She could only hope October would forgive her actions once he learned the reason for them.

Her own life was so tangled. Nothing could make it worse than it already was. She had to help Shelly Kate. She was, after all, blood kin. Nothing was more important than that.

Besides, Gila stifled a chuckle, I took on the responsibility of seeing to her safety when I chose not to smother her with that swaddling cloth.

The fluttering in her stomach brought a smile to Gila's lips even as a curious but somehow necessary tear rolled down her cheeks. "Yes, darling," she whispered to her unborn baby. "Blood kin is more important than McCandless pride or McCandless greed."

# Chapter Eighteen

✦✦✦✦✦

THE JUNE DAY was a scorcher. Beads of perspiration lined Gila's neckline and temples. The repetitious plodding of approaching hooves and the sharp odor of sweating horse drew her away from the base of the saguaro. Why was Garrett here instead of home helping his father?

She shielded her eyes with red-stained hands, carefully avoiding her forehead with the pulpy juice dripping down her wrists. "Yes?"

Garrett dismounted and placed a possessive arm around her waist. He bent to kiss her, but she turned away, allowing the kiss to graze her cheek. The lookouts would think Garrett was only being neighborly.

"Stop that," she warned as she moved away from him. "You know Thorne sends men out to protect me while I farm. Tell me what you want, so I can get back to harvesting."

Garrett's eyes turned a smokier shade of brown. "I want you, Gila. Not in a year or a month, but now. Don't tell me that you haven't wanted me, too."

Gila turned away, unable to look at him directly. Her disgust would show and ruin all her efforts of the last two months. The moments stolen to be with him, the long, lingering looks during Sunday meals shared with the O'Malleys, all had played a part in her plan. Fortunately morning sickness had given enough explanation for her moments of illness when she had felt revulsion at his returned affection. And her pregnancy had kept him at a distance . . . so far. "Yes, darling," she lied, the words bitter on her lips. "I have wanted you."

Garrett reached for her and drew her slowly to him. The kiss was not gentle and she had to force herself to respond to him. His lips burned a trail down her neck and she let a well-timed moan escape just as his hand reached up to cup one breast. She would have preferred to kick him in the groin and hear *him* moan.

"Oh, darling Gila," his voice rasped, "I've wanted you for so long, but . . ." He pulled away.

"But what?" she asked, pretending to pout. What stroke of luck had ended his passionate assault? Whatever it was, she was grateful. She was uncertain how much further she would let him explore just for Shelly's sake. And it wasn't as if he hadn't roamed this section before.

Garrett let go of her. In frustration, he ran a hand through his sandy hair. "I can't stand the thought of you carrying his baby. What if he doesn't choose to leave?"

"Oh, he'll leave," Gila assured him as her heart sank at the thought. "Just as sure as we're standing here, he'll leave."

"And the child?"

Gila took firm control of her temper. "The child is McCandless. Mine. The baby stays with me. No matter what." What sort of woman did Garrett think she was?

Garrett threw his hands up in annoyance. "I didn't come here to argue or even to talk about this now. I need your help."

"What's happened?"

"Father has trouble and if we don't act fast, we'll have every Apache in the territory riding down on us. Can you saddle up now?"

Gila looked at her tools and the red saguaro pulp drying in the sun. She would lose this batch if she didn't get it into the accordion sheaths within the hour. "Would you send one of the lookouts for Book and ask him to finish up for me? I can't lose today's work. I'm going to be short of salve as it is."

"Yes, yes, I will," he said impatiently.

Gila gathered all but the tools Book would need and placed everything else in Wee-People's saddlebags. She set the paint free from the travois that carried her supplies, then carefully mounted him. There was a real trick to straddling such a broad horse since she was becoming fuller with child. "Book knows what to do with the rest. I guess I'm ready to go. What's so urgent?"

Garrett mounted his dun and reined half-quarter. "We've got trouble with Mexicans. Take some of your salve."

Garrett refused to answer any of the questions Gila asked until the lookouts had been told of her leaving and the need for Book's assistance with the harvesting. Both taken care of, Garrett proceeded to tell her of the afternoon's trouble. Gila grew increasingly nervous with each mile they left behind. She knew she was safe while on Thorne's land, but the Shamrock's border was drawing near. From the sound of things, O'Malley land might not be such a wise place to be at the moment.

"Why don't you send for someone who speaks Spanish? At least she can ask this wounded Mexican where the pain is located. All I can do is doctor what I see."

Garrett blew out a long breath. "It would have taken too long to send to Tucson, and we don't want him to talk to anyone. We just want you to doctor him and get him out of here as quickly as possible."

"You've broken Cochise's pact, haven't you?" she asked with dread. She should have suspected something bad was happening when Octavio had to act as interpreter weeks ago. "You know you can't get away with this, and Thorne must—"

"Your father can mind his own damn business!" Garrett's eyes flashed with deep-seated hatred. "'If he had kept his word in the first place, this would never have happened."

Gila despised the man Garrett O'Malley had become. A sixteen-year-old boy trying to be what he thought was a man was one thing. But Garrett was no longer playing a boy's game. He was dealing with Apache. Apache who would rape, murder, destroy.

"If I'm to help you," she said, "then I think I should know everything that has happened. Maybe I'll be able to explain to Thorne, and he won't feel compelled to hand you over to Cochise."

Irritation set Garrett's jaw. "I told you everything. We were financing some Mexican gunrunners. They got a little too deep into Cochise's territory and killed some of his private stock. Now—"

"What was that?" Gila interrupted, reining Wee-People to an abrupt halt. The light flickering in the distance stopped as quickly as it started.

"Keep moving," Garrett warned. "Don't let them know we've seen them."

Conversation was thin for mile upon mile until, at last, Gila broke the silence. "Why don't they attack? There're only two of us."

"Yeah, and that red hair of yours can be seen for miles," Garrett grumbled. "Why didn't you braid it? It looks like a flag. We might as well send smoke signals."

Gila ignored his insult. Her hair was probably their only protection, provided the signallers were Cochise's men. There was no mistaking the McCandless mane. "Why won't you tell me the truth?" she implored, trying hard to control her terror. Her hands held the reins tightly, and her knees were ready to nudge Wee-People into a fast gallop should the Indians attack. "If I'm going to be killed for something you did, then I want to know the truth."

Garrett gazed into the far horizon. "You don't want to know, Gila. If I tell you, you won't work on the Mexican. If the bastard dies on O'Malley land, Cochise will think we were mixed up with Rodriguez. Then that bloody savage will take his vengeance out on us."

Gila stroked Wee-People's neck, gentling him with soothing words. The paint had apparently sensed her apprehension and was beginning to tense beneath her. "Why wouldn't I work on him?" she asked.

"He killed a squaw as she was giving birth."

Gila swung her reins tightly to the east, but Garrett had anticipated her move. His hands grasped the reins in one swift movement and prevented her from urging Wee-People into a gallop. She fought to steady the paint as he reared and pawed the air, but Garrett held firm. "Let him go!" Gila yelled. "Let him go!"

"No!" Garrett shouted above the ruckus of flailing horse against horse. Finally the paint grew still, though his labored breath took several more minutes to calm. Garrett continued to hold tight the reins. "Don't make me pull a gun on you."

"You'd do that, wouldn't you?" Gila dared him.

"If I had to," he said, conviction—or was it desperation?—flickering in his eyes.

Instinct told Gila that the real danger was not from the men who were signaling in the distance. Rather it was from the man who rode beside her, the man whose wife she might have been. "Let me go. I won't run."

"Give me your word."

"You have it," she said in resignation.

He relaxed his hold on the reins. Wee-People pranced nervously beneath her, but she cooed words of reassurance to him. When she was certain the horse was sufficiently calm, she asked, "Why aren't they riding down on us this very minute?"

Garrett wiped his brow with a forearm. His gray Confederate uniform and sandy brown hair would help him blend in with the countryside should they have to make a run for it.

Another thought sent a shiver of fear through Gila. Her red hair wouldn't help if the watchers were renegades. And what if she and Garrett became separated?

Her best bet was to ride with him to his camp.

There she might enlist one of the men to help her get a message to Thorne. "I'll go with you," she told him, "but I'm not going to doctor the Mexican." Any man who killed a defenseless woman didn't deserve treatment. Just like the Mexicans who had attacked her mother those many years ago, so did this Mexican deserve to die.

"I know you're remembering your ma," Garrett said. "But that was then. This is now. If you don't help, I'll send a message to the Imperialist Patrol at the border that a certain Don Cordoba is alive and well in this territory. Since he was arrested for trying to assassinate Maximilian, we'll see how long your precious October remains in the Gadsden."

"You're pathetic," Gila said, haughtily tossing back her hair. How fortunate she was that the marriage to October had kept her from marrying this horrible excuse of a man. "You've known about October all along and waited until just the right moment to play your hand, haven't you? If he tried to kill Maximilian, then he must have had a good reason. Your mindless games are the actions of a child. A spoiled child."

Still she knew she must doctor the Mexican. If the murderer died in Garrett's camp, many innocent people would be killed by Cochise's wrath. If he lived, Thorne would keep his word to Cochise and deliver him to the Apache. "I'll go," she finally agreed.

Several miles lay behind them when Garrett signaled for a halt. In the distance the purple peaks of the Galiuro Mountains rose into the

turquoise-colored sky. Early summer shimmered
its heated beauty on the horizon. It was a
bewitching—but dangerous—scene. Beyond the
parched beauty lay death in many forms, as Gila
well knew. "Satan's Eden," she whispered
grimly.

"It will be if we don't get to the Mexican
soon," Garrett confirmed. "It's not much farther.
Let's just hope he's still alive."

Garrett headed south, and Gila finally realized
their destination. "Are you camped at Tenniman's?"

Keeping a steady pace, Garrett hollered over
one shoulder. "Yeah, I was afraid to move him.
There's cover at the tank, in case of attack."

Tenniman's Tank was the only water hole for
several hours' ride. The slope of the Santa Catalinas had created an offshoot at the beginning of
the great saguaro desert. The unexpected rise
formed a natural sinkhole for water storage, an
oasis from the burning heat. It was the ideal
place to camp, if a man rode out this far. But
why was Garrett in this part of the San Pedro
Valley?

When Tenniman's became visible in the distance, the dun's pace became more urgent.
Wee-People seemed to sense that water was
near, too. The ride had taken the better part of
the afternoon, and Gila was certain the horses
were as tired and thirsty as she was.

A weariness had settled into her muscles, and
she knew there would be no rest until she had
performed her doctoring duties.

Garrett gave a shrill whistle and stopped, then

whistled again as they neared the camp. His signal was returned in exactly the same manner. One long. Pause. One short. A tall man stood up from behind a boulder and waved them in.

"He's still alive, boss. Barely," a rail-thin man said as they passed through. He gave a brief nod of acknowledgment to Gila and bid her, "How'do, Miss McCandless, ma'am."

"Cordoba," she corrected. "Mrs. Cordoba."

Two more lookouts indicated their positions. With three guarding point, there had to be at least the same number guarding the rear. One or two must be attending the Mexican. That accounted for about half of Sean O'Malley's men. If so many of his wranglers were in on this dirty business, then the old man was, too. He wouldn't let half his outfit off his ranch for no reason. She had wished Garrett was in this alone and that Sean was not tangled up in his son's double-dealing.

They arrived at the center of the rugged enclosure. Gila dismounted and immediately hurried to the prone figure near the rocky trough. One glance told her the job of saving his life would not be an easy one.

An arrow pierced the man's right shoulder, and he appeared to be near death. She doubted the salve could help at this late date, but somehow she had to save him. "Garrett, get over here and pull this arrow out," she ordered. "It will take more than my hands to get it."

As the wooden weapon was yanked from his body, the Mexican screamed in agony, then fainted. Thankfully the arrow was still in one piece. Had it splintered, she could have done little. At least now the infection would be in one concentrated area.

"Make a fire," she demanded. "Get some water heated."

"It will just draw attention," Garrett complained.

"Hell, they knew this is where you'd come before you got here," Gila argued. "Why not act natural, and they won't think you're trying to hide something? Now get me some clothing that I can shred for bandages."

Gila tore her own blouse, using the sleeves to sop up the profuse flow of blood. The Mexican awoke, moaning at each of her ministrations. The skin around the ripped shoulder showed signs of life-draining infection. Already the blood was tinged with greenish pus. Gila felt the revulsion tighten in her stomach and rush to her throat, but she forced it back down. Now was no time for her to get sick.

She took a few deep breaths, trying to regain her composure. When she felt in control once again, she hurried to Wee-People. While groping inside the saddlebags, she noticed there remained a few of the saguaro wraps she used to protect the pulp. If the accordion liner would preserve meat, pulp, and milk, why wouldn't it seal medicine into a wound?

Excitement propelled her back to the Mexican. It was all she could do to control her impatience as she waited for the water to boil. She busied herself with mopping the blood until, at last, the water was ready.

After thoroughly cleansing the wound with hot clean bandages, she applied a generous amount of salve. The ointment's numbing effect soon claimed the man and eased him to sleep. Gila placed two of the saguaro wraps on either side of the man's shoulders, then bound the cactus bandage together with a long piece of sinew that she had cut from the saguaro trunk. "There. That ought to do," she said proudly.

She felt the Mexican's forehead and was not surprised at the raging fever. "Get my saddle blanket," she ordered. "We've got to sweat this out of him."

Many times during the evening she replaced the cloth on the injured man's forehead with a new one. She was exhausted and her back ached with the constant stooping. She thought she could bear no more when Garrett arrived with a plate of food.

"Here's a biscuit and jerky," he said. "I'll watch him while you eat."

Food was the last thing she wanted, but it might be the last meal she would have. The last meal any of them would have. And some time to herself would give her a chance to stretch, wash, and maybe close her eyes for a minute or two. "Call me if he wakes up or gets rowdy."

Garrett brushed back a tangle of auburn hair from her mouth and gently touched his lips to hers. "You've done a good job, Gila. I promise I'll show you my appreciation when you aren't so tired."

Gila did not turn away from the kiss. She tried to imagine October's lips rather than Garrett's. If she were going to die in this hellhole, then she would hold onto whatever shreds of human feeling there were left between her and Garrett. Saints and begorra, she was just too blamed tired to care. She knew she would never collect his promise because of a promise long ago given to October. Shelly Kate or no, she would never again feed Garrett's ego. She could only hope she would make her sister see the truth about this man. And if she couldn't . . . well, she simply didn't care at the moment.

The urgent shaking and the sound of Garrett's voice jarred Gila from a troubled sleep. "Wake up!" he ordered.

When had she dozed off? What was wrong? Garrett helped her to her feet, his grasp too tight to be considerate. He was angry. Angry and unkind. Well, she could be just as belligerent!

"Begorra! I merely fell asleep," she complained, yet was actually glad that he'd awakened her from the nightmare she was having. She'd dreamed the Indian *had* actually raped her. "I think I deserved a little rest like the lot of you. After all, I'm the one who's saving all your hides."

"Not if you don't get over there and rebind that dressing," he bellowed. "The Mex yanked it off a few minutes ago. He was pretty feisty, but we got him settled down. Had to stake his arms to do it, though."

"You fool," Gila muttered. "You may have undone all the good I've done." She hurried to the injured man and cut the rawhide that bound his arms to the stakes. A deep crimson tide flowed from under the edges of the wraps.

She untied the sinew and quickly removed the dressing. She cleaned the wound again, added more salve, and rewrapped the man's shoulder in the saguaro wraps, which Garrett had cleansed with boiling water.

Her patient opened his eyes and looked up at her from the depths of pain. "*Gracias,* señorita," he said. She was about to offer a soothing word when Garrett drew near. The man closed his eyes instantly.

"Will he survive?" Garrett asked with a hint of desperation in his voice.

"No thanks to you," Gila accused. Why didn't the man want Garrett to know he had come to his senses? Did he know Garrett wanted him off his spread as soon as possible? Surely everyone in the territory knew about the pact Cochise and Thorne had. But what if the Mexican didn't? Was there some other reason for the man to be frightened of Garrett?

Suspecting she had not been told the truth about the incident, she kept silent about the man's consciousness. Perhaps in her broken Spanish, she could get more information from him. But for now, she needed information from Garrett.

"He's calm now," she said, pulling the blanket over the man's shoulders.

"How long will it take for the fever to break?" Garrett asked impatiently.

"Who knows?" she hedged, planning to let it

take as long as she needed to get some answers.

"I think our best bet is to load him up before dawn and try to make a break for the Circle-Shamrock. The Apache won't strike until then. Thank God for their savage superstitions."

Gila looked into the far eastern horizon. The deep shadows of night were streaked with softer hues of gray, signaling the approaching dawn. She had an hour at the most, if that long, to learn something from the Mexican. Somehow she had to get Garrett busy and away from them. "Listen, why don't you round up the others and I'll try to rouse the Mexican? Maybe if I knew his name, I could repeat it over and over until he hears me."

"It's worth a try," Garrett admitted. "His name is Rodriguez. Emilio Rodriguez."

When Garrett was gone, she placed Rodriguez's head in her lap. In her best Spanish, she asked him if he were awake. For a moment there was no answer. Had she said the right thing? Her nerves tightened with each passing moment. Barely able to control the urgency in her voice she repeated, "Emilio, are you awake?"

Brown eyes opened and stared up at her.

"It's okay. I am your friend." Realizing she had spoken in English, she added, "Amiga."

"S-sí."

Relief flooded her. Saints and begorra, he trusted her! Despite the delirium, his mind must have registered that she'd doctored him. Now if she could only get him to tell her what he knew. She stole a glance toward the eastern edge of the enclosure. A billowing cloud of dust lightened the horizon, telling her riders were approaching. Garrett would be here any moment! She fumbled for the right Spanish words, but the man interrupted her.

"I speak English," the Mexican said. "I did not want the rebel to know."

"Thank heaven and St. Patty," Gila said gratefully, then asked her question.

"I was not gunrunning," Emilio corrected. "I brought news. Your presidente . . . Lincoln . . . was shot. Two months ago. The rebel tortured the squaw. He say I did the evil thing. He say I killed her."

Why was the Mexican trying to pin the blame on Garrett? she wondered. Yet if the Mexican were telling the truth, how did he become wounded? "Were there more Indians? How did you get shot?"

"No." Emilio breathed heavily. "The squaw was alone. Her baby, dead. The rebel shot me." Emilio slumped back, drained by his effort.

The sound of thudding hooves in the desert sand brought Gila to her feet. It took every ounce of willpower to keep from getting her knife so she could hurl it into Garrett's cold, cruel heart. To have intentionally killed a woman, much less a woman who had just given birth to a stillborn child, was the worst crime any man could commit.

Disgust and hatred filled her soul as Garrett rode up to her, but now was not the time to confront him. If she spoke now, it would be so easy for him to kill her and do whatever else he was capable of. If she didn't play her hand right, the whole territory would be a bloodthirsty battlefield. No, she could not accuse Garrett until Thorne was nearby.

"Can he ride?" Garrett asked as he dismounted.

"If you tie him on," Gila said. "I'll ride next to him and hold the reins. He won't have the strength."

"We've got to ride hard. Can you control both horses?"

Anger fueled her words. "I can outride you or any other man, and you know it."

"Settled." He ordered two of his men to put Emilio on a horse, then waited until she had mounted Wee-People. "Guns ready? Let's move out."

Morning peeped over the Galiuro Mountains as the O'Malley party galloped toward the Circle-Shamrock. They all knew they would never make it back to safety if the Apache chose to attack.

She looked toward the northern horizon with longing, wishing desperately to once again see the stern face of her father or the tilt of Shelly Kate's pampered chin. And dear beloved Book. How she would miss the joy of his love and friendship. Dublin. Who would take care of her Dublin?

A pain knifed through Gila as she thought about October. How long had she loved him this dearly? When had her mind accepted what her heart and body had known from that very first night, from that special promise that she'd seen in his eyes? Now she might never be able to confess her true feelings for him.

And what of the baby? She would never touch its sweet face or feel its warm breath as it suckled at her breast. Why did it have to end this way, before she could tell her husband and the world how very wrong she had been about her prejudice? Just as she'd been wrong about Emilio, so had she misjudged the Mexican nation by a few men's actions.

Orange fingers of dawn spread across the desert sky like tentacles of doom. Though no dust cloud indicated the Apache's approach, Gila knew they followed. A tenseness filled the air. Wee-People seemed to sense the urgency that filled her and sprang into full gallop. Gila would have lost her patient, but Emilio grabbed the reins to help her keep control. The action did not go unnoticed by Garrett.

"So! He's much better now, is he?" Garrett said. "Let him go, Gila. Let him ride on his own."

"But he might—"

"I said, let him go." Garrett's look was as sharp as his command. Reluctantly she did so.

Gila didn't like what was happening. As long as she was near Emilio, there was a chance for her to learn the whole truth, but if they were separated, the Mexican's life would be in danger. Suddenly Garrett's plan became all too clear. Of course he didn't want the Mexican to die at the tank. He intended to kill Emilio in full view of the Indians so he could say he was merely

honoring Thorne's pact with Cochise. He could
save himself from both Thorne's and Cochise's
wrath, and no one would be the wiser. Except
herself!

The Chiricahua were in sight now, but not
close enough for her to know if they had donned
war paint. Why worry about paint? Their presence alone was enough to scare a sane person.
The Apache knew exactly what they were doing.
They would push the outfit to near exhaustion in
the scorching heat, then attack when she and the
men were at their physically weakest point. It
might happen at any moment or it could be
hours from now, but one thing was for certain.
The savages would strike before they reached
McCandless land and safety.

Anger welled within her as she thought about
the circumstances surrounding her approaching
death. She deliberately slowed the paint to a
trot. Let St. Peter wait a little longer! If she were
going to die, then she would do it at her own
pace.

Garrett turned and gave her an irritated look.
With an air of indifference, she returned his
frown. Let him be angry! Why should she have
to die for the atrocity he had committed? Neither
should Emilio be punished. "You're the one
who should be punished," she yelled at Garrett,
letting her temper get the better of her.

The look that marred his handsome features
warned her that she'd spoken too soon. Well, it
wasn't the first time her tongue had gotten her
into trouble. What did it matter whose hands
she died at—the Indians' or Garrett's?

Garrett reined to a halt and allowed Gila and Emilio to catch up to him. "So, our little Mexican has told you, has he?"

"Yes, he has," Gila retorted. "And I intend to see you hang for your filthy deed. You are lower than the most savage—"

"Lower than the savage who raped you?" Her gasp widened the sneer upon his lips. "Oh, yes. I've known your secret."

Garrett would never believe that it had only been an attempted rape. Hell, she couldn't convince her own father. How could she convince a madman? "How did you find out?"

"You."

"*Me?*"

"This morning you were talking in your sleep." He looked extremely pleased with himself. "Now all the pieces fit together. Your sudden marriage to a Mexican. Your father's willingness to let me court Shelly. He knows he owes me, owes me a great deal. Especially if I'm going to keep my mouth shut."

"He'll never stoop to your demands," Gila retorted.

"He won't have to," Garrett taunted. "But you will. You wouldn't want your father and your precious Oriental to look like fools, would you? What would people say if they knew the great Thorne McCandless knew—knew mind you—that an Indian had raped a white woman and did nothing about it? Don't you think they would question exactly what Thorne's treaty with Cochise involves?"

"How can you do this, Garrett?" Gila asked.

"How can you do this to two men who've done so much for you? Especially Book."

"Book. Oh Book, how could you?" he mocked, evidently echoing the words she had uttered during the nightmare. "How could you agree with Thorne? A prisoner. I can't marry a prisoner." Garrett's eyes glinted with the cruelty of his words. "Not so noble, this Cordoba fellow? How many men did you try before him? How many others know your secret, I wonder?"

Her hand lashed out, but he anticipated her move and grasped her wrist tightly. "Don't tempt me, whore, or I'll kill you."

"What will you tell my father?" she challenged.

"I'll just say Rodriguez made a run for it and got my gun. He shot you before I could kill him. Simple."

"You meant to kill him all along," she said. His smile sickened her. What had the war done to him? He had no compassion for human life. No compassion for those he once had claimed to love. What had this civil war bred? A man who no longer cared about brother, kin, or friends?

"Will you do what I want?" Garrett demanded.

Gila became nervous and angry all at the same time. "I'll spit on my mother's grave before I let you touch me again."

"You would, wouldn't you?" he said as he released her wrist. "Don't be so vain. I want what is rightfully mine. The north section and Shelly Kate."

"I'll not bargain away my sister, you bastard."

His eyes flashed a hint of warning. "Too bad

you didn't let me win one of our heads and eagles games. I would have the land already and all this unpleasantness wouldn't be necessary."

At thirteen she had foolishly bet her land on the toss of a coin with Garrett. Fortunately she had won. At least she had thought she was fortunate at the time. Had she lost, Thorne would have been merciless. Now she wished more than anything she had lost that day! "I'll give you the land," she told Garrett squarely. "Keep Shelly out of this."

"Oh, but I can't." Greed brightened his eyes. "She is my road to power in this territory."

Gila wished the Apache would attack now. Then at least October would be free to go and Thorne's and Book's honor would be saved. And Shelly Kate wouldn't have to marry Garrett.

Indecision washed over her as she considered the alternatives. There were reasons to turn Garrett over to Cochise and reasons to keep her silence. If there were only some way to save Emilio, then perhaps she could find a way to trap Garrett in the web of his own deceit.

A ripple in the air thundered through Gila's thoughts. She glanced up to see columns of dust spiraling in the distance. Riders. Many riders. Riders not seeking to hide their numbers. Either Apache or . . . Thorne! Thorne had come to help!

"Look," she shouted and motioned toward the north. Already Garrett's point riders were waving and shouting. What were they saying? She strained to listen and caught only one word. McCandless. She was right. It was Thorne.

As Garrett's attention was momentarily drawn to the distance, Gila whispered to Emilio, "Here, it's all I've got. Use it." She handed him the last sinew from her saddlebags.

"*Gracias.*"

A movement to obtain the knife sheathed in her boot would draw Garrett's attention. The sinew wasn't enough to kill someone, but if aimed correctly and whipped quickly, it could delay a man for some time until the sting wore off. "Aim for the eye," she counseled.

The McCandless party topped the rise. Garrett's hand went for his gun. Emilio let the sinew fly, his aim direct but not quick enough to thwart the deadly shot. Gila screamed as Emilio fell dead from his horse. Garrett's scream of pain mingled with hers. Before she could think, Garrett turned a bloody face to her, cupping his hand below his half-protruding eyeball.

"I'll swear I shot him while he tried to escape. And you better do the same, bitch, if you want to save your precious October." Then, as if he had a second thought, he added, "You don't want your brat to grow up being mocked and ridiculed, do you? You know what happens to half-breeds."

What good would the truth do but hurt the people she loved most? The McCandless name would be saved if she kept silent. Shelly Kate would marry the man she loved. October would be safe from Garrett's accusations. And her baby would have a real life without ridicule, without prejudice. Did she have a choice? She could not bring Emilio, the squaw, or the stillborn child back to life, but she could make the lives of the living more bearable. Everything inside her screamed that the silence would be wrong, but logic forced her to ignore her emotions.

And there was one grim consolation. From the looks of Garrett's injury, he would not go completely unpunished. He would lose his eye.

Octavio was the first to catch sight of the O'Malley riders. Relief coursed through him when he saw Gila's flaming red hair in the distance. She sat tall in Wee-People's saddle.

Gunfire startled him and a moment of horror blurred his sight. He saw something strike O'Malley, then the man riding next to Gila fell from his horse. O'Malley's hands went to his face and a piercing scream filled the air. Garrett or Gila? He was uncertain.

Garrett leaned toward Gila and looked as if he said something to her. From the way she flinched, Octavio was certain she'd thought O'Malley was about to strike her.

Octavio spurred his horse into a gallop, thundering toward the grizzly scene. What had happened? Why had the two men attacked each other? Was Gila hurt? *Madre Santísima*, the baby!

Moments stretched into eternity as he closed the distance between them. At last he reined to an abrupt halt in front of the circle of men who surrounded Garrett and Gila.

Gila looked up from the dead man. Seeing Octavio, she flung herself into his arms. As deep sobs overtook her, Octavio stroked her tangled tresses and kissed the moisture from her eyes. "I am here, *dulce mia*, I am here."

She clung to him as never before, trembling, holding him so tightly he could scarcely breathe. Why was she so frightened? He'd never seen her this vulnerable, even after White Bear's attack. Fury, cold and lethal, enveloped him, and he knew he would kill Garrett O'Malley if he were the instigator of Gila's fear. He tried to push Gila away, deep seething anger urging him toward his quarry.

"Don't leave me," Gila pleaded, refusing to let go. "Please, don't leave me."

"I am here." Octavio sensed that she was not talking of this moment, but their future. Still he would not lie and say he wouldn't someday leave, no matter how great her need. The needs of his beloved Mexico were greater.

After Gila was calmer and her sobbing had eased into an occasional sniffle, Octavio finally asked, "Can you tell me what happened?"

"Let Garrett tell you," she said, her tone low and evasive.

Her body tensed in his arms. So! She was purposefully avoiding his question. What had happened in the night alone with the rebel? "I'm afraid he won't be able to tell us anything for a while," Octavio said. "He's going to lose that eye. He's not coherent at the moment."

"I won't doctor him," she said fiercely. He waited for her to say more, but she kept her silence. As he was about to ask if there were anything she wanted to tell him, Gila repeated, "I won't doctor him."

"You don't have to," he assured her. "Book will tend to his needs."

"The Indians? What are they going to do?"

"They are talking with Thorne. Now will you tell me what this is all about? Why were you with Garrett O'Malley? Who is that Mexican, and what made them try to kill each other?"

Gila didn't look at Octavio directly when she gave her sketchy account of the incident. He suspected she was not telling the entire truth. And why wouldn't she doctor Garrett? She'd been extremely friendly toward him the past two months. Had she refused Garrett's advances? He wanted to believe it was so. Though she was Cordoba in name only, there were times in the past few months he had doubted he could endure the sight of his wife openly flirting with Garrett.

And why would a Mexican steal a piece of sinew from Gila's saddlebags rather than a gun from one of the wranglers? Something didn't make sense.

A high-pitched scream made Octavio remember that the youngest of the McCandlesses had come along. Shelly Kate had been riding with the rear guard in the event of attack.

"Garrett! Where's Garrett? Someone says he's hurt!" Shelly Kate ran to the circle of men and broke through. Falling to her knees beside the rebel, she took his hand in hers and pleaded, "Garrett. Darling. Darling, it's me, Shelly. Can you hear me? Are you alive?"

Out of the pain of his injury, Garrett moaned

and acknowledged Shelly's presence. She burst into tears. Book tried to calm her, but she ignored his soothing words and stomped over to Gila and Octavio.

"Did you do this?" Shelly asked, pointing an accusing finger at Gila. When Gila refused to answer, Shelly turned back to the men and demanded, "How did this happen? How did he lose his eye?" Her black eyes flashed with hatred as tears rolled down her cheeks. "Now are you satisfied, Gila? You couldn't have him, so you didn't want me to."

Gila reached out to comfort her sister, but Shelly Kate refused Gila's touch. "No, let me be. You're no sister of mine! You don't know what it is to love. You don't really know." She broke into hysterical sobs.

Gila's shoulders sagged at the accusation and Octavio felt a deep sadness wash over himself for Gila's sake. Shelly was young and didn't understand that whatever had happened, Gila may have only been acting out of love . . . for whomever.

"She's overwrought," he said and put a comforting arm around Gila's shoulders. "She doesn't mean what she's saying."

"Yes, she does." Gila sighed. "And I'm not so sure she's wrong."

# Chapter Nineteen

❖ ❖ ❖ ❖ ❖

GILA WAITED ALMOST a month to confront Garrett. He had not adjusted well to losing his eye and was too disagreeable to approach on many occasions. But this evening seemed different.

Shelly Kate sat beside Garrett in the porch swing practicing her embroidery. Gila sat idly. She should have been knitting something for the child, but her hands seemed to go askew with anything that needed patience.

Octavio walked around the corner of the house, his hair still wet from his evening swim in the waterfall. "Am I interrupting anything?" he asked and sat down beside Gila.

She scooted away. These days she had to keep her distance from her handsome husband to keep from blurting out her true feelings. "No, you didn't interrupt anything terribly important. I just asked Garrett how he had known Lincoln was going to be shot before it actually happened."

"And what did you mean by *deepest* South?" Octavio added, his gaze hard and interrogating.

"That letter was meant only for Gila's eyes."

Gila couldn't tell Garrett that she had not shown it to anyone until he had made his threat on Octavio's freedom. She had hoped knowing about the letter would help October should Garrett ever decide to talk to the border patrol. Of course, she couldn't tell October of Garrett's threats, but she had been able to draw her husband's curiosity with the letter that spoke of Lincoln's death and Mexico's possible involvement. After all, what was deeper south than Mexico?

"Does the letter mean what it implies?" Octavio asked as Gila removed it from her pocket.

Garrett jerked the paper out of her hands. "You're the spy, you tell me."

"I believe you are involved somehow with Maximilian, and in that involvement, you and your Confederate officers have murdered the greatest statesman this country has ever known."

Garrett leaned back and folded his arms in front of his chest. "You read the paper. That actor named Booth did it."

Octavio leaned forward. "Booth was merely the pawn, you and Maximilian were the conspirators of this assassination."

Garrett jerked to his feet. "You have little room to criticize me, señor, when you are guilty of the same crime!"

Suddenly Octavio remembered where he had seen Garrett O'Malley. "You are the man who told Governor Vidaurri about my knife."

So, Gila thought, Garrett had been responsible for October's capture! She looked from one to the other, wondering what was going on in their minds. Would October try to kill Garrett?

"I believe I owe you an apology," Garrett mocked. "I should have let you kill Maximilian. When he heard about Lee's surrender, he withdrew his offer to help the Confederate cause. Said he needed American trade since the French would lend him no more money or troops. Fortunately, the demise of Mr. Lincoln was already set in motion and he couldn't stop it."

Gila jumped to her feet and stared down at Octavio. "Are you just going to sit there and listen to this without doing something about it?"

Octavio placed a reassuring hand upon hers. "Calm yourself, Gila. Every fool has his day. Garrett will have his."

Shelly Kate threw down her embroidery. Grabbing Garrett by the hand, she said, "Let's go where we are appreciated." She pulled him toward the house.

"Hey, you're going the wrong way," Gila jeered. "The hog wallow's that way."

The incident with Emilio Rodriguez lay several months behind them. Gila had kept her word to Garrett, taking satisfaction in knowing that he'd lost one eye for his evil deed. Though Shelly Kate's and Garrett's wedding date was set, Octavio seemed reluctant to believe Gila no longer cared for her former fiancé. He brought up the subject often but never accepted her professed indifference to Garrett. "Do as you will, but do not disgrace my family."

His insinuations infuriated Gila because they echoed her father's words. But with her new-found patience she held her tongue, reaching instead to her bulging abdomen and stroking it lovingly. "I don't want to ruin anybody's name."

Now the day of Shelly Kate's wedding had arrived, so different from Gila's own. Would she and Octavio ever close the great gap between them?

Gila stood before the mirror and gave her hair several strokes, then retied the ribbon at the crown of her thick, burnished tresses. Lately, her reflection never failed to surprise her. Her hazel eyes appeared larger now that her face had thinned. She had a definite cheekline. The healthy glow in her skin made her look soft as fleece, and the rosy blush on her cheeks added a prettiness she secretly welcomed. She was still no beauty, but impending motherhood had made her passably pretty.

"Gila, the guests will be arriving shortly," Thorne said from the hallway. "Are you dressed?"

She patted her stomach once more and smiled to herself. "Yes, we're dressed." She took one last glance at the shapeless yellow cotton dress that encompassed her ample waistline and grimaced. It would just have to do. "We're coming."

With a critical eye she inspected the bedroom once more, making certain everything was in place. Lately she'd gained an unusual penchant for tidiness and could not stand the thought of anything out of order. Book had told her that her mother had been that way during her pregnancies. Gila hugged herself as she headed for the door. At least she'd inherited something from her mother.

She met Thorne in the hallway. He offered her his arm and she took it, but she wondered as they walked who was supporting whom. To her,

Thorne seemed to have aged almost overnight. Of course, none of the other wedding guests would notice. He appeared to be the same vibrant giant of a man who had come to carve out an empire in the sand more than twenty years ago. Yet the signs of age were there. Wrinkles at the corners of his eyes and mouth, a slackening jawline, and more streaks of silver in that glorious mane.

How sad and distant he seems, Gila worried. Why should he be so unhappy? Tonight Shelly Kate would become Garrett's bride and Thorne's bargain with the O'Malleys would be met. His dreams of a McCandless-O'Malley empire would, at last, be fulfilled.

They walked toward the parlor. "You'd best be attending to the guests, lassie. The men'll expect the liquor to be flowing, and I plan on keeping my eye on the winter supply."

Gila expected his usual laugh at his bit of funning, but Thorne could not even muster a chuckle. What was bothering him? Kathryn! Of course, that had to be it!

Thorne was giving away his youngest daughter in marriage. Shelly Kate looked so much like their beloved mother. It must seem as if he were losing Kathryn all over again.

What could she do to comfort him? Nothing, she realized sadly. Thorne would never admit to anyone, least of all himself, that he was grieving over the loss of his wife. Small wonder he looked old tonight. Blinking back the tears that moistened the corners of her eyes, she patted his forearm and whispered, "I love you, Father."

There! She'd finally said it. And it had been much easier than she had ever expected it to be.

Thorne stared at her a few moments, then a strange expression came over him. He started to say something, then hesitated. In that moment, Gila knew that more than Shelly Kate's marriage was bothering him. She was stunned. Never before had she seen fear on her father's face.

As they approached the throng of people who waited in the parlor, she asked herself over and over what or who in St. Patrick's name Thorne McCandless could fear?

Octavio stamped the cheroot with his bootheel and blew out the last ring of smoke. He watched the buggy's progression as the O'Malley party was escorted to the Circle-Shamrock. The desert flora was already changing to its autumn shades of dark green and brown. Indian summer had lasted into late fall.

Octavio's attention was drawn to the tall horseman riding alongside the black carriage. His gray uniform blended with the distant horizon, making it difficult for Octavio to study Garrett O'Malley. Garrett's sand-colored hair lent a ghostlike quality to his appearance. Yet Octavio felt Garrett watching him just as he watched Garrett.

Book's voice startled Octavio. "A man who fights for love must battle himself first."

Octavio reprimanded himself for not hearing the samurai's approach. "You must teach me the Silent Way," he said and bowed.

Book returned the acknowledgment.

Octavio noticed the Oriental's hair had begun to show signs of gray, yet his beard was still as black as his all-seeing eyes.

"You know of the Silent Way?" Book asked.

"Some."

"And do you agree or disagree with what you know of its teachings?"

"I cannot say that I fully agree with assassination, though I have tried it myself."

A momentary flicker of concern marred Book's face and it startled Octavio. Never before had the samurai let down his mask, failed in his Bushido. What could make a trained warrior forget himself long enough to give a hint of anxiousness?

"Has Gila spoken to you of assassination? What has she said? I must know."

Octavio was surprised by Book's question. "Why should Gila ask me about such a thing? She does not know the entire truth behind my confinement."

"You do not understand," Book said quietly and motioned for Octavio to follow. "We must talk." Without further explanation, the Oriental headed for the waterfall. Once they reached their destination, Book sat on the ground cross-legged. Octavio did likewise. The black eyes looked long and hard at Octavio until he felt as if Book were conducting an unspoken test of his worth. He stared back, unblinking, matching his will to Book's.

"Good." Book nodded approval. "This is good. I must tell you now what no one else can hear." He bent his head in thought, his voice low and compelling.

Book reached for a handful of sand and opened his palm to the sky. The grains scattered in the wind. "Words spoken to many are as grains of sands. Drifting with the breeze, they gather again, in greater numbers than when they first began." He bent his head closer to Octavio, a silent command for attention. "It is wiser to tell only one who will protect the grain from the winds." He gestured toward the waterfall. "This will keep all but your ears from hearing the truth—a truth no one else must ever know."

Octavio listened intently as Book told the story of his involvement with the McCandlesses.

"My real name is Bukamoshi Minamoto. My clan was overthrown, my father murdered in his sleep. No longer was I to be the next shogun— that for which I had trained my entire life." Book's chest seemed to swell with aristocratic pride. "When my fellow Ninja and I were left without our shogun, we followed the path of the warrior to prove ourselves worthy to the Fates. We learned to kill effectively, with an ease uncommon to most. Soon we were hired by others to rid themselves of troublemakers. Since these troublemakers were outside the law, we felt justified in ridding the world of them."

"I'm sure Gila would understand all that happened long ago and—" Octavio was halted by the closing of Book's eyes.

"No." The Oriental voice was exact. "It is not over. It never will be."

A knot of dread formed deep in Octavio's stomach, and he fought back the bitter taste that constricted his throat. "Tell me," he urged.

"We lent ourselves for hire to the British government in '43," Book began again. "I was sent on a double mission. Shannon MacGregor, Kathryn's father, originally had wanted to purchase my services as his daughter's personal guard. Thorne was frequently away with the Young Irelanders. Kathryn was left alone for days at a time. A young woman alone in the country was a likely target for plundering rebels.

"As time went by, Thorne's group engaged in battles with the British soldiers. When Daniel O'Connell was thrown into prison, many of his supporters were tracked down by my fellow samurai and killed. As a friend of Daniel's, Thorne thought it best to flee to America lest he meet the same fate. Little did he know as we sailed away that I was the one assigned to kill him."

Book nodded slowly. "Yes, I was assigned to assassinate Thorne by his father-in-law."

"Why would Shannon MacGregor do such a thing?" Octavio asked. "It has been twenty years or more, hasn't it? What kept you from completing your assignment?"

"Shannon hated Thorne," Book replied. "I was to kill him and bring his daughter back to Ireland. According to Shannon, Thorne had defiled Kathryn's soul—swayed her from her religious beliefs. Thorne is Catholic and Shannon Protestant."

"How did he win her hand in marriage?

Wouldn't Señor MacGregor have forbidden it?"

Book gave a halfhearted smile, as if he were remembering something that made him happy as well as sad. "They eloped. Kathryn was much like Gila, headstrong, willful. Thorne was dashing and vibrant, with a boyish dimple that won the lady's heart."

"If you were supposed to kill him, why didn't you?" Octavio knew he was delving into dangerous territory, but felt he must know why the samurai had broken his word.

"Fortunately Shannon did not set a time limit for the deed. That was left to my discretion, for which I have been most grateful." Book tossed a pebble into the foaming water. "You see, I fell in love with Kathryn almost from the moment I saw her. Each day it became more difficult for me to be near her and not profess my love. I wanted to touch her, to hold her as a man does his woman, but I could not. Not long after I came to serve her, she discovered she was with child."

"Gila?" Octavio asked.

"No." Book shook his head. "A son. The son Thorne always wanted but was not to have. The filthy conditions on the coffin ship killed the unborn child. Kathryn almost died of heartbreak at the loss of her babe, while Thorne never quite forgave her for losing their son."

Octavio tried to read the samurai's expression but could not. Did he dare ask the question he had wanted to since he'd met Book, or was it best left unsaid?

"No, she is not," Book answered quietly. "I

am not Gila's father, nor Shelly Kate's. I am a eunuch. I cannot father children. I offered myself to The Way when my father was killed and I no longer needed to sire sons to carry on our shogunate. I never once regretted the decision until I could not fulfill my deepest love for Kathryn.''

Book's face became a mask of pain and Octavio wished he did not have to witness the anguish of this noble warrior.

"And so you chose not to kill Thorne as you agreed?''

Book exhaled a long breath. "I wish it were that simple. Already Kathryn was grieving herself to death with the loss of her son. By the time her heart had turned bitter toward Thorne, Gila was well on her way. We were traveling cross-country. Thorne scouted ahead many days and nights. Love began to blossom between Kathryn and myself, and my resolve to indifference wilted beneath the fragrance of her smile, her lips.'' His back suddenly straightened.

"Gila is Thorne's seed, but she was formed with Kathryn's love for me. It was I who saw the first kick of life, I who sang the ancient lullabies, I who delivered the breath of our love. Thorne but planted the seed. I nurtured her into full blossom. Gila is mine.''

Book closed his eyes and was silent for a long moment. Then he half-opened them, as if he were reluctant to wake from whatever he was dreaming. "I promised Kathryn I would not complete the assignment until our Gila was married. Until she was grown, she needed Thorne, and all that a man of his destiny and insight could afford her."

Book halted Octavio's next question with a warning palm. "I told Kathryn myself that I had been hired to kill Thorne, but I did not tell her by whom. She had to know my intentions if I were to protect the love between us. She had to know that I would not kill Thorne out of jealousy."

Book's attention was instantly drawn to the paloverdes lining the pathway to the homestead. He seemed to listen intently a few moments, his muscular body tensing. "I thought I smelled something peculiar. The water plays tricks upon the senses."

Octavio drew in a deep breath. All he could smell was the roasting mutton that had been prepared for the wedding feast. One thing puzzled him concerning all that Book had told him. "Thorne seemed very much in love with Kathryn. Every time he speaks of her, it is with great respect."

Book's jaw tightened. "Thorne is like most men of ambition. He found out too late that he truly loved her. When she was alive he wanted her only to satisfy his lusts and share the throne of his sought-after empire.

"After Gila, she lost another child, then Shelly Kate came a year later. Four babies in five years was too much. Had she ever recovered from her pregnancies, Kathryn might have been strong enough to survive the Mexicans who attacked her. I spared Thorne only to have him kill her

with his desire for a male heir. Only my promise
to Kathryn kept me from killing him after she
died."

Octavio absorbed the statement fully. Compassion for Gila filled him as he realized why her
hatred for his countrymen was so intense. "You
fear Gila knows you will kill Thorne?"

Book nodded.

"No," said Octavio, "I don't think she does. If
she did, she would be frank enough to ask why.
She would also ask why you've waited until
now."

"She must never know," Book said, almost
pleading. "I must honor my obligation to Kathryn's father, even though Thorne is now more
friend than foe. It is The Way. My immortal soul
will not rest if I defile my word."

"Are you not afraid he will kill you?"

Book turned away from Octavio and lifted his
tunic above his shoulders. "I pray that he does."

Nausea rose from the pit of Octavio's stomach;
he swallowed it down painfully. Black sores full
of yellowish pus scarred the broad back. Much
of the skin was eaten away, evidence of long
suffering. "*Madre Santísima!* What is that?"

Book slipped the tunic back into place. "The
West call it incurable lesions. In the East, we call
it The Long Death. I would much prefer death at
Thorne's hands than this slow torture."

Octavio had to turn away from the hunger he
saw written on Book's face. Hunger for rest and
relief from the ravaging disease. He forced the
next question to his lips. "Does Gila know of

your sickness?" How could he tell her if she did
not? How could he *not* tell her?

"She suspects, but is uncertain."

A great sadness descended upon Octavio as
the weight of this knowledge hit him full force.
Why did he have to be the one Book confided in?
Could he hide the truth from Gila . . . and
Thorne? Was he certain that he *wanted* to keep it
from them?

He looked into the probing Oriental eyes and
almost asked Book to take back this knowledge,
take back his trust. "I don't know if I can
promise to keep this from Thorne. A man has a
right to know of danger."

Book smiled patiently, almost in acceptance,
and motioned for them to return down the
pathway to the house. "Thorne knows," he said
flatly. "But Gila must never know."

# Chapter Twenty

✦ ✦ ✦ ✦

GILA SHIFTED FROM one foot to the other, trying to
find a comfortable position. She wished her
discomfort were merely from standing so long in
one place, but the minor nuisance of playing
matron of honor to Shelly Kate was not the only
cause of her annoyance. Gossip. Homegrown,

overstuffed parlor gossip was the other culprit.

She eyed Shelly Kate standing before her, radiant in a cream-colored wedding gown. The string of black stones around her sister's dainty neck, the matching earrings dangling from each fragile earlobe made a striking contrast to the delicate lace. The sparkle of happiness in Shelly's ebony eyes dulled the Apache Tears necklace. Apache Tears. How ironic, Gila thought. I should have worn them on *my* wedding day.

As Gila admired Shelly Kate, she glanced at her own protruding abdomen, then lifted her chin proudly. "Just let everyone talk," she whispered. "I don't care."

Earlier, when Gila greeted the O'Malleys at the door, Garrett's stern-faced mother marched into the McCandless home as if laying claim as its mistress. "Putting on a wee bit of weight you are, Gila my girl," she said, untying her bonnet and handing it to Gila as if to a servant.

Gila bit back the rush of foul words that hurried to her mouth. Early in her pregnancy she had promised herself that the child would never hear bad language from her lips. Shelly Kate and Thorne were skeptical that she could ever keep such a promise. They'd mocked her effort, telling her an unborn child could not hear.

But she believed differently. The baby knew her every mood. When she was irritated, the life inside her tossed and turned as it was doing now. When she was calm, she had to nudge her abdomen to rouse the wee one from its peaceful state.

Sheer willpower kept Gila's temper in check. She merely nodded at Sherilyn O'Malley and said, "Yes, I have put on a bit of weight with the child's term drawing near. What's *your* reason?" She plopped the bonnet back atop Mrs. O'Malley's mass of blue-black hair.

"Ladies. Ladies!" Thorne stepped between the two. "This is a happy occasion."

"It couldn't be otherwise," Gila said honestly. There was reason to be happy. Now the old buzzard would not be *her* mother-in-law. Poor Shelly Kate. There were many things Gila wished upon her sister, but relationship to Sherilyn O'Malley was not one of them.

Her confrontation with Mrs. O'Malley was only the first of the evening's vexations. Throughout the past hour or so, several other guests had made snide comments about her condition. Being the daughter of the wealthiest man in the territory made her a prime target for gossip. Coming home suddenly with a husband no one knew had only added fuel to the fire.

She had turned away the malicious remarks without breaking her ban on swearing, but the guests' thoughtless words had disturbed her. She still felt uncomfortable with her back turned to them. Each whisper, each chuckle seemed aimed at her personally, rather than at the nervous mistakes of the bride and groom.

Gila searched the room out of the corner of her eye and caught sight of October sitting in the front row of chairs. He looks so handsome in the black whipcord suit I bought him, she thought. His blue eyes met her own. She blushed beneath their intense inspection and turned away, pretending to listen intently to the padre. October's thoughtful deeds of late were like a rope of possession that had lassoed her heart.

When she woke this morning, she found a beautiful cradle in her room. It was carved from the wood of her own saguaros. The intricate design at the headboard was magnificent, and she knew it had taken October months to produce such a fine piece. The elaborate *C* on the headboard irritated her momentarily, but her anger was quickly quelled when she noticed the equally ornate *M* on the footboard.

How had he found the time to produce such a masterpiece? Not only did he have his regular duties but he had completely assumed the chore of caring for Dublin, saying the job was much too strenuous for her in her condition. She hated to admit he was right, but he was.

A sharp pain in her ribs startled her. She clutched her side, momentarily winded.

"Are you all right, *dulce mia?*" Octavio whispered as he stood and placed a steadying hand upon her shoulder.

"It's just the child. He's kicked me again," she said and pulled away. A ripple of murmurs sounded behind them. "The guests. They'll—"

"They'll what? Talk? Do you care, my sweet?"

Gila turned to look at him, unsure of his thoughts or mood. She smiled at him and allowed herself the pleasure of hearing several disapproving clucks from the visitors. "No, I don't care," she said. Suddenly she felt happier than she had been in a long time. She really didn't care!

"Good!" Octavio exclaimed. "Then you won't mind my standing next to you."

Gila laughed again as his strong, reassuring arm slid possessively around her waist. She fit snugly against his shoulder, his chin resting at her right temple. She could feel the indignation of all those prim and proper ladies who sat behind them. This would certainly give the biddies something to gossip about.

The padre's chant lulled Gila into a strange contentment as she watched Shelly Kate and Garrett exchange vows. The rapturous look that radiated from her sister's eyes touched Gila deeply. She was happy Shelly was marrying for love and not merely to make good Thorne's bargain with the O'Malleys.

She looked at Garrett and saw happiness of another sort. He was finally getting what he'd wanted all along: he was marrying into the richest family in the entire Gadsden. How shocked he would be when he learned of Gila's wedding present to them! She'd had the contract written only a few days ago, giving him and Shelly the north section. She could imagine Garrett's thoughts as he estimated the worth of the property and the gold he believed it contained. She placed one hand to her mouth, suppressing a chuckle as she wondered how long it would take Garrett to discover the ore was merely fool's gold!

"Are you going to be ill?" Octavio asked with concern.

Gila lowered her hand quickly to reassure him. "No, I'm all right." His thoughtfulness brought back a rush of memories. Memories of his consideration for her. Despite his anger that night in Tucson when she'd said she didn't want the child, despite his absence from her bed since that day, despite his belief that she and Garrett had done more than argue at Tenniman's Tank, Octavio's waking hours had been spent performing tasks to insure her comfort. He'd harvested the last saguaro crop and helped bottle the cures. He'd taken over for her in the kitchen when she was too tired to cook. This she loved him for the most. She knew what determination it took to withstand the ribbing he received from the wranglers. A man whose ancestors were Spanish noblemen performing menial kitchen tasks, cooking for men whose station in life was lower than his own, was certainly a sight to see. Yet each time October did so without even the slightest protest. He acted as if he knew she was carrying his child.

Many nights she had lain awake watching him sleep on the davenport. How many times had she wanted to go to him, tell him she had been a fool ever to say she didn't want the child? She wanted this baby—his baby—but could she make October believe it? No. He would never believe her feelings could change so totally, so vehemently.

Yet approaching motherhood had done just that. This life within cried out for love she could not deny. Motherhood held as many surprises as the painted desert. Only at the birth of her wee one would October see her true change of heart. Only then.

Holy St. Patrick! Gila's throat fought back the knot that threatened to lodge there. The baby's birth was little more than two months away. Two months in which to cram a lifetime of loving. Soon after that, October would be gone.

The thought of October's leaving wrenched her soul. A feeling of utter loss shook her from temple to toe until she thought she would collapse under its force. Yet she knew she would let him go without telling him the baby could only be his. She would not keep him from his destiny. If he were ever to love her, she wanted it to be by choice, not obligation. Freedom to love was the greatest gift she could give him, no matter how much it broke her heart.

Garrett was lifting the veil and kissing Shelly Kate, but Gila paid no attention. Lost in her own sad thoughts, she felt tears stream down her cheeks as she tried to memorize everything about her husband. The way his hair flowed in ebony waves to his collar, the one lock that sensually teased his forehead. The aristocratic nose that was a sign of his true nobility, the lips that had kissed her so passionately. She leaned into the crook of Octavio's shoulder, wishing she could mold herself into him and never be released.

"Tears, *dulce mia?*" Octavio asked, his resonant tone sending waves of grief coursing through her. After he was gone would she remember the distinct timbre of his voice? Would she be able to walk into a crowd and not turn her head to see if the voice she heard might be his?

And what if it should be him one day? Could she bear the sight of another in his arms? One he loved? *Modesta?*

Silent tears burned her cheeks with the misery she now felt and would feel all the days of her life. October cupped her chin in one hand and wiped away a revealing tear. "Sentimental, querida? I would not have guessed." He searched her face as if he too were memorizing. "A kiss? For the bride and groom."

Her lips parted as her eyes beseeched him. His mouth met hers in slow tender possession. The need for his touch simmered deep within her and ignited into zealous flames. Too long had this volcanic passion she held for him lain dormant. If she were destined to be without love for the remainder of her life, then she was determined to have him, all of him, now before he fulfilled his own destiny and was no longer a part of hers.

Words from a night not so long ago came to her. "Let's give them something to remember," she had told him. Tonight she wanted October to give her something to remember . . . to cherish. And so she did what she had vowed she would not do.

As their lips parted, Gila pressed her cheek against his own and whispered, "Come to me, Octavio." She gazed into his eyes for a long moment before purposefully moving toward the hallway. Would the use of his true name startle him? Never before had she spoken it to him. Gila could only hope he understood how dear that name had become to her and what it had taken for her to beg.

Gila stood before the mirror and slowly lifted her dress above her shoulders. As the garment reached eye level, another pair of hands helped relieve her of its folds. Octavio's lips gently caressed her neck and shoulders, sending waves of warmth surging through her. She sighed with contentment as his arms reached around her protruding abdomen and cradled her into the contours of his own body.

A longing, sweet and tender, engulfed her as he pressed his cheek against her own and slowly rocked her from side to side. His warm breath urged her lips toward his. The kiss deepened and she was intoxicated, not so much by its taste as by the powerful sense of belonging that overwhelmed her, the powerful love that possessed her.

Her hands seemed to have a will of their own as they caressed the hard, sinewy muscles of his shoulders. Her fingertips, already afire with her own desire, seemed cooler to the touch than his flaming skin. As she wound his ebony tendrils around her fingers and pressed his lips closer to her own, a moan escaped him, and she felt an incomparable triumph.

His lips left hers and blazed a trail of white-hot flame down her throat. They lingered at her breast, his hungry tongue teasing a swollen peak. Her pulse seemed to echo from every part of her, a steady drumbeat to her rising passion.

She fumbled with the buttons on his jacket as he nibbled delicately at her other breast. She felt as if she would melt in his arms the way his eyes, now clouded with desire, beseeched her for that which she desired most to give.

Through barely parted lashes she stared back with equal intimacy. "Let me feel you, Octavio," she whispered.

Even as he undressed, her hands caressed the hard muscles of his chest. He drew her to him.

"Love me," she pleaded desperately. His lips were full and moist from their contact with her swollen nipple and it sent a ripple of desire through her. "I need you."

She kissed him fully, a kiss that promised all she could give and more. No longer could she deny she was woman, for she knew now she belonged to this man. She was a part of the whole. They were one breath. One soul.

Octavio pulled away and looked at her questioningly. Was he uncertain? she wondered. He had never seemed so before. Could it be that he wanted to tell her he merely desired her and nothing more? That she was not to expect him to return the love that cried out with her every heartbeat?

No! Those eyes had made a pledge to her on their wedding night. She'd believed that promise and knew that her love for him had begun the very first time he held her in his arms. She would gamble on that silent vow, just as anyone gambled who lived in this death-dealing desert.

"Octavio, I love you," she whispered as she peered into his piercing blue eyes. A smile caressed her lips as joy filled her soul. Tears of happiness trickled down her cheeks as she spoke aloud the truth. She wept to hear it with her own ears. "Don't you see? I love you!"

With fearful anticipation she waited. One sculptured finger rose and touched her lips, then moved downward to nestle under her chin. "So, my little prickly pear," he whispered softly, "at last you blossom. And now I, Don Octavio Diego Cordoba, have been pierced by your thorns."

Gila looked away, uncertain of his meaning.

"No, my sweet. Do not turn away when I am about to profess how much I, too, love you."

Joy rushed through her veins, as tumultuous as the rapids at Oak Canyon. She could not take her eyes from him, capturing, memorizing every detail of her loved one.

He drew her to the bed, where they lay entwined for many moments, enjoying the newness of their discovery. His finger gently twisted an auburn curl while the other hand brushed back the moist tendrils from her forehead.

"Darling," his voice was more caressing than the endearment itself.

"Beloved."

"Querida."

"My own." Each returned the other's affection until Gila knew she had to do something or else faint from wanting him. But first there had to be no more secrets between them. "When Garrett and I were fifteen, we—"

"Sshh, *dulce mia*," Octavio murmured as his finger outlined the swell of her lips. "It doesn't matter. You love *me* now, don't you?"

"Forever." She began to move slowly against him, at first teasing, then enticing, now demanding.

"Cease, my sweet," Octavio commanded with a husky chuckle. "Perhaps you are choosing a confrontation you cannot win."

"Oh, I'll win," she said invitingly. "Even if I am the only one who fights." She rose and positioned herself astride him, guiding his passion to meet her own. "Because I intend for you to surrender all of your love to me, sweet stranger."

Blue eyes locked with her intense hazel gaze as her fingers massaged the flat muscles of his abdomen and traced a flirtatious trail across his broad chest. Rapture enhanced his features as she began to make love to Octavio slowly. At first it was as she said; she was the conqueror relishing his pleas to end her merciless taunting. Then just as quickly the conqueror was conquered, yielding to the thrust and parry of her relentless adversary until, at last, their battle cries echoed in sweet union.

Neither Gila nor Octavio could sleep after the lovemaking. They could not get enough of the other and both explored the pleasure points of their chosen love. Finally spent, they reveled in holding each other with a familiarity only true lovers know. A thrill flowed through Gila as his arm came to rest across her hip and possessively embraced her.

"I love you and you love me," Gila whispered aloud, touching her lips as she spoke to make certain this was no phantom dream. "I never thought . . . I never hoped—"

Octavio kissed the tips of her fingers, then threaded them with his own. "I think I fell in love with you when you walked through the door wearing that ridiculous wedding dress and those oversize boots." Together they laughed, once more sharing a long, lingering kiss.

Gila snuggled against his chest. His lips pressed gently against her temple. Would it always be this way—so wonderful, so warm? she wondered.

His voice took on a more serious note. "I never dreamed when I struck a bargain with your father that one day it would be like this. I intended for you to be a catalyst for my freedom. And now I know that you are more than any bargain, any destiny I thought I had."

Gila rose abruptly and stared into his smoky blue eyes. "No! No, my love. I won't have you if you do not fulfill your destiny." The puzzlement and hurt she read in his expression was like a dagger in her heart. Still, there was a hint of something more in his look.

"Don't you see?" she continued. "If you don't complete this fateful mission you've set out on, you'll always wonder what could have happened. I won't have you living a lifetime wondering if you made the right choice. Mexico has waited for you. I can be patient, too. If you're destined to be mine, then I shall have you. And if you aren't, then I will have you until you must go." She could not stop the tears that fell in silent fear of the future.

"*Dulce mia.* My darling Gila," Octavio whispered, his voice breaking with emotion.

"Señora Cordoba," Gila corrected, the name fading upon her lips with his kiss. She trembled with the sweetness that engulfed her, her spirit soaring as he, too, shivered under the power of their love.

A light rap on the door shook the lovers from their rendezvous. "Gila, are you all right?"

Thorne! The guests! "Yes, Father," she replied hurriedly. "Just a little tired." She felt as if she'd been naughty and he were scolding her. Which he should have been. She'd left all the duties of hostessing to Shelly Kate on her wedding day. "Are all the guests gone?" Gila asked hesitantly.

"All that aren't staying over," Thorne answered. A long silence followed, yet Gila knew he remained outside the door. Just as she was about to ask if there were anything she could do for him, Thorne spoke again. "Katie and me . . . I lost my baby tonight, lassie."

Octavio squeezed her fingers reassuringly. He had caught the sadness in her father's tone and thought—as she must have—of the day when a child of theirs would marry.

"Not lost, Father," Gila reassured Thorne and herself. "Never lost."

"Goodnight, daughter." Thorne sounded so old, so distant.

"Father?"

"Yes, Gila?"

"I love you."

"And I . . . you. Goodnight, lassie."

"Goodnight," she whispered to his fading footsteps. That was the closest Thorne had ever come to expressing his feelings for her. He might not have said the words *I love you*, but she felt his love all the same.

Her soul shouted with the glorious love she had gained this night. Love of her husband and her father. Was it fair that she should be so happy?

Suddenly an unexpected tremor ran the length of her spine and settled coldly around her heart. One of Book's sayings raced to mind. If an eagle soars too high, his breath plunges to earth.

She chided herself for being silly and nestled closer to Octavio. Nothing could take away her happiness. Nothing.

# Chapter Twenty-One

✦✦✦✦

A SHAMROCK OF light woke Gila at dawn. She turned on her side to avoid the morning glare. Warmth of another kind coursed through her when she glanced at Octavio. His loving eyes were closed in slumber now, but his lips held a hint of fullness, a pleasant reminder of the previous night's intimacies.

She suppressed a giggle as she brushed back a

lock of hair that nudged his forehead. His nose twitched back and forth as if she had touched it with a feather. Feeling wicked—and enjoying every moment of it—she traced a path from his nose to his lips, then down toward the victim of her intentions. She shivered with delight as a quiver rippled through him. She realized with a thrill that even in deep sleep he could not deny his love for her.

Her happiness suddenly dulled when she caught sight of his scarred thighs. What terrible torture had he suffered, and why? Though his injuries were well healed, she felt freshly wounded. Anger swelled within her until she thought she would burst with fury. Who dared defile her beloved this way?

Was it Maximilian? she wondered. Had he ordered this savage means of torture? Had he thought himself better than Octavio because he was an Austrian and Octavio was not? How could one man believe himself better than the other?

Or one woman, she silently condemned herself. Hadn't she harbored such a prejudice? Hadn't she ridiculed and condemned Octavio as her inferior, when at every turn he had proven more caring, more forgiving than she? Her heart heaved with humiliation as she remembered the countless times she had degraded him with her harsh words.

Prejudice such as her own might have given him the lesions on his thighs. Each wound could have been a lash from her own biased tongue. Each scar would be an everlasting reminder of her self-righteousness. Bitter tears brimmed in her eyes.

"I'm sorry, darling," she whispered. Unable to control the guilt that engulfed her, Gila rose from the bed. Never had she felt so ashamed. Even the near-rapes she had suffered had not left her feeling such revulsion. Those attacks had been beyond her control, but her prejudice was of her own choice. Scouring baths had helped wash away her attacker's foul smell. Now, could a bath help remove the stench of her own unfairness?

Gila slipped into the yellow shift she'd worn the night before. The task of opening the barred entrance to the pool had become more difficult with each passing month of her pregnancy. After several hard pushes, she succeeded in lifting the barricade. Octavio would most likely be angry when he woke and saw that she had gone into the pool alone, but her need to feel clean once again outweighed any other consideration.

She proceeded through the passageway to the pool. The underground tunnel was cool, already hinting of the approaching winter. Once inside the cave, she welcomed the warmth that greeted her. Steam from the swirling pool rose and flushed the air. As she lit the lantern, she wondered about the strange odor that assailed her memory. Gila twirled and peered into the shadowy recesses of the cave. Nothing was amiss.

How foolish, she thought. She turned away from the pool and grabbed the hem of the yellow shift to lift the garment overhead. Beads of water splashed her legs. She turned. Powerful, violent arms closed around her. Streaks of red and gold flashed before her eyes. She screamed, but a foul-smelling hand clamped over her mouth and pulled her down into the whirling water.


Octavio woke shivering and fumbled for the sheepskin coverlet. Pulling it over his shoulders, he sought the reason for the sudden chill. The cave. Gila must have decided to bathe and left the door ajar. The draft whistling through the passageway was enough to cool the room considerably. Should he get up and push it closed? The thought of leaving the warm bed was answer enough, and he decided Gila would not appreciate a closed door between them, especially after last night.

Such an odd pair they were, yet undeniably one. Her lips had given all she possessed and his had taken gladly. The promise had been kept.

Daring the cold, Octavio rose and entered the passageway. The warm water would rid him of the chill. Even better would be Gila's warmth. Darling Gila. Passionate Gila. His alone.

As he hurried through the tunnel, he wondered if the urgency in his steps were caused by the frosty air nipping his flesh or by his desire to hold Gila in his arms once again. The next few months he would spend making love to her, getting to know her every mood, her every thought. Their budding love must blossom fully, and he intended to sweeten the nectar with trust and understanding.

*"Dulce mia?"* he called out as he entered the cave. He gazed at the water and saw no disturbance at the surface. No frock or robe lay near the edge. Deciding she must already have bathed, he assumed she was in the kitchen cooking.

Octavio looked down and laughed aloud. The imprint of Gila's feet trailed from the doorway to the water's edge. He placed his right foot in one print and marveled at its tiny size. How different her feet had seemed the day he saw them in the large boots. How was he to know she'd deliberately bought them too large? "Such big *zapatos*, my sweet."

A cold breeze from the passageway reminded Octavio that he was naked and his plans for warming himself had been waylaid. He ran through the tunnel, hugging his shoulders. Once inside their bedroom, he chose not to dally with bolting the door and instead pushed the barrier into place, quickly shutting off the autumn breeze.

This task is too hard for a woman in her condition, he decided. He must remind her not to open the door by herself. Though he did not object to her independence, he found Gila too often stubborn. Her iron will both interested and irritated him, but from this day on he would not allow her self-sufficiency to interfere with her health. She belonged to him now. When she hurt herself, she hurt him.

He dressed hurriedly and tiptoed to the parlor, hoping none of the wedding guests were early risers. In his haste, he had forgotten his boots. No matter, he decided. He would coax Gila out of the kitchen and back to bed. This way he would have less clothing to remove.

*Madre de Dios!* Terror suddenly knifed his spine and plunged deep within his heart. The footprints had gone in only one direction! He raced through the parlor, shouting Gila's name.

"What's wrong?" Garrett asked, stepping out into the hallway. Octavio brushed past him without answering. Seconds might make the difference.

Octavio rushed into the bedroom and jerked the shelf away from the wall. Bottles, baskets, and decanters fell with a nerve-shattering crash. He ran through the tunnel and into the cave.

A swift glance at the footprints leading to the water's edge confirmed his fear. He plunged into the swirling pool.

Though the water was warm and inviting, icy fingers of dread gripped him. His ears thrummed to near-bursting. His lungs burned for need of air, but he stayed in the dark whirling water, groping, searching, waiting to touch, but finding nothing.

Gasping for breath, he surfaced, then dove deep again, this time toward the underwater barrier to the cave. In her condition, it would be hard for her to fit through the two rocks. But if she hadn't, it meant she was—No! She can't be. I won't let her be!

After several more futile attempts, Octavio

climbed out of the whirlpool, struggling to slow his breath into a steady rhythm. "Gila," he screamed with all his might.

Massive hands jerked him to his feet. "Where is she, October? Where's Gila?" Thorne demanded.

Octavio confronted the challenge in the hazel eyes. "She is my wife, señor, as well as your daughter. If you will remove your hands from me, I will continue to look for her body. I fear she has drowned."

A gasp from the cave's entrance drew Octavio's attention. He turned in time to see Shelly Kate faint in Garrett's arms. He turned back to Thorne. "Now if you please," he said and pushed away the now-slackened hands.

Book brushed past and without a word dove into the pool. "He need not bother," Octavio said brokenly. "I've searched the bottom several times and checked the barrier. She's not there."

"Then she may not have drowned," Thorne said, his voice taut with hope. "The lassie's probably outside feeding Dublin or Wee-People, she is. And you're a fine sort, scaring the living daylights out of her father this way."

Anger welled within Octavio until he could not control his thoughts, his actions. He pushed Thorne's massive chest once, twice. "Do you dare dispute the word of Don Octavio Diego Cordoba? Do you dare waste precious time quibbling while the life of my wife is in question?" Octavio's right fist swung and connected with Thorne's bearded jaw.

Thorne collided with the earthen floor. He

shook his red mane, then reached up to inspect his jaw. "That'll be the first and only time you raise your hand against me, son. Now tell us what you think has happened."

Octavio was as surprised as Thorne by his action, but the deed was done and could not be undone. Now was not the time for the two of them to fight. They must unite if they were to recover Gila's body.

Gila's body? Beloved Gila. Passionate Gila. Grief overwhelmed him. His heart ached, his loins throbbed. His feet felt as if a cannonball were tied to each one. His mind ceased thought, ceased caring. Who were all these strange people? Why were they glaring at him, almost daring him to speak? Did they know he would never again have a reason to live, would never again kiss his beloved's lips?

"Damn you, man, talk!" Thorne demanded as he rose to his feet.

Thorne's roar brought Octavio to his senses. "I came to join Gila in the pool. I found her footprints, but they only went *to* the water, not back. She must have fainted or gotten a cramp while she was bathing."

Octavio motioned to the large wooded fence that blocked the outside entrance to the cave. "I searched the opening between the rocks that I told you about. She's too far into her term and . . ." His voice trailed off weakly.

Book surfaced. The Oriental's sudden appearance startled Octavio, making his heart leap. Had he been afraid it would be Gila's body rippling the water? Could he face the inevitable?

What in the Holy Mother's name would he do when he found her?

Octavio offered a hand to the samurai, helping him out of the pool. He'd been so consumed with sorrow that he hadn't noticed the samurai had been underwater for so long. No one could stay under that long. Had he checked beyond the barrier and into the waterfall?

As Book waded out of the water, Octavio caught sight of a bright yellow piece of material clutched in the Oriental's hand. Though certain of the answer before he asked, he had to hear it spoken aloud. "That's part of Gila's dress, isn't it?"

Book nodded.

Dread surrendered to resignation as Octavio muttered, "Where?"

"On a yucca. A mile downstream. On the hillside. We must saddle the horses and get provisions. She's alive for the present."

Had he heard correctly? The Oriental nodded again and confirmed, "Kidnapped."

Gila abducted? By whom? The words had no time to form on his lips before Thorne placed a reassuring hand on Octavio's shoulder.

"It could be anyone, laddie. Anyone. A rich man knows many enemies. I only wish I had heeded your warning. I did post more lookouts near the waterfall, but I didn't think anyone would use the stream itself as an entrance. I should have closed off the opening, but it seemed unwise. Should there have ever been another raid inside the house, I wanted to use the waterfall as our means of escape. Don't worry, son," Thorne added with conviction, "We'll get her back."

"It was the Indian." Book's statement halted the procession through the passageway. A tenseness passed between the Irishman and the Oriental and did not go unnoticed by Octavio. Why had Book said *the* Indian? What Indian?

Octavio started to ask Book to repeat the statement, but Thorne demanded they not tarry. By the time Octavio reached Gila's room, Thorne's booming voice was barking out orders to every man within hearing distance.

"Get the horses saddled. Billy, get enough grub on those pack mules. Yes, yes. Get your tail to Cochise and tell him what's happened. He'll be knowing how best to track the renegade. Saddle up Wee-People. He'll find her before we do. Dublin, too. I don't care if you don't see the need. Can't you see Dublin knows? Let him loose, man. Let him loose!"

Octavio changed into dry clothing and grabbed a rifle. Thorne clanged the triangle six times and the call to arms resounded across the Circle-Shamrock.

"Here." Thorne handed Wee-People's reins to Octavio. "No one else can handle him."

The paint reared and bucked when Octavio mounted him, but soon settled down under Octavio's expert handling.

Thorne's fiery brow arched in surprise, then lowered into a look of renewed respect for his son-in-law. "Ready?" he asked.

"Ready." Octavio nodded. Odd how one word could sum up the tide of determination rising with his every breath. He was ready. Ready to do whatever he must to save Gila. Ready to kill whomever he must.

# *Chapter Twenty-Two*

✦✦✦✦✦

GILA'S FEET ACHED with each step as rocks and cactus thorns tore her bare soles. Her arms hurt with the constant jerking motion of her captor's Appaloosa as they traveled up the mountainside. Her crossed wrists were chafed by the rawhide that bound her to the pony's mane. If the Indian kept this pace, it wouldn't be long before the pain would cease and her hands and feet would be numb.

Her feet! What did she care of them? How long would the red devil keep her trotting beside his fast-moving pony? Didn't he see she was near her term? How much longer could the child withstand this torture?

Gila eyed the Indian, catching only glimpses of him through a haze of noonday sun. What a fool she'd been to think White Bear had been the same Indian who had tried to rape her the first time. What a fool! He had not come to commit the crime a second time at the Colossal Cavern. His attack was his first. And she'd been foolish enough to think she was no longer in danger,

that the arrow Cochise sent through White
Bear's heart had ended all her worries.

Now she stared at the warrior who had tried
to take her unwillingly that day seven months
ago. He slowed his pace and stared down at her.
She met his estimating gaze, looking at him
closely for the first time. His nose was long, with
flaring nostrils. His eyes were dark and piercing.
His cheekbones were finely chiseled and painted
with wide streaks of red and gold. His mouth
was straight and unforgiving.

She continued her inspection, noting the
sharply corded muscles of the warrior's arms
and legs. She wondered how recently he had
collected the scalps hanging on his waistband.
Her attacker noticed her horror and broke into a
yellow-toothed grin. With a savage tug, he
pulled on the rawhide that bound her to the
pony. The pain was fierce, but she would not
give him the satisfaction of crying out.

Instead she threw her weight against the
Indian's right leg and bit down with all her
might. Blood and grease-soaked skin sullied her
teeth. Furiously, he kicked her away with a
sharp blow from his moccasin. She fought to
keep her footing as the Indian once again urged
the Appaloosa into a trot.

On and on she ran, stumbling, slipping, gasping for breath. Occasionally she caught sight of
the nasty bite she had taken out of her captor's
leg and it gave her the courage to keep going.
Had he wanted to kill her, he could have done so
at any time. But he hadn't. How long was he
going to spare her?

Would she be sold to another tribe as a slave? Worse, would he keep her for himself? "Octavio," she whispered, "come for me, please."

Octavio searched the trail with a discerning eye. The signs told him the Indian had been moving steadily for hours. Each of Gila's bloody footprints gave him a sharp, cruel pain in his heart. How much could she endure in her condition? How soon would the devil tire of his slow-moving captive? How long before they found her mutilated body lying in the sand? How long?

As if it were not enough to deal with Gila's kidnapping, Octavio found Book's and Thorne's silence unbearable. "Will no one tell me of this Indian?" he raged. "Will no one tell of the danger this man means to my wife?" Thorne ignored his question. "Can you tell me?" Octavio implored Book.

"There is no time to spare." Book motioned toward Thorne, who nodded. "I will tell you as we ride," the samurai promised.

Octavio listened intently as Book related the events prior to the marriage ceremony in Nogales. His heart sickened at the knowledge of the degradation his beloved had endured. Degradation at the hands of her own father, and yes, even himself.

Hadn't he thought of her as his "American whore" in the beginning? Yet out of ignorance he had misjudged her. Darling Gila. Brave Gila was the innocent one in their relationship. At least he'd been given a choice about their marriage. Whether or not Gila had been raped by the Indian, she had lost her freedom—freedom to give what was only her husband's to take. No! Only hers to give.

Octavio was filled with an even deeper love for her than he thought possible. Not once during all those months had she uttered a word about her father's cruelty. She chose not to seek his sympathy and instead had won his heart by her own right. She was the very woman he had sought all his life. A slim seductress like Modesta Hidalgo could hold no claim on him now. He wanted only Gila. Hot-tempered, honest, pure Gila. How he loved her! And now no one and nothing would keep him from fulfilling that love. He urged Wee-People into a gallop as he shook his fist to the far horizon. "I, Don Octavio Diego Cordoba, swear this."

Gila shivered as the cool breeze of evening blew across her face. Perhaps now her captor would stop his torturous journey to God knew where. For the last few hours they had climbed up from the base of Mount Lemmon. A piercing wind whistled through the juniper and oak. She'd expected the redskin to take her along the San Pedro into the desert. Here in the foothills of Mount Lemmon, there was chance for survival if she could escape.

At this moment she was not thinking of escape. She was praying the Indian would not be so much of a renegade that he would forget the superstitions of the Chiricahua. Through her exhaustion she struggled to remember all Book had told her about the tribe.

"The Chiricahua do not wander beyond their campsite after sunset." The memory of Book's voice comforted her. "They call themselves Men of the Rising Sun. They revere the sun. When it sets, they believe evil walks the earth. They fear that the spirits of those who have been wronged seek vengeance during the hours before sunrise."

"They believe in ghosts?" Gila had asked, amazed that such fierce men would fear anything.

"Not the ghosts of which white men speak," Book replied. "But spirits that inhabit the elements, or an animal. A hooting owl, for instance, means impending death for the Apache who hears it. A snake is bad luck. You were very fortunate the day you were attacked. The Indian must have believed a spirit had entered Dublin's body and was determined to save you. The white buffalo is sacred to the Chiricahua. That is the only reason your life was spared."

"Then why did the Indian knife Dublin?"

"He probably sensed Dublin's presence and threw the weapon before looking. When he saw the buffalo was white, he knew he had committed the worst of crimes. He had to retreat.

"You must beware the revenge of the renegade. He will be back to punish you for his ill fortune. And he will probably attempt to kill Dublin as well."

"But why?" she had asked, concerned for

Dublin's safety. "You said he committed a crime
by harming Dublin. Why would he want to kill
him?"

"Chiricahua legend says that great hardship
will befall his people until he brings them the
entire hide of the white buffalo. Only then will
their tribe never again hunger. Only when the
hide hangs in the circle of honor will his camp be
free from the sickness that comes with winter."

A jerk at the Appaloosa's mane brought Gila's
thoughts to the present. The renegade was untying her hands. Immediately an ache settled
into her armpits, making her arms fall to her
sides as if they were weighted down. She
slumped to her knees, incapable of walking
further. Gently she positioned herself on the
ground, wincing as pain knifed through her,
then dulled into sheer exhaustion.

Recollection of Book's words had given her
the reason behind the kidnapping. The savage
was smart, all right. He'd intended for her loved
ones to come after her. That's why he ran her
alongside the pony. He knew Thorne would
send Dublin to follow her trail. It would be easier
to follow her climbing Mount Lemmon than
crossing the Sonora. How long had he watched
the ranch to plan his revenge?

Gila knotted her hand into a tight fist and
struck the ground beside her. "Why in hell don't
you get it over with?" she shouted. "Why?"

He sat across from her, unmoving, his dark
eyes laughing at her fear. Anger surged through
every inch of her tired, aching body, straightening her back with indignation. "Kill me now,

Redman. What are you waiting for? Dead or alive, they'll come after you. And don't think you'll get Dublin. He beat you once, he'll do it again. Do you hear? Coward! Coward! Coward!'' Her voice rose with each word, yet she fought the hysteria racing to consume her.

The glint of metal moving from the rawhide sheath at his waistband sobered Gila into calmness. Without flinching, she met his gaze, preparing herself for the inevitable. Let the renegade see what a McCandless, a *Cordoba* was made of. Then he might hesitate challenging the rest of her family.

Gila tilted her head, staring haughtily at the Indian. She waited as the army-issue knife slowly neared her throat, then dropped to toy at her right breast. She faced her captor's death-dealing gaze, thinking that his eyes resembled two black moons. Evil moons. "Moons are a part of the night, Chiricahua. And I swear by the God Almighty moon I will haunt you till the end of your days. Beware the spirits of the night, Redman, for one of them will be me." She spat in his face.

His stoic face contorted with insane fury. He pushed her backward, pressing the blade sharply against her abdomen.

"Oh, my God!" Gila whispered hoarsely. "Please, please, not the baby!" She dared not struggle against him. Any sudden movement could send his weapon deep within her womb.

"God . . . ple-e-ease," she prayed aloud, repeating her desperate pleas over and over.

Her prayer was answered, for the Indian

stood and walked away. She took several moments to slow her breath to a regular pace. She had escaped death for the moment, but how many times would she be so lucky? Her nerves felt as tightly strung as the deer gut on the Chiricahua's bow. Dread pulsed with her every heartbeat.

The child lay quiet within her, and this frightened Gila most of all. The baby had been so active these past months. Now she felt not even the slightest movement. Had she saved her child from the Indian's blade only to have it born dead? Or worse, what kind of life would it have?

The renegade skirted the edge of the camp and disappeared into the darkness for several moments. Gila tried to sit up, but her strength was gone. How can I escape when I can't even get up? She pulled her knees to her chest and began to rock gently back and forth until she gained enough momentum to sit. But even if she could get to her feet, she would not get far. The moon was too high overhead. The Indian would be able to track her easily. She would have to think of another plan.

A deepening shadow warned her of the Indian's return. To her surprise, he took the riding blanket from his Appaloosa and dropped it beside her. Carefully she wrapped herself in its folds. The stench of man and horse emanated from deep within the material, but its warmth was more potent than the disgusting odor was foul.

Gila's stomach rumbled with dissatisfaction as

she watched the Indian take nuts and berries from a deerskin pouch and feed his horse. She hadn't eaten since before Shelly Kate's wedding the previous night and she was ravenous. Her hunger overcame her caution.

"Hey. Is there any more? I'm hungry, too."

The Indian gave her a warning look and let loose a string of harsh, guttural words. He was silent for a moment, then held out his palm to her. It held three piñon nuts and several mulberries. Was he being civil or merely tempting her, she wondered. Fighting back the fear that threatened to overwhelm her, she reached for his offering.

She struggled to open the podlike shells of the nuts, but her strength was not up to even this smallest of tasks. Her breath caught as the Indian wielded his knife, slicing the miniature pod in two pieces without leaving a mark upon her opened palm. She shivered with dread. His skill with the weapon was alarming.

She ate the berries and one of the nuts, but slipped the last two piñons into the single pocket of her dress. She could not know when—if ever—she would be given food again.

Exhaustion crept through her like a scouting party in enemy territory. She pulled the blanket tightly around her shoulders and let the numbness of sleep ease her pain and fear. Tomorrow she would plan her escape. If there was a tomorrow . . .

# Chapter Twenty-Three

✦✦✦✦✦

GARRETT O'MALLEY GRABBED up his war bag and blanket. "I still say it's a waste of good man-hours, Ben. There's no point in all of us missing our sleep. With two of us on watch, we could keep an eye out for trouble."

"You going to be one of the two?" the trail boss asked. "No? I didn't think so. Well, bud, ain't none of us going to sleep good till we get Gila back. So why don't you just quit your mouthing and get to your post?"

Garrett grumbled under his breath but didn't argue. Someday Shelly Kate would inherit the Shamrock and he would have his revenge on Ben. Anybody in his right mind knew they weren't going to get Gila back, and if they did, they wouldn't want her after that Indian had finished with her.

He swung his leather goods up into the juniper branches, out of reach of the desert coyotes. He rolled out his blanket and made himself as comfortable as he could. Damned hard ground. Too bad they weren't further up the mountain, where the pine forest was thicker. It would make for better bedding.

Keep an eye out for signs of the Indian. That's a laugh, he thought as he removed the black patch he wore over his useless socket. Gila had already taken one eye from him, now he was expected to use the other for her safety. Folding his arms behind his head, he looked up at the

314

sky. The moon was three-quarters full and surrounded by a pale mist.

"Storms acoming," he muttered. "Damn, I
hope it doesn't rain tonight. That's all I need."

Well, I'm not going to worry about it till my
boots get wet, he decided.

Moments later Garrett was sound asleep,
dreaming. He saw Shelly Kate dressed in black,
standing over a grave. Her eyes were puffy from
crying. He had been right! Gila was going to die.

Why was Shelly shaking her head no? What
was she saying? "I don't want it. You keep the
north section."

Garrett called out to her as she handed Thorne
the deed to the land. As a tear fell down Shelly
Kate's face, Garrett felt a splatter upon his
cheek. Then another.

Cursing, he rubbed away the moisture with
the back of his hand. His eyes gradually opened
and he focused on the low overhanging clouds.
"Wouldn't you know it would rain?"

Garrett reached up to wipe away another drop
and suddenly caught sight of the blood smeared
across the back of his hand. Too late did he look
up to see the fresh scalps hanging from the
Indian's waistband. The Indian's upraised knife
plummeted toward Garrett's throat.


The burial was brief.

"Oby, Garrett, Jose, and Stefan O'Rourke."
Thorne intoned the dead men's names. "All four
with their scalps gone. That Indian's becoming a
real nuisance, Lord. Not on my land. If this is

your purpose, to rob me of a daughter and a son-in-law, not to mention three good hired hands, I don't see the jest of it."

Thorne took off his broad hat. "Now, I would be the first to get down on my knees and say Amen and praise your holy name, if you let me find my Gila alive. Innocent people have suffered enough for wrongdoings."

With that declaration, Thorne McCandless bent to his knees in prayer. All other Circle-Shamrock knees did the same.


The McCandless party crested the lower hills of the Santa Catalinas as the noon sun burned its wrath into their skin. Ahead, Thorne's raised forearm signaled he had found something. Octavio urged Wee-People into a fast trot, then halted near a large oak where Thorne was peering down at the ground. The Irishman pointed to the empty piñon pods. "They spent the night here, 'tis for sure. At least we know he means to keep the lassie alive for a while longer. He would never have left the pod here otherwise."

Octavio's face mirrored his puzzlement. "Why is he leaving a trail? It's almost as if he's taunting us."

"He is," Book confirmed. Inspecting the edge of the campsite, he lingered at one of the mulberry trees. "He's baiting us. He lets us see Gila's trail but not his own. He wants us to follow without knowing how many are with him. He could be alone. Or not."

Thorne stood and shielded his eyes, directing

his gaze further up the mountainside. He studied for several moments, then announced, "We'll camp here."

Octavio gestured in frustration. "Why? Why stop now when we're so close? They'll just get farther away."

"I said dismount, Cordoba. The horses won't take much more pushing and neither will the men." He placed a firm hand on Octavio's shoulder. "We'll catch up with them tonight while they're acamp. You'll have her by morning, son."

"If she lives that long," Octavio added defiantly, meeting Thorne's disapproving gaze.

Thorne remounted and reined his horse half-quarter. "I'll be back in a while. Dublin's too far afield. He'll be knowing she's close." He nodded to the wrangler who led the two pack mules. "Billy, get out a jerky and a sourdough for each man. Not more than a cup of water for each. The springs are dry from here to Mammoth." He spurred his horse into a fast trot.

"I'm going with him," Book said.

Octavio jerked to attention, forgetting the task at hand. Wee-People could be hobbled later. He tried to read meaning into Book's words, but the Oriental features disclosed nothing. He watched the dust stirred by the horses' hooves as Book hurried after Thorne, wondering whether he should go with them.

But what good would it do? Was he willing to come between a samurai and his word?

Octavio brushed back an ebony lock from his forehead and took a deep breath. Squaring his shoulders with purpose he realized he had no choice. If Book fulfilled his promise now, he might destroy any chance of rescuing Gila. He must go!

A pain low and deep in Gila's back nearly took her breath away. After a searing moment, it subsided. She knew it would come again, just as it had every few minutes the past several hours. Her abdomen felt as if there were a ball and chain strung around it and the next step would tear her stomach away from her body. Deep breaths seemed to ease the ache momentarily, but when the pain began again, she could do little but grit her teeth and wait for it to end.

The Appaloosa continued to climb the hillside. Gila's shoulders were so tired she felt as if she had carried the horse on her back. At least the renegade had slackened his pace this morning and she was able to follow without stumbling.

Several times, as the painful contractions came closer together, she fell to her knees. Gila wondered how much longer she could last, knowing the Indian would not stop his trek until nightfall.

Her stomach tightened into a hard knot. Something inside broke loose. Water gushed down her legs. "Not now, Lord," Gila cried aloud, "please, not now. Ohhh . . ." Agony wrenched through her entire body and she screamed with its fierceness.

With one swish of his blade, the Indian cut her bonds. Gila sank to the ground, grateful for the

respite. She could barely raise her head to look at
the renegade. Why had he let her loose?

He sat there, unmoving. Was he going to
watch? No. Book had said something about
Apache squaws going off on their own.

Another violent pain rippled through her. Gila
scrambled to her hands and knees, frightened at
the prospect of being left alone. She was only
seven months along. What if there were trouble?
What if the baby came wrong? What if—?

She doubled over, feeling as if she were being
torn in half. Her thoughts went beyond caring,
beyond questioning. Her body writhed with the
spasms that tore at her abdomen.

In a blur of agony, Gila took in her surroundings. Nothing. There was nothing to help with
the birthing. No water. No cloth except the filthy
horse blanket and the torn shreds of her sheath.
She rolled on her back, hoping to relieve the
contracting spasms, but the hard earth was little
comfort.

Through a haze of blistering sunlight she
gazed at the looming horseman above her. What
would he do once the child was born? Surely he
would not leave her and the babe to die on the
mountain. Or would he? Would he resume his
maniacal march as soon as her ordeal was over?
How could she survive? If she didn't live, what
of the baby? How in St. Patrick's name would
the baby survive?

She turned slowly on her side, then struggled
back to her hands and knees. Ignoring the
excruciating cramps in her stomach, she crawled

forward. A juniper tree was only a few yards away. She could make it. She must!

She crept toward the tree, her breath coming in rasping gulps. Finally she collapsed at the base of the juniper, weeping with exhaustion. Forcing her arms to encircle the tree trunk, she braced herself for the next contraction. It came too soon, obliterating any thought of time or place, leaving only the vague memory of fading hoofbeats.

Octavio followed Book and Thorne at a reasonable distance. He knew the Oriental was aware of his presence, for the samurai had stopped once and stared in Wee-People's direction.

On and on Octavio rode. The strong sun did little to warm him. He had been cold since the moment he knew Gila had been abducted.

Abruptly he reined Wee-People. Several yards in front of him Thorne McCandless was bent over, studying his horse's hind hoof. Dublin was grazing a short distance away.

Wee-People tossed his head and snorted. "What's wrong, boy?" Octavio asked and patted the horse.

Dread slowed Octavio's breath as he caught sight of the samurai creeping through the trees, circling to Thorne's right. As Book quietly stalked his prey, Octavio stared in horror—and respect—for the samurai's progress. Could he warn Thorne in time, he wondered. But what if calling out distracted Thorne long enough for Book to make the kill? Octavio became angry

with his indecision. If the samurai truly loved
Gila, he would not even think of doing this now.
He should be trying to save her, not trying to kill
Thorne!

Book leapt toward Thorne. Before Octavio
could shout a warning an Indian appeared in the
oak branches above Thorne. Octavio found his
voice. "Above you!" he shouted.

Book's sudden movement had knocked
Thorne out of harm's way. The samurai's back
took the full length of the Indian's blade. He
staggered under the impact, the gray tunic turning crimson.

Octavio unhooked his lariat from the saddle
horn and knotted it securely. He had only one
chance and he had to make it count. He pressed
his knees hard against Wee-People, and the
paint sprang forward.

Thorne recovered and threw the full force of
his weight against the renegade, preventing the
Indian's attempt to scalp Book.

The renegade flipped Thorne over his back
and gripped the massive Irishman's throat. They
rolled over and over, the larger man unable to
free himself. Thorne's face began to match the
color of his hair; still the Indian refused to
relinquish his hold.

Octavio whirled his lasso above his head, his
flexing wrist matching the beat of Wee-People's
galloping hoofs. The Indian turned, let go of
Thorne, and ran toward Wee-People. Octavio let
fly the noose and prayed it met its mark.

The rope fell effortlessly around the black-
braided head. Octavio jerked the noose tight and

reined Wee-People to an abrupt halt. Then he signaled the paint to retreat. The Indian struggled to free himself but could not. Octavio ran Wee-People at full speed until he was certain the Indian was dead. He left the savage lying amidst the creosote and rushed to where Book had fallen.

Already Thorne had regained his wind and was bending over the motionless samurai. Octavio jumped from the saddle. He hurried to Thorne's side and searched the pale Oriental features for signs of life. "Is he alive?"

Octavio was surprised at the open grief displayed in Thorne's face. "Not for very long," the Irishman muttered.

As Thorne stood and walked away, Octavio's respect for the man grew. Despite the fact that the rancher knew Book had every intention of killing him, he could still grieve for the loss of a decent man, a man who had been his friend for many years.

Gently Octavio grasped the samurai's right hand with his own. No longer could he feel the powerful life-force that had been so much a part of the fallen warrior. "Book?" he called softly.

Book's lips pressed together several times. His lashes fluttered open, yet the ebony eyes appeared unseeing.

Octavio said the name again. Book's eyes turned to gaze directly into Octavio's. A rush of breath and a whisper escaped Book's lips. Octavio bent closer. "S-s-same."

"Same what?" Octavio asked, peering into

Book's eyes once again. Already the light of understanding was fading from the ebony pools. The massive chest quivered.

"Rape."

Octavio searched his mind for the meaning of the two words. Same. Rape. Same rape? Of course! The Indian. This was the same Indian who had tried to rape Gila!

"Gila's nearby!" Octavio shouted. Pressure against his right hand confirmed he had guessed Book's meaning.

Looking up, Octavio saw Dublin start to scramble up the hillside. He must have picked up Gila's scent, he reasoned. Thorne ran off after the great white buffalo.

A loud resounding cry from further up the hillside startled Octavio. Another cry quickly followed. "The baby!" he exclaimed and looked to see if Book had heard as well.

Book squeezed Octavio's hand again. A wide smile stole over the dying man's face, even as the twinkle dwindled in his ebony eyes.

A sharp hiss of breath told Octavio the samurai had breathed his last. "Forgive me, my friend, for doubting you. A swift journey," he whispered. With some difficulty, he lifted Book and placed his body across Wee-People. Leaning close to the paint's ear, he said, "Find the others," and swatted the horse's flank. Wee-People took off down the mountain.

Octavio raced up the hill, moving in the direction of the baby's cry. The trees broke open into a clearing. Gila lay at its outer edge beneath the branches of a juniper. She was weeping, weeping uncontrollably. The babe. Where was the baby? Had it been too early for the birth?

Octavio surveyed the area and spotted Thorne. He had taken off his shirt and torn it in two strips. He was using one piece to clean the tiny baby he held in one arm. When he finished, he swaddled the infant in the larger piece.

Octavio rushed to Gila's side. She reached for him, desperately clutching him to her. "Shhsh, *dulce mia.*" He cradled her in his arms, trying to comfort her. "I am here."

"I love you. I love you," she repeated over and over until his lips met hers. She clung to him desperately. Cooing words of love, he rocked her back and forth, reassuring her, promising never to leave.

When she was calmed, Octavio told her gently about Book. Tears brimmed in her eyes and spilled over in silent grief. She lay against his chest, quiet and unmoving.

He brushed back the tangled auburn strands from her forehead and raised the blanket to cover her shoulders. Thorne would need to find the others soon. Night was already approaching. She and the babe needed more than this filthy blanket and a piece of Thorne's shirt to keep warm.

Gila fell into an exhausted sleep. Thorne urged Dublin to lie down beside Octavio and Gila, providing a windbreak. "I'll go get the others," he said. "And I'll take my grandson with me. She needs her rest."

Octavio nodded. Grandson? A boy. The pride

in Thorne McCandless's voice when he said *grandson* was undeniable. Thank the Holy Mother, the child would be welcomed. He had not thought of the baby or its gender once he caught sight of Gila. He was ashamed of that, knowing he had promised to love the child as his own because it was of Gila's blood. When she awoke he would confess the transgression and beg her forgiveness. He had been so worried about her, he had been unable to think of the child.

Octavio held her for more than an hour. His arms began to cramp and his back ached from sitting in one place for so long. He was grateful when he heard the sound of approaching horses. To his surprise, Cochise and several braves rode alongside Thorne.

Thorne dismounted and untied Wee-People from behind his own horse. "We've brought blankets and food. Laughing Water prepared medicine for Gila." He searched through the paint's saddlebags and brought out a deer-gut pouch. "Have her drink this."

Octavio placed Gila's head in his lap. "Gila. Wake up, *dulce mia.* You must drink this."

Gila was a willing patient. She drank thirstily. "Enough, my sweet. You'll be sick if you take too much."

"My son. Where is my son?" she whispered hoarsely and struggled to look around. Her body tensed at the sight of the Indians, but Octavio hurried to reassure her.

"Don't be frightened. These are Cochise's men. Thorne sent for them when he found you were abducted. He thought the chief would help us track you since the renegade was a Chiricahua."

"The baby? My son?" she begged.

Thorne bent down and took her hand into his own. "My grandson is fine and healthy. He's a bit of a wee one but that's because he's like his mother—always in a rush to do things his own way. You've got your hands full this time, lassie."

Octavio was pleased at the love displayed in Gila's eyes. At last Gila and Thorne had a common ground on which their love could grow.

Thorne nodded downhill. "He's about a mile down the mountain with the rest of the boys. Laughing Water's nursing him. She had a little one herself a few days ago and she's got plenty of milk. It was Cochise's idea to bring her along."

Octavio nodded a silent thank-you to his blood brother. Cochise said something in Spanish.

"What is it?" Gila asked. "What's wrong, Octavio?"

Octavio did not realize he'd grown so tense when he heard the chief's offer. The concern in Gila's voice was unsettling, and he was uncertain how to answer her. How could he tell her Cochise wanted him to go with the Chiricahua now? That Cochise wanted to escort him to Juárez.

No! He would not. He would not leave her when she needed him most. His love for Gila was more important than any day of reckoning with his destiny. He told her so.

Gila placed a trembling hand upon his arm. "Tell him you will go," she whispered. He searched her face.

"You must go," she told him. "For me as well as for yourself."

"I cannot leave you." He shook his head slowly. "I cannot."

She withdrew her hand. "And I cannot abide a man who won't keep his word!" Though the hazel eyes flashed with anger, Octavio was touched by the trembling that beset her. He, too, felt an ache tearing at his heart. How difficult it must be for her to tell him to go, when her every heartbeat, every touch asked him to stay.

"P-p-please go. Go with Cochise now . . . before I won't let you go."

Octavio bent to kiss her. Their lips confirmed the love they held for one another, promising that Destiny would not defeat them.

Octavio's gaze lingered on his beloved. "I will come back to you, *dulce mia*. I will come back."

"I love you, Octavio."

"I love you, *querida*."

Octavio walked away, unable to look back. Cochise offered the reins of one of the horses and Octavio mounted. The sound of Gila's weeping pierced him like an arrow. He fought back the urge to hold her in his arms, never to let go. He reined half-quarter and said, "I'm ready."

As the Indian party headed for camp, Octavio was thankful for the shadows of nightfall, for they hid the shadows in his heart.

# Epilogue

✦✦✦✦

*May 1867*

OCTAVIO HAD WAITED for this moment for more than a year and a half. This dark and cloudy night would decide his destiny. Tonight he would capture Maximilian!

He had been a part of General Escobedo's forces since early in the month, when they had surrounded the sprawling city of Querétaro and cut off its food and water supply.

He'd even had the pleasure of seeing Vidaurri, the governor from Monterrey who had arrested him at the ball, captured along with twelve hundred Mexican Imperial cavalry. An official state order for books and wine was found in Vidaurri's possession. Now the Juárist republicans were certain that Maximilian was hiding in Querétaro.

Octavio had positioned himself on the *Cerro*

*de las Campanas,* the Hill of the Bells. Something in his bones told him this was the place to be. Perhaps the sight of the flame-tipped prickly-pear blossom had drawn him to this spot.

The flower reminded Octavio of his darling Gila. It dared to grow wild and free in the shadow of the great church, just as his beloved wife dared to live wild and free in the shadows of the giant saguaros.

The rough clackety-clack of wheels drew Octavio's attention to the lonely-looking carriage that teetered on its rocky path toward the chapel on the hill. It was shrouded in funeral black and driven by a friar.

There was something vaguely familiar about the driver. The tilt of his head. The hardened physique. Suddenly the clouds parted as if on cue, shedding moonlight upon the padre's face. Tomás Mejía. Maximilian's generalissimo. Maximilian must be in the carriage!

Octavio gave the signal that he and all the other Juárists had awaited for more years than they cared to remember.

As Octavio raced toward the carriage, the bell rang in the chapel's tower. Passing the flaming prickly pear, Octavio reached out to pluck the blossom. He raised the flower to his lips. "Do you hear it, Gila? Do you hear the bell of our freedom?"

\* \* \*

Gila bent over the bank of the seep and washed the red pulpy saguaro fruit. A spray of water splashed her face, sending sweaty strands of auburn hair down into her eyes. "Diego Bukamoshi Cordoba, you stop that this minute!"

Gila brushed back the hair and stared down at her mischievous son. His blue eyes sparkled and the dimple in his left cheek quivered with laughter. She shook a warning finger at him. "How many times has Momma told you not to go near that water hole, you little imp!"

The pout on his lips and the crease frowning his forehead tore at her heart. How much longer would it be until Diego knew his father? She tussled his ebony locks playfully. "That's all right, Diego. Momma needed to cool off."

Diego suddenly pointed. "Horsie."

A whirl of dust preceded the rider. Thorne McCandless reined to a halt and dismounted quickly. He opened his arms wide and little Diego toddled off the bank and into his grandfather's arms. "I see you're up to your shenanigans again, laddie. Now just what is your granddad gonna do with you?"

Gila laughed. The sight of her father's arms wrapped lovingly around her son was something she would never tire of.

Thorne stood, holding Diego in one hand and rummaging in his saddlebag with the other. "Here it is," he said and tossed Gila a folded newspaper. "Got something you'll want to read."

Gila opened the June 1 edition of the *Mesilla Times*. The headline proclaimed:

MAXIMILIAN DEFEATED. VIVA JUÁREZ!

Gila looked up from the newspaper and saw the smile that lit Thorne's face. "Does this mean—?"

Thorne nodded. "Yes, daughter. And this letter came with it this morning." He reached down into the saddlebag and brought out an envelope.

The sight of Octavio's handwriting on the letter made Gila feel as unsteady as if she were standing in the quicksand of Devil's Canyon. She tore open the envelope and unfolded the single sheet of paper. A flaming red blossom slid from the inner folds. She read the words slowly, lingering over each one.

*My Darling Gila,*

*The deed is done and I am coming home. Home to you, my beloved wife. Home to our son.*

*I send the blossom of the prickly pear that grows beside the church here in Querétaro. It reminds me that the brilliance of your smile belongs to me, the flame of your lips is mine to touch, and I am pierced by your love.*

*Forever,*
*Octavio*

Gila closed her eyes and whispered, "He's coming!"

"No," Thorne corrected. "He's here." He pointed to the tall figure sitting atop the rise. At the wave of Thorne's hat, Octavio kneed his horse into a gallop.

Gila ran toward him, tears of happiness falling down her cheeks.

Octavio reined up short, dismounted, and ran to take her into his arms. Their lips met amidst a mingling of tears and joy. A longing sweet and tender filled them both and they knew they had finally obtained the world's most precious freedom. The freedom to love.

Gila watched adoringly as Diego Bukamoshi Cordoba toddled up to meet his father.

Octavio lifted the boy and gathered him into his arms. For the first time he noticed the child's eyes—eyes the same hue as his own. Joy as great as any he'd ever known filled him and he swallowed the lump of pride knotting in his throat. "No more shall I be a stranger to you, my son," he swore and encircled Gila's waist with one arm. As he looked into the hazel eyes filled with love, he renewed the promise given those many nights ago. "I surrender my love and my life to you, *dulce mia*. This Don Octavio Diego Cordoba swears!"

## *About the Author*

The authenticity of DeWanna Pace's novels springs from her love of the Southwest in general and Texas in particular. Readers of her historical romances will find themselves caught up in an era of reckless bravado. With passions that deny their prejudices, the heroes and heroines of DeWanna's novels rush headlong into conflicts that would send most of us scampering for cover. Yet their pride and sense of justice carries them through the most difficult situations; and the embers of their desires burst into flames that will ignite the hearts of romance lovers everywhere. When she isn't plotting or researching her novels, DeWanna enjoys art and reading. She lives in Amarillo, Texas, with her husband and daughter.

# The End?

The end of a book is never really *the end* for a person who reads. He or she can always open another. And another.

Every page holds possibilities.

But millions of kids don't see them. Don't know they're there. Millions of kids can't read, or won't.

That's why there's RIF. Reading is Fundamental (RIF) is a national nonprofit program that works with thousands of community organizations to help young people discover the fun—and the importance—of reading.

RIF motivates kids so that they *want* to read. And RIF works directly with parents to help them encourage their children's reading. RIF gets books to children and children into books, so they grow up reading and become adults who can read. Adults like you.

For more information on how to start a RIF program in your neighborhood, or help your own child grow up reading, write to:

**RIF**
Dept. BK-1
Box 23444
Washington, D.C.
20026

**Founded in 1966, RIF is a national non-profit organization with local projects run by volunteers in every state of the union.**

THIS SUPER-SELLER FROM
PAGEANT BOOKS WILL
CAPTURE YOUR
HEART!

Annie Ellis is a lady's maid in her mistress's clothing,
but the outfit is a wedding gown! Coerced into a
marriage meant for her mistress, Annie leaves
Chicago for the sandhills of Nebraska with her new
husband. Their hardworking days and sensuous
nights soon evolve into grand passion—but can
Annie shield the dangerous truth of her iden-
tity? Or will her new husband forsake her to shield
his wounded heart?

ISBN: 0-517-00623-5   Price: $3.95

AVAILABLE AT BOOKSTORES NOW!